MW00609112

...R OF MA...

MAUVIAS

TZU TIHAS
AND
FORTRESS T'VULUS

T'SKEL MOUNTAINS

KISOHI'S
FORTRESS

FORGOTTEN
VALLEY

SETMESH
RIVER

CASTLE
ERRASITKA

KALITOOMBA

NORTHERN
YENDU

URTAK

SAREI

LAKE
MAIYAN

...RN

CURSED BARRENS

PRISONER OF MAUVIAS

BOOK I OF THE GOD'S GAME SERIES

THE GOD'S GAME SERIES

PRISONER OF MAUVIAS

BOOK 1 OF THE GOD'S GAME SERIES

TIFFANY BRAZELL

REGALIS
PUBLISHING

Regalis Publishing, LLC
New York, NY 10000, USA

This is an original publication of Regalis Publishing, LLC.

This is a work of fiction. Names, characters, places, and incidents either are the product of the author's imagination or are used fictitiously, and any resemblance to actual persons, living, dead, or undead, business establishments, events, or locales is entirely coincidental. The publisher does not have any control over and does not assume any responsibility for author or third-party websites or their content.

Copyright ©2020 by Tiffany Brazell.
Text Design by Julie Larsen.
Cover Art by Jason Engle.
Cover Design by Tiffany Brazell.
Map by Tiffany and Ryan Brazell.

All rights reserved.
No part of this book may be reproduced, scanned, or distributed in any printed or electronic form without permission. Please do not participate in or encourage piracy of copyrighted materials in violation of the author's rights. Purchase only authorized editions—otherwise it's very hard for the author to pay her bills.

The crown logo is trademark of Regalis Publishing, LLC.

First Edition: January 2020
Library of Congress Cataloging-in-Publication Data
Brazell, Tiffany
    Prisoner of Mauvias / Tiffany Brazell—1st ed.

ISBN 9 780989 447423

1. Teenage girls—Fiction. 2. Brazell, Tiffany 3. High Fantasy—Fiction
4. Epic Fantasy—Fiction

Printed in Canada

10 9 8 7 6 5 4 3 2 1

FOR
MY PARENTS,
JEFF & MARIANNE

PROLOGUE

PLAINS,
SOUTHERN YENDU

Hazc tore into the fabric of time. Darkness filled his eyes as he stepped through the rift to the stagnant realm outside of time. Voices echoed in the dense space around him, intensifying as he drifted forward, filling his mind with their pleas, their longing. The voices increased to a howling crescendo, plucking every fiber of his person until he vibrated like a harp string.

He knew they were a part of him, but he didn't know them. He couldn't know them, not yet.

He focused ahead, lifting an arm and flexing his fingers, and opened another rift, breaking the bond.

The cries fell silent, and wind touched his face as he stepped from the rift with nothing but air beneath his feet.

Hazc fell into a mud hole in Southern Yendu, which sucked him in up to his chest. It would not have been an annoyance if his gnome body, standing just over two feet tall, weren't so pathetic. It had a plump, white face, beady eyes peeking from beneath frazzled brown hair, and, worst of all, it possessed a massive gut that interfered with even the most basic tasks.

The pungent odor of fertile earth replaced the stinging bitterness of the sulfuric environment that he had just abandoned as he strained to free himself of the suns-warmed mud on the other end of the portal he had made through time.

Hazc clawed at the wet dirt that ringed the lip of the pit and caught hold of a handful of silky, black grass. With a final grunt, he heaved himself free, and staggered to his feet.

Wiping his brow, he squinted against a rising zephyr. The rippling grass stretched on for miles beneath the dark sky before an elegant villa broke the flat horizon a small ways off. The green of the churning cloud cover reflected off the slick, black stalks, providing relief from the intense light of twin suns.

The wind quickened, snatching loose dirt from the field and tossing it into the air, where it began to spiral. Hazc shielded his face from the increasing squall as rain pounded toward him across the plain.

Lightning charged through the clouds above; thunder cracking as the lightning painted the field blue. Twin funnels burst free, smashing into the ground and winding toward the villa, shredding and hurling fistfuls of dirt like an impetuous child.

Well, he thought, *it might be in my best interest to see to those before they damage the house.* He scowled. *Asha will blame me for it if they do.*

He pulled his cloak over his face as he strolled through the squall. Turning parallel to the swirling funnels, Hazc sauntered across the uneven ground to reach the house, making his way up the paved walkway as swirling destruction bore down on the structure.

Hazc turned back toward the tornadoes, raising his brows at them. "Off you go."

They each stopped, as if in contemplation, then veered away in the opposite direction. There.

He turned back toward the house and hopped up the marble stairs. Pausing in front of the doors, he commanded the mud and water from his body, and they flew from the veranda into the garden behind him without touching a spot on the polished stone.

There was nothing in the wide universe that he detested more than filth and clutter. Not even his fat gnome body, which sat quite near the top of his loathsome list.

He looked up at the house. Warm plaster and stone composed the tastefully aged building's exterior. Charcoal-colored vines swathed its sides, bright green edging each pointed leaf. A pair of elegant, arched windows flanked the doors on the first story while similar windows and two half-circle verandas occupied the upper—all in perfect symmetry. Brown ceramic tile comprised the low-pitched roof. The veranda, upon which he stood, jutted from the front doors.

The ornate wooden doors swung open at his whim, and he strode in. Then the doors clicked shut behind him.

Within, glossy black marble covered the floor, a staircase curved out of sight toward the upper story in front of him, and two, arched doorways led into separate chambers opposite each other, one on the right and one on the left. Without hesitation, Hazc chose the right, which led into a private armory filled with relics from his long-time smithing hobby.

As he walked, he could see the villa, all its constituent parts, and every living thing in it. He saw where wind and rain lashed and trickled down the outer walls, rattling glass in the windows and trickling into new holes where there had been tile before the twisters had pulled them free. Tiles moved back into place, cracks disappeared.

His mind shoved through the thick marble, ran up the polished stairs, coursed through the ornate cushions adorning the furniture, and slipped through the floorboards beneath where Fargon, the housekeeper, kneaded bread in the kitchen.

Content that all was well, Hazc pulled a worn leather-bound book from an inner pocket. A glowing crescent moon hovering over the seat of a tall throne embossed its silver-lined cover.

Approaching a low cabinet beside a workbench, he pulled the handle, and the door silently swung open. Shelves of books and carefully rolled sheets of music waited within— some of their pages glowing with a soft, ethereal light. Moving some of the contents aside to make room, Hazc added the leather-bound book that he had brought with him to the collection.

Satisfied that the protections he had placed on the cabinet and its contents were undiminished, he selected another leather-bound book, identical to the one he had arrived with, from the shelf inside. Should his hunters reach their goal, at least there would be these to aid his allies. Not that there would be anything left for them to fight for should such a disaster occur.

Now that the more important matter of the two he had come to settle had been dealt with, he would go and see to Asha and her beasts.

Fargon walked through the entry toward the armory. His hoary head bowed, and his knobby hands hanging down at his waist. He hadn't noticed the gnome. That was why Hazc had elected to reside in this body most of his days—no one ever noticed him until it was too late, if ever. That, and he deserved punishment for his many misdeeds. No one else could punish him, so he punished himself.

The old man shuffled into the arched doorway and froze when he spotted the master of the house. His pale eyes widened, and his sagging lips trembled. Fargon whimpered and, with an animal cry of terror, fled back the way he had come. Hazc chuckled.

Well, Asha thinks the old clod takes fine care of the house.

The woman had sent for him when her beloved dragon's pregnancy had gone wrong. Jaidyn's travails and offspring should have been of little import, but something had drawn him here, something he could not ignore.

Asha had taken leave of her duties, north in the empire, to assist in the birthing months. The prime female had finally conceived after half a century of failed spawning. As a master of husbandry, Asha cared for the empress's finest stock. The prime's line was one of the only pure ones left, descended from beasts that the destroyer goddess, Vias, had created to carry her troops into battle so long ago. Of course, that was before their voices and wings had been taken …

Hazc had raised Asha from infancy, following her fool parents' deaths. Worlds later, he still didn't know why he elected to take her from ruined Digaria when the gods had abandoned it. He sometimes supposed that it had to do with the idea of freeing her from a war-torn life, but when he had such notions, he had to remind himself that chaos and war followed him wherever he went. By sentencing her to a life in his vicinity, he had not spared her that. Still, few things succeeded in entertaining Hazc, for his existence consisted of endless ennui, and to see Asha happy had become one of his few pleasures.

Rare dragons, like Jaidyn, were still full-blooded northern beasts and lived there. Asha had brought the dragoness south when her pregnancy had started showing signs of slowing down. At first, she had reported improvement, but now...

The dragon won't die until after I get there. But I suppose I should get moving.

He reached out and, grasping the air in front of him, tore time.

With Hazc's tiny, gnome fingers, he wrenched the entrance hall aside as though it were a hanging sheet and stepped into the rift. The voices filled his mind once more, and darkness enclosed him. He then opened another rift and stepped through, appearing in the birthing caves, five days' ride to the south.

Colossal stalactites, colored deep purple, hung from the cave's distant ceiling. Trickles of water dripped from their tips into puddles upon the shimmering ground. The luminous emerald veins scoring the dull gray stone of the cave floor provided the only light source in the bowels of the mountains.

Somewhere nearby, a stream carved its way through the rock. Its tinkle filled his ears, and cold humidity spattered his face and throat. He turned and approached the narrow rivulet.

As he attempted to ford, he slipped on a stone. He snatched ahold of a jagged outcropping as he fell toward the water, his bulk pulling on his little hand and driving the sharp stone into his palm. It pulsed and seared, and a small trickle of blood coursed down his wrist and into his sleeve.

Deplorable body.

Why did he subject himself to this form? He chuckled despite his pain. *Why? Because I deserve it.*

Hazc thrashed his stubby legs and, with a grunt, scrambled back ashore.

He looked down at his bleeding hand as it began to swell and yellow. Dragon venom. What were the odds that dragon saliva had ended up on that particular rock?

He scowled. A wound like this would have been the end of most. Not him, though. He had ways of cheating death.

"Hazc?" Asha's stern voice cut in from behind him and echoed in the vaulted ceiling as she called after him.

He looked up at her as she crossed the stream in an easy step to kneel down beside him. Even then, she towered over his gnomey body.

She was a lean, powerfully built woman, over seven feet tall, which was typical of a person of her breed. Of mixed races, Asha was one of the last of either—mersa and zermai.

Exquisite brown skin covered her warrior's body, and black hair reached to her waist in a tight braid. Eyes of bright jade lay between a pair of soft, doe-like ears that protruded from her fine locks, a trait that betrayed her mersa heritage. She wore woven leather armor colored bronze. Several daggers hung around her hips, and a slender katana rode her back—all tools necessary for her station as Mu'Zhai, or protector, of the empress.

"Hello, Asha, my dear," Hazc said blandly. He tucked the gruesome hand behind his back to conceal its increasing inflammation. He would suffer the venom a little longer, for he deserved it for his lack of attention.

Stars, but it is good to see her after so many weeks alone among mine insensible royals.

"I called for you weeks ago. What took you so long?" she asked.

Hazc raised a brow. "Perhaps you should be concerned by your messenger's rate of travel, not mine."

"Now that you're here, you can come and see Jaidyn for yourself. Hurry." Asha rose and brushed past him. She strode into a dark portal carved from the rock before them.

Hazc wandered after her at his leisure, focused on ignoring the sensation that his hand would burst at any moment. He followed the slick tunnel that sloped farther into the mountain.

The passage opened into a second cave. The stream fell from an opening high in the sheer wall of black rock opposite Hazc.

He frowned. The chamber should have been crawling with dragons this time of year.

"During Jaidyn's last episode, they fled to another set of caverns on the east mountain," Asha said in answer to his unasked question. "She came crashing out here yesterday, screaming and rolling around. She's fighting her own unborn. She's in that chamber now." Asha pointed to an opening beside the waterfall.

Hazc nodded.

She beckoned him on, gracefully navigating the slick ground to the far side, next to the lake, where she faded into another tunnel.

Hazc trotted after her and nearly knocked into the backs of her knees when she halted. However, he stopped in time to peer around them instead.

Jaidyn lay in a sprawling heap, entrenched in a rut in the cave floor. Her breaths came as labored rasps as she thrashed her muscular tail with pain.

Tough, black skin covered her thick body. Each of her four limbs ended in several pearlescent claws. Her massive head, resting on the end of a short, thick neck, lay in a pool of blood that oozed from her fanged mouth. Venom mingled with the crimson fluid, which made it steam and bubble. The metallic scent, mingled with the stench of bile and urine, permeated the chamber.

The beast groaned and tried to lift her head from the puddle, but the muscles in her neck barely twitched. Her bloodshot eyes rolled back, and she bellowed, her deafening screech rattling the cavern.

Hazc's knees buckled, and he toppled backward onto his rump.

Shaking his head, he could see the life leaving the dragoness and that healing her with the thing inside of her would be a fruitless task.

"Methinks it is much too late to save her. Perhaps we should cut the spawn from her to spare it," Hazc said, cradling his hand in his lap as he stared at its gross size, now nearly equal to his face.

Asha didn't turn toward him, still more concerned about the black monster. He could see that her slumped shoulders trembled with quiet sobs. She loved the creature.

Jaidyn continued to writhe and scream as the bulge within her stomach thrust violently outward, all of the skin stretching taut around it until it took on a recognizable shape.

A foot. A tiny foot.

But not a dragon's foot ...

Hazc narrowed his eyes, and his hand ceased to bother him for a moment.

"Ash—"

"I see it!"

Jaidyn roared once more, the bone-shaking sound rattling the ceiling's stalactites. Several fell and hit the poor beast.

Asha stumbled back, almost stepping on Hazc.

A great tearing sound interrupted the last echoes of the roar and, from between the dragoness's rear legs, a gory mass of limbs tumbled heavily to the cave floor.

Asha edged forward, and Hazc craned his neck to see around her.

"Hazc," Asha whispered, tears flowing down her brown cheeks.

Something writhed within the shredded womb, struggling to free itself. Clawing its way from the remains, a bloody form scrambled onto the rocks with a low hiss. Its two arms and legs came first. Five fingers. Five toes. A humanoid body of flesh.

The small creature inspected Hazc with almond-shaped eyes of deep emerald, filled with primal hunger. They had diamond-shaped pupils, like a dragon's. Hair hung around its face and neck to their shoulders. He could have discerned its color had it not been so covered in blood. Its skin was black as pitch, like its mother's, and a fleshy tail snaked out behind it.

It crouched down and cocked its head, regarding him intently, hungrily. Hazc simply stared back, withholding a smile.

"It is a girl."

Asha started as the creature lunged at him. She snatched the newborn's arms and wrenched her backward. The child snarled and snapped.

They performed an awkward dance, one snapping and one dodging, until Asha managed to force the dragon-child to the floor. The little creature uttered another low growl as she struggled to throw Asha off.

Hazc watched them for a moment. The creature couldn't have touched him against his will, anyway.

He left Asha to her wrangling and made his way Jaidyn's head. Although her eyes were mostly closed against the pain, he could see an emerald glow between her lids. The old dragoness's eyes had always been amber. How had Asha failed to mention the change to him? Furthermore, how had he not noticed until now?

He sensed a familiar presence, one that he had last encountered the night that King Yulari shackled Vias the Destroyer seven millennia ago.

Hazc approached the tattered womb, nudging a heavy fold of flesh aside with one of his booted feet. Green stained the tissue there, as well.

Embedded in the wall of the womb was a fist-sized emerald with many octagonal faces, each with a thin scratch through its center. With both hands, he could barely contain it as he pulled it free from the slimy tissue. Using his cloak to wipe it clean, he turned back to Asha.

The child lay on the cave floor, her eyes closed. Sweat streamed down Asha's face from her struggle with the unruly newborn. She sat on the dragon princess with her eyes on the object Hazc held.

"What's that?" she asked.

Hazc hoisted the ancient talisman aloft so that she could see it better. Veins of green covered his hand and snaked down his wrist and arm from where he touched it.

He smiled at the heinous thing that had brought him all this way, masking the sorrow and hatred it stirred in his heart from Asha's sight.

"The cause of all this racket," he said.

CHAPTER ONE

BHEVIR,
SOUTHERN YENDU

Fading moonlight shimmered through scattered boughs of lofty cedars to sprinkle the forest floor. The air hummed with glowing insects that hovered over a glassy pond, suspended like the invisible stars above the needled canopy.

Luminescent creatures surrounded a raft constructed of thick twigs and sap. Its sides curved up to cup a sixteen-year-old girl who sat cross-legged, engrossed in a leather-bound book that filled her lap. The light from the bugs shimmered over her lush auburn tresses where they hung around her lovely face. A blanket lay in a rumpled heap around her middle, forgotten. The warm glow of a hooded lantern illuminated the book's large pages as she rapidly flicked her intelligent eyes—golden, like the greater of the two suns—over the text.

Salmaara paused and rubbed her eyes, wondering how long she had been reading. She gazed through the thick wood around her pond into a nearby break.

As the first lavender light of dawn crept over the dark grass and across the narrow trunks and mossy forest floor, she gasped and thumped the book shut. Snatching the gnarled branch that lay beside her in the twig-raft, she rowed to shore.

There, she extinguished the lantern with a short gust of breath then scrambled from the raft. In her haste, she knocked the lantern sideways with a foot, and it rolled onto the light blanket of needle-like leaves on the forest floor.

Snatching the lantern back up, she hugged the book to her chest and sprinted through the dark foliage toward home until she broke from the trees, panting.

Her father, Illun, would not be pleased she had read another night away. *We have much to do today, and I've had no rest.* But Salmaara could never find a good stopping place. She needed the books' wondrous tales like she needed the light of the suns. She needed their haunted castles and insane lords, elegant ladies and bright festivals. They filled her like nothing else could.

She bit her lip as she gazed ahead.

Where the forest ended, a whitewashed fence began. It encompassed a weathered two-story house and bisected the property at the house's center into separate front and back yards. Blue paint peeled from the house's shingle-covered sides, and a white veranda encircled its front.

The barren backyard was far too dangerous to traverse, so she followed the fence around until she reached the front gate. She slipped in and softly pulled it closed behind her. Then she dashed up the flagstone path and onto the veranda. Its warped boards squeaked.

Squeezing her eyes shut, she froze and shook her head. When her father didn't burst through the heavy front door, she edged up to it and peered in through the square pane of glass set into it.

Nothing moved within.

Setting a slender hand on the knob, she twisted it, and the door glided halfway open. She squeezed through the crack and into the humble entrance hall.

The familiar scent of clay from the studio to her right struck her immediately. The entire house smelled of it. There was no smell she loved so much as the damp earth and pungent minerals Illun used for glazes.

She swiveled the knob so that the latch wouldn't click as she closed the door behind her. Dancing on tiptoes over the wooden floor, she crept past the steep staircase, and down the hall to a narrow door halfway down the corridor.

Inching the door open, she paused for a moment, straining her ears to detect any sign of movement.

Silence.

When she slipped through and down the bare stairs that descended into her father's library, she wiped a trembling hand across her brow.

The chamber was long and rectangular. Dilapidated bookcases crowded with old volumes covered its walls, and a simple blue rug adorned the cold, wood floor in the room's center.

Salmaara moved forward in the dark chamber, shuffling her feet, feeling for the edge of the rug in the dim light. She then slid the heavy book back into place on its shelf with reverence and darted back to the stairs.

In a moment, she was on the second floor and in her bedroom. An exhausted haze covered her vision as she peeled her muddy frock off, folded it, and then set it on a tall chest of drawers. Crawling into the inviting white covers that awaited her, she closed her eyes.

Salmaara awoke a short time later, her fluffy down blanket resting against her chin as she traced the ceiling beams with her golden eyes, her auburn curls arrayed in a halo about her face.

She sighed and squinted at the bright sunlight pouring into the round window beside her bed and sat up. Her father would already have eaten breakfast and be at his wheel, no doubt.

Father. Illun wasn't really her father. He was the lucky person who had extracted Salmaara from a river when she was five years old, or so he said, as often as occasion permitted. But she'd saved him, he insisted.

Salmaara remembered nothing of her life before the river. But, she had always had a feeling that her body in the water had not been an accident. Lately, she was having a hard time ignoring the questions no one seemed able, or willing, to answer. *Who am I? Who are my real parents? Where do they live? How did I end up in that river? Did they ever search for me?*

As she did on more mornings than not, she felt the urge to get up and leave Bhevir behind to search for the answers to her questions.

She glanced over at the pack she kept by her dresser. Every time she thought she would pick it up and walk through that door in search of her family, she just left it there. She couldn't leave her father. It would break him.

Shoving the heavy blanket from her legs, she swiveled and placed her feet upon the smooth floor as she rubbed the sleep from her eyes. Taking to her feet, she made the bed and smoothed the wrinkles from the soft coverlet.

She glanced at her reflection in the mirror as she passed to ensure she was presentable. People told her she was beautiful, but Salmaara couldn't help but notice that her fair skin, red hair, and eyes as golden as one of the suns were nothing like everyone else's exquisite dark features. That observation always led to the same question: *Does everyone look like me where I come from? I look so different.*

She hauled a clay-spattered smock from her closet, and over her head.

Tying the sash, she moved to the mirror and re-braided her thick hair where it had come loose. She made sure to grab a green sunshat as she walked out the door.

Salmaara wandered down the hall to the staircase, where she rode the banister to the bottom, hopped off, and skidded across the floor.

She hung her sunshat on a peg by the door, saying, "Father, I'm up."

"In here," Illun called out as she entered the tiled studio.

Clay caked every inch of its floor, walls, and long tables. She had no idea what color they had originally been, as only layers of gray, brown, red, and black splatters were visible. She loved it.

In the midst of the studio sat a suns-browned man of medium build, clad in a rough tunic and apron, and as covered in clay as the room around him. He had chestnut hair flecked with gray and a stubbly hint of a beard on his strong chin and neck. He always wore a warm smile, but his cobalt eyes harbored a chronic tinge of melancholy. With his callused hands, he formed marbled black and red clay into a graceful vase upon the potter's wheel, grating gently as it rotated between his knees.

She inhaled the humid scent of clay as she crossed the room to watch him from behind, ever amazed at how effortless he made his craft appear.

Many generations of Illun's family had enjoyed the wheel, each passing the art to their children. While Salmaara was proud of her own work, the intricate vases, bowls, plates, and other things that her father created revealed him a master.

Each morning before they went out to face the suns and toil in the shop where he sold his pottery in Bhevir, Illun and his daughter created their wares side by side.

Salmaara wedged a ball of red clay on a plank. She turned the clay over and over then thrust the heels of her hands into it until satisfied it was free of air pockets. Carrying it to a second wheel at Illun's side, she slammed the clay upon the wheel's center so that it would stick. Fetching a small bucket of water and soaking her hands, she sat down and pumped a pedal with her foot that spun the wheel between her knees.

"Did you sleep well, Maara? You look weary," Illun said, gazing over at her. His little smile wavered, as when he was concerned.

"Yes, quite well," she replied, cupping her hands around her clay. She forced it upward into a cone and eased it back down into a flattened cylinder with her thumbs.

She swallowed. She needed to discipline herself to come in earlier. That would help.

"You're sure?" he pressed as he dipped his hands into his own bowl of water. Easing his fingers back around the evolving vase, he moved one hand outside and the other in, caressing it gently. It yielded to his experienced touch, growing taller and more slender.

Does he know I was gone all night? I hope he's not worried. What is he thinking?

As she pondered the questions, Salmaara could suddenly feel him, or some sort of aura that she knew was him. She was usually aware of it when her father was nearby and had never thought it out of the ordinary. It was soft yet cool, reminding her of silky clay waiting to be molded.

With her clay cupped in her hands on the wheel in front of her, she wondered idly what might happen if she touched the clay sensation that told her that Illun was there—well, if she could touch it. It was not a visible thing, but something she felt, something that was simply there as surely as the potter sat at his wheel.

Curious, she reached for the cool, soft sensation that was her father and brushed it with imaginary fingers. As she did so, Illun's voice sounded although he had not spoken aloud.

"She has circles under her eyes. I thought I heard her sneak in this morning.

She's sleeping in later some days, too. Well, she's coming of age ... Could it be a boy? That Kelaren lad has been making eyes at her more and more lately."

Salmaara's breath caught in her throat, and color filled her cheeks.

When she released the clay that was her father, she also let go of the real clay that rested in her hands, stomping on her pedal. The clay, which she had just raised into a tall cylinder, twisted wildly and part of it tore away from the rest, and tumbled from the wheel, hitting floor with a wet splat.

Illun stopped his wheel and turned to her. "What?"

"Um ... Nothing." Her cheeks flamed. *He thinks I'm sneaking out to see a boy? He ... he thinks ... He didn't say ... He thought ...*

"You want to go ahead without me? I'll catch up," she said, shaken. She stared at the heap of clay and stopped her wheel.

Illun narrowed his eyes. "If you wish it."

He remained, looking over at her, waiting for her to explain.

She opened her mouth then closed it. Her face must have been the color of a ruddy sunset.

An uncomfortable moment passed. With a soft sigh, the potter wiped his hands on his apron.

Salmaara scratched an itch on her forehead, forgetting that clay covered her fingers.

Illun stood without another word and strode to one of the counters, where he fetched a square plank of wood then returned to his stool. He deftly slipped the wood beneath his completed vase and removed it from the wheel with experienced ease. He set it on a rack by the window.

Tense silence hung between them as they scraped the muddy wheels with blades then thick sponges.

Illun glanced back at her one more time and shook his head. "We'll talk about this further when we get home, my little miss," he said quietly. Dropping the loop of his soiled apron on a rounded peg nailed into the studio wall, he hesitated once more in the doorway, and, when she didn't say anything, strode from sight. Heavy thumps marked his ascension of the stairs.

Salmaara went to the kitchen at the back of the first story and set a small fire in the oven. Over the flames, she fried an egg and, once done, added a handful of spiced olives to her plate. Cooking completed, she sat on a three-legged stool, alone and unsettled.

Salmaara had made the kitchen her pride. She always found a deep satisfaction in making it shine and couldn't stand the thought of her father having to keep the house clean on top of everything he already had to do. The floors and counters sparkled in the sunlight that streamed through a window, an astonishing contrast to the splotched pottery studio.

She finished her food then glided across the smooth floor, her eyes riveted on the dark reflection she made in its well-loved planks. Reaching the sink, she rinsed her dishes and pan then crouched down and opened a cabinet near the sink, where she stored a hefty sack of feed and a few ears of corn.

He did not say those things aloud. I know it! But I heard them clearly, perfectly. Salmaara's books told of a race that spoke only with their thoughts. *But I'm not one of them. Perhaps it's getting to me ... and the lack of sleep.*

A boy, indeed! And what he noted about "that Kelaren boy ..." Her cheeks flamed at the thought. She had not noticed any such attention.

She hefted the sack from the cabinet and craned her neck to see out the window.

The decrepit llama outside had been her grandmother's, Illun had told her. Llamas were rare beasts the world over, so how one had come into his mother's possession, the potter didn't know.

Most of the time, the nameless beast had been given full run of the barren paddock behind the house, but more and more often, they had to tether it. It usually lurked in the thick bushes against the house's walls—the only vegetation foul enough to survive the beast's appetite. It waited to ambush the next unfortunate soul who bore the sustenance to sustain its insatiable villainy.

Salmaara stood by the window and poured a portion of feed into a badly dented pail. She and Illun used to have a feeding trough attached to the kitchen window, but after several incidents, her father had removed it and barred the window.

Her father kept the llama because he didn't know what to do with it. More often than not, he was too busy to so much as look at it, let alone care for it. So, since Salmaara loved animals, she had taken it upon herself to see to its care.

She often wondered if giving it a name would lessen its malice, but nothing she had ever thought of seemed to fit, so nameless it remained.

She was uncertain why it hadn't already died. Salmaara knew llamas didn't typically survive through multiple generations of owners. This one had been through three at least, according to her grandmother.

Her heart fluttered at the thought of opening the back door. Every time she thought she had a plan, the mad creature thwarted her, its ratty head lashing out of nowhere, like a great snake, impossible to charm.

Leaning against the windowsill, she scanned the thinning shrubs for a sign of heaving beige.

Sucking in a steadying breath, she set the bucket beside the door. She unfastened the first of three latches and flinched at its metallic *snap*. The second and third locks followed before she carefully set her hand, white-knuckled and quaking, on the weathered silver knob. She took a long, deep breath, and cracked the door open.

Nothing.

Exhaling, she leaned over to push the bucket out the thin opening, and …

The llama's fuzzy maw, bearing crooked, yellow teeth, launched through the small opening.

Salmaara, her face exactly at the height of its bulging eyes, shrieked and toppled backward, flying with the bucket through the air. The feed cascaded over the shining kitchen floor in a wave.

The llama unleashed a shrill bray of triumph.

Salmaara's head slammed into the cabinet from which she'd removed the food. Black spots dotted her vision as the skeletal llama, scrambling on twig legs, rampaged around the kitchen. It tore the cupboards open, strewing their contents on the floor. Pots crashed, dishes shattered. It brayed wildly until it tripped on its fallen caretaker and toppled head-long into an open cabinet, breaking its door into splinters. Then the llama collapsed, having rendered itself unconscious.

Salmaara groaned. Her head throbbed, and a sizable bump was already forming on the back of her skull.

The llama lay before her, motionless, its thick tongue jutting from slimy lips like salami.

"Oh, I hope you're not hurt, you mad thing," she whispered.

Rubbing her arms, she stood and reached for its head to check for injury. When it twitched and growled softly, she withdrew her hand and gingerly took ahold of the llama's two front legs. With a grunt, Salmaara dragged it to the open door and laid it on the stone step outside. The mangy heap moved with regular breathing but still appeared insensible.

Inside, she hastily swept up the feed then carried the bucket back outside, setting it beside the llama.

Closing her eyes, she took a deep breath. The room swayed back and forth, and she had to blink to regain her bearings.

She shut the door quietly, and locked it quickly for fear that the fainted savage might rouse.

After putting the kitchen back together, she headed into the entry, where her father's satchel no longer hung on the hook beside the door.

I know I heard him speak in my mind. I ... connected to him ... somehow. By touching that feeling.

Slipping her feet into cloth sandals, she collected her green sunshat from the hook, opened the front door, and stepped out onto the white veranda.

From the dirt road, she gazed downhill to where Bhevir waited, cradled in the grassy hills. It was the only settlement in view.

Most of the older townspeople had come from outside, fleeing violence and destruction. Whenever she had pried, they either forbade her to ask more or quickly changed the subject. After that, those she had questioned avoided her and whispered together when they thought she couldn't see, shaking their heads and eyeing her darkly. Besides them, only a handful of smugglers ever moved in and out of Bhevir, and they never spoke of the outside world, if she could get them to talk at all.

The blue sky held scarcely any clouds. Two suns, the golden one larger than one tinged with red, nestled near one another, shining intensely on her as she meandered down the path toward town. The salty scent of the sea wafted on the breeze from the south, the water itself hidden by the hills. And an array of wild blossoms in violet, white, and yellow stood out from the glossy black grass that surrounded her as she made her way nearer the dense collection of buildings down the hill.

A white rose lay in the grass to the side of the road, glowing in the sunlight. She looked around for rose bushes but saw none.

She scooped the flower up with a smile. It was too sad to leave it there to wither with no one to see it— a perfect bloom unappreciated.

So, she tucked it into her hair, carefully replaced her sunshat, and picked up her pace, hoping not to leave everything left to do for the wedding to her father.

Although isolated, Bhevir was a good-sized town. The stone-paved streets, filled with people going about their business, stretched out before her, encircled by the outlying homes that crawled up the surrounding hills. The smell of freshly baked goods and exotic spices smuggled from somewhere west of Bhevir joined the tang of the sea in the morning air.

The fairer-skinned outlanders who survived the journey to bring their spices covered themselves from head to foot with tunics, gloves, pants, and boots with curved toes. They hid eyes so dark that it was impossible to tell their color beneath wide-brimmed hats.

Salmaara marveled at them every time they came, as most in Bhevir had skin as dark as the good soil they lived on. But the fairer outlanders had complexions closer to Salmaara's.

No one in Bhevir seemed to know where they came from. Approaching them had produced wry smiles and head shakes, and a search of her books didn't reveal their secrets, either.

Salmaara stepped from the dirt path and onto a cobblestone street, where buildings of brick, of plaster, and of wood engulfed her as she strolled toward the heart of the town. No two were alike, none exceeded five stories, and most were new.

People filled the broad street, going about their business. Salmaara waved to or greeted several as she passed them.

A round plaza waited at the town center, paved in deep green marble, with white stone benches surrounding an immense and intricate fountain.

The dry fountain always made Salmaara a little sad, for none remained who knew how to make the water flow.

Behind the fountain lay the ruins of what had once been a building said to have been of unmatched grandeur. Seven towers had circum-scribed it, but all that remained of them now was a single marble ring set into the ground, directly behind the fountain. The townspeople had found the stone foundations of the building and towers immovable, so they eventually built over them where they could.

The beautiful plaza had continued to decay throughout her young life. Although the townspeople scrubbed and polished the marble, the once ornate mosaics made of glass, tile, and inlaid precious stones on the fountain's exterior crumbled more with every passing season. Still, on the mural surrounding the base of the fountain, she could discern the tall men and women in long, colorful robes, each holding a book in one hand and a small ornamented pen in the other. The precious stones that had adorned the covers of the books were long gone. She often wondered what could have been written in them.

No one in Bhevir, except her father, owned books, and Illun had always told her that she had to keep them a secret. The books were pre-cious, he said. And dangerous. She never mentioned them to anyone.

Salmaara entered the plaza that had wooden poles erected in a circle around the benches and fountain, topped with pale ribbons of blue, white, and violet holding bright flowers. Enough long tables had been set out to accommodate most of the townspeople. Groups of men and boys still carried in the necessary benches and chairs.

Salmaara and her father had worked for two months in preparation for Torone's—the governor's son—wedding to Rianne, the oldest of six born to Relaro, Bhevir's physician and Salmaara's best friend. Not only had Salmaara and Illun made all of the cookware, plates, cups, and the ceremonial vessel, but they had also made many vases for every flower Rianne insisted she needed.

As Salmaara strode across the plaza, someone called out to her.

Turning, Salmaara spotted Rianne running toward her, waving an arm.

"Good morning, Maara."

Although five years older than Salmaara, Rianne stood two heads shorter. She was a beautiful girl, with the earthy dark skin characteristic of someone born and raised in Southern Yendu. She wore a tunic and pants similar to Salmaara's, but in blue instead of green and sleeveless. Her brown hair, she wore in a loose braid, with no hat.

Upon reaching Salmaara, she spoke in a rush. "I saw your father pass by and wondered where you might be. Is the train ready? With you as my train-bearer, at least that will be perfect. You're good luck, after all. Everyone knows that."

Salmaara smiled. "Of course it is—every button. My father and I finished the last of the vases and the ceremonial vessel yesterday. How is everything else coming?"

Rianne heaved a great sigh. "You know people—they can't do anything right. They think pink is blue and up is down. They even got the wrong wine, but I think they have it now. Ah, but somehow we have gotten something together. It'll have to do." The bride-to-be looked around nervously. "They'll be ready by the day after tomorrow, don't you think?"

"I think everything will be just as you've hoped and better."

"Because you said it, I believe it. Maara." She dropped her voice to a hushed whisper and stepped closer. "They've been staring at you since you got here."

"Who?"

Rianne nodded over Salmaara's shoulder, trying to hide a devious smile.

Salmaara turned her head just enough to see five boys, all her age except two, standing across the plaza. They alternated between staring at the girls and ribbing each other. They laughed and pushed one boy forward—Rianne's younger brother, Hend Kelaren. He was sixteen, tall and muscular, and shining with sweat from carrying furniture around all morning. Hend was also the one whom her father had noticed was "making eyes" at her lately.

He smoothed his dark hair back as he made his way toward them.

Cheeks flaming, Salmaara pulled her sunshat down so the brim covered her eyes. Mortification taking root, the potter's daughter prepared to flee. "I'd best get to the shop. Father and I have much to do today."

Rianne pursed her lips over Salmaara's shoulder, and her brother froze.

"Shameless. Absolutely shameless, aren't they?" she said loudly so he would hear. "He doesn't care if his own sister is watching!"

Hend resumed his approach and stopped in front of them.

Rianne folded her arms under her breasts, and Salmaara looked up at him, hoping the sunshat covered the flaming color her face must have been.

Hend shouldered Rianne aside. "Chirno, Maara. Want to dance with—"

Rianne smacked his arm. "It's not time to dance! It's time to finish setting up the chairs."

The handsome boy rolled his eyes at his sister then turned his dark eyes to Salmaara. "At the party after the wedding?"

"If you'd like," Salmaara said quickly.

Hend lifted the brim of her hat so that their eyes met. He cocked his head with a charming smile. "Promise?"

Rianne hit his arm again. "Leave her alone, Hend!"

Salmaara placed her hands on her hips, trying to ignore her pounding heart and the heat blossoming in her face. "It's quite all right. I'll dance with him. I said I would, didn't I? Even if he is your brother."

Hend grinned and turned away, apparently satisfied.

Salmaara watched him retreat and rejoin his friends. The others were all gleeful smiles as they patted him on the shoulders.

Salmaara pulled the hat brim back down, trying not to think of how he had looked at her.

He only did it because his friends told him he had to. That's all … But then there's father's observation. Hend couldn't possibly … It took great restraint not to finish the thought.

Rianne twisted her lips sourly. "Such a showoff. You don't have to dance with him if you don't feel like it."

Salmaara cleared her throat. "Thanks, Rianne. I'll see you later."

The bride-to-be nodded as Salmaara made haste from the square.

Brightly glazed pots, cups, and vases filled the bowed front window of her father's shop at the end of a narrow street stemming from the fountain plaza. She mounted the stone steps that led to the double wooden front doors and opened them. A small bell tinkled above as she walked in and removed her sunshat.

Mined from nearby, pale gray stones floored the shop, shelves of bright wares for kitchens and decorations lined the room, and a long counter of faded, black oak occupied the back wall. A skinny passage behind it led to the back of the shop where Illun kept the kilns, his commissioned projects, and did repairs. The scent of clay and newly fired wares hung heavy in the air.

"There you are. I was beginning to worry you'd lost yourself," Illun said jovially as he stepped from behind the counter to embrace her.

"This is pretty," he said, brushing the rose where it perched in her auburn curls with his fingertips. None of his earlier worry marred his clay-smeared face.

"Yes. It made me sad to think that it should wither in the suns with none to enjoy its beauty."

"I'm glad you saw it," he said with a warm chuckle. He examined the bloom then shifted his attention to one of her arms that had started darkening with bruises. His smile dimmed. "Did it get in?"

"Yes, but only for a moment. Everything is fine. Well, except for a cabinet door. We'll need a new panel." Salmaara pulled her sleeve down to cover the darkening bruises.

He shook his head slowly. "I've loaded the cart. Now we just need to get it all to the plaza."

She had known he wouldn't spare any more words for the poor llama.

The potter's daughter made her way behind the counter to stand beside Illun. "Father?" she said quietly.

"Hm …?"

"I awoke this morning thinking about the family of my birth," Salmaara began.

"Did you?" Illun was behind the counter with a checklist balanced on one of his sinewy arms. He stood by a wheeled cart of gleaming new wares, fresh from the kilns: a stack of triangular plates with royal blue accents, mugs with two shades of red glaze, and several oval serving platters in sea green, all overlaid with rich geometric patterns. Illun counted the items with the end of his charcoal-stick.

Salmaara knew her father didn't like to talk about the day he had found her or about her lost family. She worried that perhaps it made him think she loved him less, which could never be true.

"I wonder … How did I end up in the river? Do they even care that I'm gone?"

"We've talked of this so many times, Maara," he replied. "Bhevir is a safe place. You don't remember what happened where you came from. That's a blessing most of us here can't enjoy." Illun led her into the back room, where four kilns, two set into a wall and two dug into the ground, filled the chamber.

"You once told me that I drew a picture of someone I knew, didn't you?"

With a deep breath, he turned toward her. "Not long after I pulled you from the water, you drew a picture and told me it was *the wicked man.*"

At that, Illun opened the back door that led to a small courtyard cluttered with stacks of mineral barrels and clays. A cart, as long and wide as Salmaara was tall, stood in the center, loaded with crates.

Why can't I stop thinking about my family lately? It's been getting harder and harder. She knew the melancholy would take Illun if she pressed much more, and she couldn't stand to see anyone upset, but she *had* to know.

"The *wicked little man,* didn't you say?"

Illun didn't turn. "Yes."

"Could you show it to me when we get home?"

"If you wish it." Illun fell silent then, making it clear the topic had been exhausted.

"Thank you, Father." She gave him a kiss on the cheek then, with effort, she turned to her work.

She took a cart handle in each hand. "Is this everything?"

"It is. Can you manage?"

"Yes."

Salmaara pulled the cart to a gate that connected the yard to an alley and returned to the road. Reentering the plaza, she pulled the cart to its center and looked through the crates. One held dark yellow- and green-glazed plates and goblets, another floating candle platters, while others held cream vases.

Several women approached on the other side of the nearest table.

"Why, good morning, Maara," said the first of them, the groom's aunt, a thin, middle-aged woman with straight black hair. She wore a long, gray dress embroidered with silver down the sleeves.

As Salmaara pulled a long, cream vessel decorated with both geometric and organic designs from a crate, the woman made a delighted sound. "Oh, it's beautiful!"

Salmaara smiled. "I hope Rianne will like them."

"May I help you set them?"

Salmaara nodded and carefully stacked two of the floating candle platters in the woman's outstretched arms.

One of the other women whispered behind her hand to the others, "We're just fortunate Miss Maara is here. She's good luck for the wedding."

The other ladies nodded in agreement, despite the discomfort Salmaara could feel coming from most of them.

She knew they liked to gossip about her fair skin, red hair, strange questions, and even stranger luck. Word had once reached her ears that she had been accused of being some sort of spy. For whom and to what end, no one had bothered to say.

Salmaara offered a smile, hoping to divert their attention from the growing red spots on her cheeks.

For as long as she could remember, Salmaara had been called "lucky." She loved solving problems and seeing people happy because of it. Turbulent relationships, a well poisoning—anything she set her mind to resulted in a working solution one way or another.

The only thing Salmaara couldn't seem to solve was where she had come from.

I should be content. I have a father who loves me, friends, a home, clothes to protect me from the suns, enough to eat. The books ...

And people need me here. I can't just go gallivanting off who knows where. What if I did go and find my family, and they don't want me? What if they aren't even alive? What would it have all been for? I should just stay ...

She thought the same often, and every time she did, something stirred within her heart. Something that told her she was not meant to be here in Bhevir, something that tugged at her no matter how hard she tried to ignore it.

But, where else would I be? Everyone speaks of the outside world as a curse, if at all. Those who go never return, and any newcomers say as much, as if lightning might strike them if they loosened their tongues. Everyone, even Father, says to be grateful that I don't remember my life before Bhevir. Perhaps I should be.

She walked among the long table, setting platters in place.

A little way across the plaza, Hend and his friends hauled barrels marked with the sign of Southern Yendu's best vineyard into the plaza, stacking them behind the platform. Rianne was yelling something at them.

Behind Salmaara, the ladies added the candle platters to the tables and placed the vases in a wide circle.

Salmaara loved to be in the fountain plaza at Bhevir's heart. It made her feel as though she had fallen into one of the books.

They spoke of a fantastical world ruled by a mad but benevolent god, King Yulari. In that world, they paved public areas with fine stones and had fountains that threw water into the air in elaborate patterns. A fountain was an example of the least of their technological marvels.

The books described towers of colored glass so tall that they soared above the clouds, strange wagons that didn't require anyone to pull them, and people living for hundreds of years. Best of all, they roamed free! They didn't have to stay in one place, afraid for their lives if they went beyond their borders or said a wrong word. They weren't confined. They could do and be whatever they wanted.

By the time she finished setting one of the tables to present to the bride, the suns hovered low in the late afternoon sky.

"No, no! These feathers are not acceptable. They must be longer. Where did you get these?" Rianne snapped at the town's seamstress, standing one table over from Salmaara.

The elderly woman, clad in a violet linen dress, with her thinning silver hair tied in a tail at the nape of her neck, frowned and turned the white veil over in her hands. "I'll try to find some more tomorrow—"

"Please do."

Rianne then turned to Salmaara and the table she had finished setting. She clapped her hands once. "Oh, Maara, it's perfect! The colors, the shapes, oh … everything. Everyone is going to love them." With that, Rianne glided off toward the platform.

Salmaara smiled after her. *She'll be all right.*

Once she returned everything she had brought with her to the cart, Salmaara made her way back to the shop.

Upon entering, she took a duster in hand. Salmaara loved making it tidy and clean.

Customers came in a steady flow. Some came seeking pots or plates, others came with complaints of broken mugs or vases. Some came to her for assistance, while others entrusted their needs to Illun's masterful hands.

As evening shadows stretched through the front window toward Salmaara's feet, her father joined her. She had just finished scrubbing the counters.

He smiled and rested an encompassing arm around her shoulders. "I got some vichuberries this afternoon when I went out. I thought we'd make a pie." He glanced at the small, deep orange fruits peeking from the bulky bag held in his free hand.

"I'm definitely ready." She slipped from his embrace and hung the rag on a hook.

"Let's go, then," Illun said, opening the shop door.

Salmaara went through it first, looking forward to pie and the picture.

CHAPTER TWO

BHEVIR,
SOUTHERN YENDU

After darkness had fallen, the potter and his daughter sat in their kitchen. The sweet scent of vichuberry pie filled the air, and Salmaara was aware of spiteful llama eyes at the barred kitchen window, envious of the pie.

Salmaara stood and drew the curtains together, which elicited a protesting snort from the beast. She didn't want it to hurt itself on the window bars again, and vichuberry would hurt its stomach. She would sneak it some corn once Illun had gone to bed.

She bent over to gaze at the pie in the rounded stone oven. "It's ready to eat, I think." She fetched a cloth from a nearby drawer.

Heat billowed into her face as she pulled the steaming pie from the oven and set it on the counter. Having done so, she tossed a fistful of green powder into the oven, which extinguished the fire.

A brining barrel still full of the fluid that they had soaked their supper in sat beside the pie. Salmaara took its handles, intending to take it outside and dump it.

"Now," Illun spoke from behind her, "don't think I've forgotten about this morning. You've been up all night at something. I see it in your health. You know you can tell me anything. I'll be more inclined to punish you for lying than for any other offense you may commit. Out with it."

Salmaara flushed, her heart swelling in her throat, as she set the brining barrel down. "I … I spent the night in the woods with your books over the past several months."

Illun's somber face split into a pleasant, relieved grin, and he laughed shortly. "Have you?"

Salmaara's cheeks burned anew. "Yes. I can't do without The Blue King Yulari and his Vias. There is also the evil Empress Velanoma Zamazcus who took over the whole world singlehandedly and rules with an iron fist!" She brought her fist down on her palm. "But I can't seem to find the ending anywhere."

"Ending? Perhaps someone can stand against the empress." Illun sighed. "You know, my grandfather entrusted those books to my care. They're original manuscripts from the lost library of Seash the Sorcerer himself. He sheltered my grandfather in his many travels over one hundred years ago. Those books were mostly written by the hands of those to whom they are about. Or, at least people very close to them."

Salmaara's eyes widened. "I knew it couldn't all be fantasy. Those people, the gods, the haunted castle, the shining city Kalitoomba? The Mauviasen empress? How much is true?" she asked breathlessly, turning to face him.

Illun tilted his chair back on two legs and rocked it slowly. "All of it, as far as I know." His lips tightened. "The times you read of in the books were gone well before I was born, though. During my time, the world has become more dark, more dangerous. The empress continues to destroy everything that came before—light, and knowledge, and freedom—cloaking the world in the cruelty that fills her homeland. It is she you can thank for making books illegal."

The melancholy rose in his keen eyes, and his little smile wavered, almost vanishing. "Everyone in Bhevir fled her violence, seeking some sort of peace. Velanoma's rebel daughter makes war with her, but the empress controls most everywhere these days."

He eased his chair back down. "The world my father knew was magnificent. The people lived with their gods. When the merciless empress threw King Yulari from his tower and seized power, everything began to decay. It still decays. Technology stamped out, condemned as corruption by the empire. And the great city Kalitoomba, jewel of our history, lies rotting and forsaken. In time, the empress will erase it altogether."

Salmaara's heart faltered. "Yulari Lordian is dead? But he can't die. In the books, he just disappeared. No, he's not dead. He is a god!"

Illun shrugged and heaved himself to his feet, stretching his arms over his head. Then he took the brining barrel. "My father and grandfather were there. They lived near Castle Errasitka, the king's home. On that dreadful morning when sunslight and silence fell on Kalitoomba after a long battle, they saw him. He lay in the castle's grand courtyard, at the foot of his tower, on what we now call the forbidden flag, then known as *Inshá Dorén*.

"As they sought something to cover him, they saw that all the flags of Yulari's kingdom that regularly flew from the castle's turrets had been cast to the ground. They looked up to see what could have felled them. Black and emerald flags flew in place of the fallen flags, harbingers of the storm that was coming. Ensign of the Destroyer, *Maliem Esculis*," he said darkly.

"When they looked again, the king was gone. All that remained was his outline, drawn with his own crimson life force, on the white of the largest flag that once flew atop *Dail Scha*, that mightiest tower."

He's not dead. He can't be.

Salmaara could see a deeper grief in Illun's eyes than she had ever seen before.

Illun carried the barrel to the front yard, where he threw the salty water into the road. Meanwhile, Salmaara cut into the pie and served two slices on a pair of cobalt ceramic plates. After several moments, Illun retuned without the barrel.

"I dug this out for you." Illun reached into his pocket and retrieved a yellowed paper folded many times over. He extended it toward her.

"Oh, the drawing! I'd almost forgotten." She accepted the paper and unfolded it. It was rudely sketched in charcoal, the scribble resembling a gnome's face.

Dull brown eyes squinted at Salmaara; she could see nothing else. Cold displeasure filled them. His thin, white lips curled upward as he gripped her by the shoulders. She lay on her back as he stood above her. He was unnaturally strong for a two-foot gnome.

Why wouldn't he let her up?

She knew what he was, but she couldn't remember …

Rope bit into the tender flesh of her wrists. She barely had time to gasp before he rolled her over until she toppled backward into frigid water.

Darkness swirled around her. She couldn't reach the surface. She tried to scream but expended her air instead.

The current tossed her end over end, banging her against rocks, trying to fill her lungs with searing water.

She fell. Down. Down. Down.

"Maara! Maara!" Illun's panicked voice filled her awareness.

Her head throbbed. She'd already bumped it today.

She opened her eyes and found herself lying on the kitchen floor, the chair she had occupied a moment earlier capsized beside her and Illun had her head cradled in his lap.

She blinked against the haze that covered her vision. She trembled still.

She could feel the water filling her lungs. Cold yet burning, burning, burning.

"Maara," Illun whispered, "what's wrong?" He stroked her cheek and kissed her forehead.

"I remember him," she croaked, barely able to speak. "He wasn't my family … I think he just wanted me dead."

"Whoever he is, he can't get to you now," Illun said fervently as he held her. "It's past, Maara. He can't hurt you now. No one can while I am here."

"But, why?" she whispered. "Why would he want to kill me?" She held one of Illun's callused hands and took comfort in its warm pulse.

She had never done anything to hurt anyone, and she never wanted to, but she couldn't forget the power lurking behind those gnome's eyes.

CHAPTER THREE

BHEVIR,
SOUTHERN YENDU

Try though she might, Salmaara could not focus on the ledger of Rianne and Torone's wedding purchases over the shrill voice—which rose in volume with each sentence it uttered— coming from the front of the shop the following morning.

Most people in Bhevir could agree that Mistress Palderi and her three sons were the most unpleasant people in town. If not for the much-needed sheep that the mistress and her sons raised and the wool they spun, Salmaara wasn't certain that the townsfolk would suffer them as they did.

The potter's daughter set the charcoal stick that she had been writing with beside the ledger and peeked around the corner from the backroom and into the front of the store.

Her father stood with his back to her, his hands folded against where his clay-spattered apron was tied, relaxed despite the onslaught of angry words spouting from the woman standing before him.

Mistress Palderi had always reminded Salmaara of a broom—all thin handled at the top, with a more than ample midsection and legs on the bottom.

She had a scrawny arm raised, shaking a cracked bowl with red and tan glazing at him as she yelled, "But you make me weak pottery, Illun! See? It has broken *again!*"

At that remark, the potter's shoulders stiffened somewhat—Salmaara's father took great pride in the quality of his work. He cleared his throat and said, "Perhaps, if you refrained from dropping them so oft—"

The woman snarled and hurled the bowl down at his feet so that he had to step back to avoid the pieces of the heavy and—Salmaara's heart sank—beautiful bowl as it shattered on the stone floor.

"Like that?" Having said so, the enraged woman spat on the broken pieces for good measure then turned toward the door.

Illun started after her. "Now, Milady," he said, his calm tone all ice, "I'm sure we can come to a more civilized arrangement than this."

A sharp knock came from behind Salmaara, jarring her attention from the scene unfolding before her. She turned to the back door and opened it, slipping outside when she saw Rianne waiting there.

"Hey, Maara, I didn't want to come in the front while ... well, you know," she said uncomfortably.

Salmaara nodded, closing the door to separate them from the ongoing spat of the couple within. "What can I do for you?"

Her friend shook her head and put her hands on her hips. "So formal, Miss Maara? *What can I do for you?*" Rianne grinned. "I just feel like it's been forever since we talked, or ate lunch together, or ... or something."

Salmaara raised a brow and grinned back. "It could have something to do with a *devastatingly handsome boy named Torone. You know, the governor's son, Maara?* consuming your days."

Rianne blushed and smacked Salmaara's arm. "I am being sincere! I wanted to do something before the wedding. You want to have lunch? I brought some bread and ... ahm, whatever these are," she said, looking down at a covered basket dangling from her arm. The aroma of freshly baked pastries wafted up from it.

"All right, I'm sure Father can manage without me for a little while." Salmaara made her way across the kiln-filled yard and to the gate that let out into an alley.

Rianne hurried after her, closing the gate behind the two of them.

Once outside, Salmaara asked, "So, is it Hend again?"

"How did you know that?"

Salmaara shrugged, starting forward down the street. "You always flee a fight, and you're carrying what I expect must be the source of the fight for our lunch."

The bride-to-be nodded grudgingly. "Yes, he and Mother and Father have been at each other more and more lately. He just ... doesn't want to be what they hope he can be, you know? They have tried so hard to groom him to take over the practice, but he won't have it, not for a bit. He shirks his studies and his duties constantly, disappearing for hours at a time. Mother will break one of her beakers over his hard head one of these days if he isn't more careful."

"And he's been sneaking to the baker's to help instead of working at home?"

Rianne pursed her lips. "Yes. Yes, he has. Father and Mother have told him the kind of life that would be for him and his future wife compared to what he could have, but he doesn't care, of course." She sighed, turning down a street lined with worn marble benches. The girls reached one, which boasted detailed scrollwork of birds and flowers across its arched top.

"Enough about him. I have a question or two about you," Rianne said, sitting on the bench and setting the basket on the seat next to her.

Salmaara sat, as well, waiting for the aforementioned inquiry.

"I would really like to know what you were doing in the woods the other morning. I was out for a lovely dawn walk—you know how I get nervous, especially with all the wedding details—and what do I see? My favorite Miss Maara barreling out of the trees with something in her arms. What is she doing? And, what is that thing she's holding?"

Salmaara's heart leaped into her throat. *That is the last thing I thought I had to worry about!* "Getting away, really. To think."

Rianne uncovered the basket and selected a pastry glazed with some sort of dark pink sauce. "And the book? You have to know you can't just go around in broad daylight—or even dawn-light—with something like that. What if it hadn't been me, but one of the Palderis, or ... or someone else? Not everyone in this town can be trusted. You and I both know we can't have books—that's just life. What do you even do with them? What could be worth a public beating ... or worse?"

"Rianne, what have your parents told you about the outside world?"

Taking a large bite of the confection, Rianne shrugged. She chewed then swallowed before she answered, "Almost nothing. Mainly, that I and my siblings should be grateful to be here, and not there. I'm content enough to leave it alone. It's all obviously something terrible, the way mother Mother gets pale and Father touches that icky scar on his neck if it happens to come up."

"Rianne, most of my father's books are about how the outside world used to be before the empress took over. Others are about her and how she secured her rule a century past. My father also chose not to say very much concerning the world to me until recently, and the more I've thought on what he said and about what I've read, the more I wonder why we are all sitting here, pretending that the rest of the world doesn't exist, just waiting for it to come and get us. If the Empress Velanoma I've read about still rules the world, she won't leave us alone forever. In fact, she *will* come for us. Suddenly, I feel like we should be building a wall around town and preparing to defend ourselves, not going about our campestral existences as though nothing is amiss."

Rianne raised her brows. "I don't know what a campestral existence is, but most people came here over a decade ago, and they don't seem worried—at all—about this empress finding us here." Rianne offered one of the soft pastries to Salmaara. "I trust them."

Accepting the cream-filled roll, the potter's daughter said, "Why then did you say that I can't trust people with my books? Why is it that, every time we try to talk to our parents, or even other people, about the lands beyond, they bind their tongues? It makes me think that there are spies for the empress among us, making sure we obey her laws or ... or something. Being beaten or killed over knowledge is silly unless someone doesn't want you to have it."

Rianne tried to smile, but Salmaara could sense her discomfort. "Books and spies ... and talk of empresses won't help either of us, or anyone else here, Maara. I'm getting married the day after tomorrow! Lighten up. Everything's going to be perfect."

Salmaara started eating her roll to cover a sigh. Her friend had never been able to handle serious topics.

Seeing me with that book must have worried her enough that she had to come and say something, though. It was thoughtful, but I should have known better than to try to talk to her about the outside world. If not her, then who? I've always been able to talk to Rianne. But she'll be married tomorrow ... Father warned me how that changes a friendship.

"Well, it's good to see you, Maara. Promise me you'll be more careful. And take these rolls home and enjoy them. I've a final fitting to go to." Rianne waited, clutching the basket.

Salmaara offered the bride-to-be a smile. "I promise, all right?"

Rianne quickly hugged the potter's daughter, stood, and dashed away down the street, toward the town plaza.

Watching her friend's retreating back, Salmaara sighed then glowered at the half-eaten pastry in her hand.

"You know, she just doesn't want anything to be wrong. She wouldn't believe it if it was staring her in the face." The masculine voice came from behind the bench.

Salmaara gasped, inhaling a piece of the bite she had been working on.

Hend circled the bench as Salmaara choked on his confection.

The handsome young man raised his hands in defense and took the seat that Rianne had vacated a moment earlier. "Sorry, I didn't mean to kill you. Are you going to be okay?"

"I probably"—Salmaara coughed—"need some"—she coughed again—"water, you sneak!" Her lungs and throat burned with the coughing, and her cheeks with embarrassment. *How much of that did he hear?*

"Don't worry! I'll save you." Hend grinned as he rose and jogged down the street toward one of Bhevir's many wells.

Frowning, Salmaara hurried after him, still coughing on the sweet snack. She reached the round well just behind him and waved the bucket he offered away, scooping the water into her hands instead and drinking until the coughing lessened.

Leaning on the well's stone lip, Salmaara looked at Rianne's younger brother— at his smooth, suns-bronzed skin, his curly, chestnut hair, and bright eyes. "How long were you listening?"

"I heard my name, so I figured I'd follow."

"So ... most of it?"

"Yeah, you could say that. But don't worry; I'm used to people talking about me that way. I was more interested in your books and talk of turning little old Bhevir into a fortress or something."

"It's not going to happen. Rianne's probably right that I should just leave it alone. I've seen how talking about those affairs upsets my father. I don't intend to stir things up for no cause."

Hend chuckled, flipping the bucket over in his hands. "You? Stirring things up? I find that hard to believe. Besides, anyone our age who's paid any attention has noticed by now how isolated we are. Anything could be out there. Why not a conquering empress?"

Salmaara tried to smile back but was certain it came off as a grimace. "Why not, indeed?"

Setting the bucket back on the well's edge, Hend ran a nervous hand through his hair. "Well, I've got to go. My mother will really have my hide if I don't return with what she sent me out for some time soon. See you around, eh, Maara?"

"See you around," Salmaara said, waving as he backed away and left her with her thoughts.

CHAPTER FOUR

BHEVIR,
SOUTHERN YENDU

Every time Salmaara reached beyond her height, soapy water ran down her arm in lukewarm rivulets that created damp spots in her armpits. There was no knowing what task her father would assign her next. What good did a smock do when the offending liquid got in her clothes and seeped out from beneath? Fortunately, the wedding wasn't until the next night, so she wouldn't have to worry too much about how messy she got now. *This window is going to be clean.*

Salmaara and Illun did not have the resources to hire anyone else for surplus chores. Therefore, as Illun helped customers and busied himself with restoring damaged pieces, Salmaara got to scrub the entire front window clean. She had already finished with the floors, walls, and the inside of the window. It seemed like she had been working on its outside for hours.

She considered fetching a chisel as she faced the bowed sheet of glass but knew it would do no good. Her arm ached and burned from her exertion.

Foggy, white streaks still covered the glass. Clay, dust, dirt, glazes, and anything that turned foul when wet ended up on the window, inside and out, no matter what Salmaara did. Scrubbing it to a sleek shine had never proven possible because, with every pass, the rag just smeared the substances across the window.

As she worked, a shadow weighed upon her, filling her with dread. She had experienced the sensation before. The last time had been on the morning before a construction project on the northern fringe of Bhevir had collapsed, killing two men and injuring ten more. Previously, if she could have figured out what was wrong before it happened, she could have prevented it. *But I have no notion of what this could be. Everything looked well on the way here.*

She let her arm fall to her side and blew out an exasperated breath. It was hopeless. The window refused to be clean. She had already emptied and refilled her bucket three times and used four of the cleanest rags that she and Illun owned.

Turning from the window, she dunked her filthy rag in a pail of even filthier water. Frowning at the opaque, white sludge, she poured the water into a drain off to the side.

At the end of the street just ahead, a small well stood outside the Relaro's infirmary and family home, the home Rianne would say farewell to tomorrow. Salmaara made her way there and set her bucket on the stone lip.

Something flickered in the corner of her eye. All the doors and windows of the two-story building were closed, but Salmaara could see a cloud of black smoke and the wild dance of flames through the window on the upper floor where the family lived.

Salmaara looked around the sparsely inhabited street. So many were still setting up in the plaza around the bend.

She shouted as loud as she could, "Fire! Relaro's is on fire!"

Salmaara rushed to the front door and tried to force it open, but it wouldn't budge. She grunted in frustration and planted a hard kick next to the doorknob. The door banged open in a cloud of splinters.

The potter's daughter coughed and waved smoke from her face as she ran inside. She could see the beginnings of the fire as it spread down the top of the stairwell and glowing veins filled the beams supporting the upper level. They groaned and cracked as fire flicked through the boards above, wrapping around them.

Salmaara coughed once. "Is anyone here? Relaro? Rianne? Hend?"

She thought she heard a faint reply, like a whisper drifting on the air, but couldn't understand it over the crackling blaze. Someone—no, not just someone—Rianne was trapped on the upper story.

As Salmaara was familiar with the clay-like sensation that marked her father, so she could feel others, as well—everyone different—when she paid attention. Rianne felt like the gentle wing beats of a small bird.

She must not be able to get to the window for some reason. I can't get up the stairs.

Outside. I have to try outside.

Sprinting from the building, Salmaara looked up. A crowd of people had arrived in the street outside, hauling buckets of water from the well. Salmaara snatched her own bucket and rag from where someone had knocked them to the ground and made her way back to the building.

Someone behind her yelled at her as she clambered up the side of the wood and brick building, using window shutters and the infirmary sign to reach the second-story windowsill. She didn't listen to them, for her friend was in danger.

Several hard hits from the bottom of her pail smashed the upper window, and Salmaara lost her balance when it broke and fell inside.

Smoke stung her eyes, and the fire burned hot. She raised her wet rag to cover her nose and mouth.

Part of the floor had collapsed, so she could see the lower level. Ahead, a dressing table and mirror had fallen over and, pinned under it, Rianne lay motionless, wearing her feathered bridal veil.

The potter's daughter took to her feet and made her way around the edge of the room. Tossing her pail aside, Salmaara hauled the table from Rianne then extended a hand to her as the building creaked. "Come with me, Rianne. We have to get out. You're to marry tomorrow, remember?"

Rianne didn't move.

Salmaara kneeled beside her and took her hands. Thankful that the other girl was smaller than herself, Salmaara dragged Rianne toward the window.

The floor seemed soft beneath Salmaara's feet. However, she kept her gaze on the window.

As she neared it, a familiar face popped into view. Salmaara recognized Torone's broad form.

"Rianne!" He leaped through the window, scooped up his fiancée in his strong arms, and returned to the window. The pair disappeared.

Salmaara climbed from the window behind them and back to the street.

Torone supported an ash-stained Rianne, who had regained consciousness. She stared at what remained of her home with wide, haunted eyes. Torone cradled her and kissed the top of her head.

A pair of arms came around Salmaara hard. "Don't ever do anything like that again!" Illun said fiercely.

Salmaara looked into her father's worried face.

He touched one of her cheeks then withdrew his fingers, showing Salmaara the soot on them. "Look at you. Let's go home and clean you up."

Salmaara opened her mouth to protest, but the sound of Rianne's shrill voice made her pause.

"Postpone? Postpone, you say? *Nothing* will stop me from having you tomorrow. Nothing …" Rianne coughed, buried her face in Torone's chest, and sobbed.

Relaro barreled toward them from around the corner with his medicine bag in hand. At a glance, he took in his home and daughter as he made for Rianne and Torone.

Behind them, most of the gathered townsfolk still labored to extinguish what remained of the blaze which, fortunately, had not spread to the surrounding buildings yet.

Once Relaro had determined that Rianne and Salmaara needed little more than rest, Illun escorted Salmaara home.

As they passed through the front door and into the entry, Salmaara inhaled the scent of clay, trying to smell something other than smoke. Her head seemed full of it.

From behind her, her father spoke. "Can you make it upstairs? I will draw some water."

"No, don't worry about it. I'll—"

"Go upstairs. Now."

"Thank you." Salmaara made her way to her room, grateful for the prospect of changing into the extra set of clothes that Illun acquired from the Palderis just a week prior in exchange for the place settings the elder Palderi had been shouting at Salmaara's father about the previous day.

Inside, she removed her blackened sandals, quickly followed by her pants and tunic. Wrapping herself in a thick blanket, she sat on the edge of the bed.

In the mirror across the room, Salmaara could see her sooty reflection. The only clean patch of skin on her face was around her nose and mouth, and she stank of smoke.

Illun entered, carrying two deep pails of water across his shoulders and an empty wooden tub in his hands.

Salmaara offered a smile. "You really shouldn't—"

"You scared us all—scrambling into a burning building before anyone could say a word. How did you know she was there? She didn't make any noise, and someone said she was in the plaza. No one was supposed to be there. Relaro had locked the place up while he and Mirana were doing errands." Illun set the tub in the middle of the floor and the water beside it.

"I saw the fire and thought someone had to have started it." *That and I just knew. I knew exactly where she was. I couldn't see her, but I could feel her there.*

I suppose it might be an unusual thing to be able to do ... She had never thought of the sensations attached to people as unusual in any way.

"Wash up. As long as you're all right, I'm going back to close the shop," Illun said.

Salmaara nodded. "I'm fine. Really," she added when he raised his brows at her. "Father," she added as Illun stepped into the doorframe. He paused, waiting. "Considering all that has happened, I was thinking we should invite Relaro, Mirana, and their family to stay, in case they have nowhere else to go."

"I'll ask them."

She waited for him to close the door before she dropped the blanket. Stepping into the knee-deep tub, she took a sponge from one of the water buckets beside her. She emptied her mind as she washed herself.

Satisfied that she had removed enough soot, she stepped from the blackened water, and dressed in a blue-green tunic and brown pants.

Finding herself alone, thoughts of the vision came flooding back—the gnome, his cold gaze, and falling into the water. *Who is he? Why would a gnome try to kill me? Was he acting on someone's behalf or for himself? I think it was him. But what would I ever have done to incur the wrath of a gnome of all creatures?*

Beside her, the pack that she kept at the ready for when she was prepared to find answers waited. She glanced down at it for a long moment and looked away. *I should prepare something to eat in case we have guests. Even if we don't, Father is sure to be hungry when he returns.*

After re-braiding her unruly hair, Salmaara went to the kitchen and found some vegetables and the silver-crested duck she had submerged in a brining solution the previous day. She peeled several pash, bulbous vegetables with yellow skins and soft red insides, and four gray-skinned lihmus, each as big around as her thumb and as long as her forearm. Several heads of lettuce with pale gray leaves, each lined in deep violet, occupied a hanging basket.

As she reached for one, the llama's patchy face popped into the window. It shoved its snout through the bars, sticking its long tongue out so it came just short of touching the glass. Salmaara sighed, turning the lettuce over in her hands. "All right, but only one. Father will notice more."

She opened the window inward, and handed a leafy head to the llama, through the bars. The creature snatched it then slunk from sight with its prize.

Closing the window, Salmaara took another head of lettuce, meaning to chop it, when the front door banged open, ushering in several pairs of feet and voices. One sounded above the others. Salmaara thought it belonged to Mirana, Rianne's mother.

"Where is she, Illun? Where is that hero girl? I must see her right now!"

"In here," Salmaara called.

The physician and his family filled the kitchen in a rush.

Mirana was a petite woman but stout. She embraced Salmaara, pulling her head down so she could kiss her forehead repeatedly as she spoke.

"You saved my baby. Oh, the rumors about your luck are true. How blessed we are! How blessed." She shook Salmaara by the shoulders and kissed her forehead again.

Somewhat dazed from the kissing and shaking, the potter's daughter managed a short, "... welcome."

When Mirana released her, Hend stepped forward with a grin on his charming face.

Heat filled Salmaara's cheeks as she tried to straighten her rumpled tunic and hair.

"Hey. Thanks for saving my idiot sister," he said.

Salmaara counted only four of his five siblings behind him. "Where is she? Is she all right?"

"Oh, Illun took her upstairs to lie down. She's still raving about getting married tomorrow. I think it may actually happen."

"If she's not well enough ..."

"No point in talking about it now. I think the smoke got to her," Hend said. "She's even wedding-crazier than she was before." He rolled his eyes and waved a finger in a circle by his head.

Illun entered the kitchen, looked around, and counted the bodies in the room with a finger. Salmaara counted with him. *There are nine of us. Where are we all going to sleep?*

Illun addressed the small assembly with a smile. "Let's see if we can find something to eat. The bird is small, but we can make do. Maara, did you bring those vegetables in yesterday?"

"Yes, and I already started cutting them," Salmaara said, indicating the neat piles on the counter. "There are more..."

Before she could say another word, Relaro and his family took over the kitchen, taking up knives, and vegetables. Relaro picked up the duck while Mirana concocted seasoning with spices from one of the cabinets.

Every time Salmaara tried to squeeze in, or offered help, they told her she must not do anything, and pressed together, so she had to do as they said.

"I'm going up to see Rianne," Salmaara told her father when she realized she wouldn't be allowed to help with supper. Illun nodded.

Salmaara found Rianne on her bed, staring at the ceiling, tears trickling down her face. She had apparently washed, but Salmaara could still see traces of soot here and there on her face and neck. The potter's daughter sat on the edge of the bed. "Hi, Rianne."

Rianne looked over, her lips trembling. She uttered a single sob. "I've ruined everything. Torone and his father may be able to help my father rebuild, but it's gone. Everything is gone! Everyone is going to see me tomorrow and say, *Oh, look! There goes the girl who burned the infirmary practically to the ground on the eve of her wedding.* If I were them, I'd be thinking, *good riddance!*"

"They're not angry. They're happy you're safe." *Angry probably comes later...*

Rianne sniffled and swiped at her tears.

Salmaara offered one of her hands, and Rianne took it. Hers trembled.

The potter's daughter offered her a warm smile. "If you don't mind my asking, what were you doing? Your parents said they had locked up, and that you were supposed to be in the plaza."

"I... I haven't even said thank you. You saved my life and the first thing I do is complain! It was a stupid mistake and completely embarrassing. It's not even worth telling."

Salmaara raised her brows. "Try me."

"The seamstress wasn't supposed to be done with the additions to the veil until tomorrow morning but finished early. I collected it and, on the way home, Torone asked if I wanted to have supper with him and his family. I went home to ready myself, but everything was locked, except the back window downstairs. I climbed in and went upstairs to freshen myself a little. I thought my eyebrows looked terrible after I powdered, so I was trying to prepare an ash-stick for them when I knocked the lamp from the table. It landed on the pile of clothes I'd just taken off, and everything went from there. I tried to catch it but had scooted the dressing table chair in too much. It all ended up on me, as you probably saw."

"Lucky for you, Maara went in there after you, or you'd be more cooked than this duck right now," Hend said from the doorway. He held two plates heaped with steamed vegetables, accompanied by slivers of duck meat. He offered a charming smile. "Are you ladies hungry?"

Salmaara nodded, but Rianne turned her nose up at him.

"Why do you always have to be so nasty?"

"Don't see any reason not to." He handed the food to first Rianne then Salmaara, to whom he offered a wink.

Salmaara pretended not to see as she accepted the food with an expression of thanks, but her heart fluttered.

Hend proceeded to speculate on how they might rebuild while the girls ate. He hoped his father would design something open, with more windows, because Mirana had always hated being in the sunless back room, mixing medicines and entertaining the outlander smugglers. Salmaara quickly lost track of what he was saying. Although everyone was accounted for after the fire, and everything was in order for the wedding, she still felt the weight on her heart. *Is something still wrong? I've never experienced it for a whole day. What could be causing it?*

The face of her gnome assailant materialized in her mind once more, squinting down at her in disapproval.

She swallowed.

"Hey, Maara, are you all right?" Hend asked. He and Rianne had both turned to look at her.

"Yes, of course. I'm only tired and know that we all have much to do tomorrow."

"We sure do. It's Ri's big day. Finally. You're still going to dance with me, aren't you?" Hend took their plates.

"I am."

"Off with you, scoundrel," Rianne said, waving a hand.

Hend grinned as he left, closing the door behind him.

Salmaara stood. "I'm going to find blankets, and whoever is sleeping in here with us."

"I'm coming with you," Rianne said, taking to her feet.

When Salmaara put her hands on her hips, Rianne held up a menacing finger. "I feel much better. I think it will be good to prove to them they have nothing to worry about. Because they don't."

"You have to be careful …"

Rianne brushed past Salmaara and into the hall.

The potter's daughter went after her and downstairs to find her friend's siblings as dread pressed upon her heart, heavier than she had ever felt, and she still found herself unable place it. *Someone is still in danger.*

CHAPTER FIVE

BHEVIR,
SOUTHERN YENDU

An odd calm settled over Bhevir and the surrounding hills as dusk fell on the night of Rianne and Torone's wedding. No wind. No sound. All seemed flat and without shadows. However, grim light covered the town in the hills. Perhaps rain was on its way.

While it rained frequently in Southern Yendu, its people didn't suffer the nearly chronic deluge that those in Northern Yendu did. Several weeks had passed since the last rainstorm.

As she, Illun, Relaro, and Rianne made their way toward Bhevir's heart, Salmaara thought she detected something new amid the usual confectionaries and other scents the city regularly produced … something bitter that stung her throat and made her stomach sore. She still couldn't shake the feeling that something was wrong.

A distant thundering broke the silence.

Perhaps a storm really is on the way,

she thought again, looking to the sky, at the clouds that drifted in the gray sphere.

If it does, it will be very ill news for Rianne and Torone's long-anticipated festivities.

My upset can't be about a storm ruining the wedding, can it?

"Sounds like a storm might cut the evening short," Illun echoed her thoughts, looking upward.

Rianne narrowed her eyes. "It had better not." She wore a gray cloak over her white dress to keep it clean, and her brown hair in braids of varying sizes, gathered atop her head in an elaborate bun. Her mother had gone ahead to procure her new veil from the city seamstress, since no one had been able to get the ash and burns out of the original.

"There's just thunder now. It could wait. You never know," Relaro said.

Glass lanterns hung from the ribbon-poles and sat on tables, illuminating the circular plaza as the small party arrived. Most of Bhevir filled the space ahead. Some sat at the long tables, while others exchanged greetings or chatted amongst themselves.

Mirana made her way through the masses with a purposeful stride, veil in hand. "Maara, Rianne, follow me. Gentlemen, make sure everything is ready for us."

Salmaara and Rianne scrambled to follow the physician's wife into one of the buildings overlooking the plaza—the baker's shop. Pale wood floored the modest chamber, and a long counter, covered every inch with bread during the day but empty now, spanned from wall to wall. The shop's mistress welcomed them inside and closed the door.

Mirana set the veil in Salmaara's hands then removed Rianne's cloak. She proceeded to fuss over her daughter's hair and a wrinkle in the bride's floor-length gown.

The fitted garment shimmered pure white with lace accents around the high neck and flowing wrists. Sweat had started to run the powder on Rianne's face.

Mirana pursed her lips. "Maara, if you will see to the train, I must find some more powder for this nervous girl."

Rianne's pretty face darkened. "I am not nervous!"

Mirana ignored her and asked the baker's wife if she had any powder. Then she followed the woman to the back room.

Salmaara set the veil on the counter and unslung the leather satchel she carried. As tradition required, she had made the train herself, in the color the bride had chosen. Rianne had requested bright yellow. A long row of buttons attached it to the back of Rianne's dress.

Salmaara could feel her friend trembling as she fastened it in place. "You're going to be fine. You love Torone, don't you?"

"Yes."

"You think he's the most handsome man who's ever lived, and you want to spend your life with him no matter what? You said that." Salmaara set the white, feather veil on her head, folding the front portion back so Rianne's face was still exposed.

"Y-Yes, but—"

"But nothing," Mirana said primly as she swept from the back of the shop with a powder tin in hand. "You are going to marry that boy as soon as I get this on you. It was all your idea, yes?"

Mirana started brushing the powder onto her daughter's face before she could reply. Once satisfied, she stepped back and smiled. She patted Rianne's cheeks to remove extra powder then pulled the veil over her daughter's face. "Perfect. Oh, you are so beautiful. I can't believe you're mine. Now, let's go."

Rianne waited for Salmaara to pick up her train before the pair exited the bakery. Salmaara followed Rianne toward the stand where Torone and his father, Governor Portranos, waited.

Outside, all the guests sat at the tables, leaving a central aisle, marked by a silver carpet, clear. A small assembly of musicians playing drums, end-blown flutes, and plucking at deep-bellied stringed instruments filled the courtyard with a festive tune from where they stood to one side of the stand, their melody one that Salmaara had heard at a handful of weddings before.

Torone grinned when he saw Rianne, and the bride straightened, her shaky walk smoothing out. She seemed to float the remainder of the distance to the stand.

Salmaara let the train fall as they reached the bottom of the stairs, and moved to the side, taking a seat beside Illun at a nearby table.

The governor cleared his throat. "We gather here, on this glorious evening, to bind the lives of Torone Portranos and Rianne Kelaren."

Torone took Rianne's hand as the officiator continued, "Do you, Torone Portranos, swear to love and cherish Rianne Kelaren as your wife before the four creators?"

"I do, sir."

"Very good. And do you, Rianne Kelaren, swear to love and cherish Torone Portranos as your husband before the four creators?"

"I do."

"By my authority, I hereby declare you as one, forever and ever."

The governor held out his hand to Salmaara, who took the ceremonial vessel from Illun. It resembled an elongated teapot with two opposing spouts and handles. Yellow and deep orange glaze colored it, and fresh, Southern Yendu wine filled it.

Salmaara stood and slowly made her way onto the platform. She extended the vessel to the bride and groom. When they each accepted a handle, Salmaara returned to her seat but couldn't sit down as the feeling of wrongness spiked. Her heart sped as though she were sprinting, and her stomach clenched.

Illun took hold of her arm and tried to pull her down. "Maara?"

"Something's wrong," she whispered.

A shrill voice overrode what the governor said next.

"They're coming!" A hoary man wearing a patched apron charged from one of the side streets and into the fountain plaza. Caem, the miner, who regularly sold Illun glaze minerals, clawed at the air as though it would speed his passage. He skidded to a halt beside the fountain, looking at the stunned faces around him with wild eyes. When no one moved, he shouted, "They're coming! They're coming! Don't you hear me? Enough of 'em to wipe this sorry place from the face of the world without much thinkin'. They're coming, and it's blood they want. They. Are. Coming!"

The plaza erupted all at once. People scrambled to gather their families, knocking chairs and tables alike over. The voices rose to a din, almost loud enough to cover the thunder. *But it isn't thunder, not this time,* Salmaara thought.

The thundering increased to a deafening roar that came from everywhere at once. And Salmaara felt people surrounding the town, thousands of them.

As swiftly as it had begun, the pandemonium in the plaza stilled, leaving only the ominous rumble of the army's march and the pounding of Salmaara's own heart.

All eyes had turned to where Caem stood, their collective breaths held so fiercely that the potter's daughter feared she might suffocate.

A solitary creature, the likes of which had only haunted Salmaara's imagination from the pages of her books, brushed past the old miner and into the crowd. He possessed many of the features expected of any man—two arms, two legs, a head, and other such things—but the likeness ended there.

Dark brown feathers sprouted from the man's scalp instead of hair and, below his sharp nose, taut skin stretched over where his mouth should have been. He possessed enormous amber eyes, shot with veins of red, and black armor of woven leather clothed his muscular body. At his waist hung a pair of kamas—wicked curved blades on short handles.

The people of Bhevir parted before him as sheep before a wolf—the wolf he surely was. Salmaara recognized him as one of the liths, a race of creatures created by Vias the Destroyer and endowed with mind powers to carry out her will in the ancient war for the world.

The lith passed where Salmaara stood frozen beside her father and strode onto the stand, towering over the trio still positioned there and his paralyzed audience alike.

Torone dragged Rianne from the platform and placed himself between the intruder and his bride.

Now alone, the lith folded his hands—huge, sinewy hands—behind his back and cocked his head.

A sensation like the cool blade of an axe resting against Salmaara's throat came upon her. Then a crisp, clear, male voice, silken as the tongue of a serpent, spoke in her mind.

"Denizens of Bhevir, kneel before its masters. We have come to this ground in the name of the empress of all, even Velanoma Privii Zamazcus."

Several in the plaza fell to their knees with faces to the ground.

Salmaara's gut twisted in revulsion and fear.

The lith's cold, amber eyes slid over the crowd and, after a moment, found Salmaara's, fixing her with his gaze.

A shudder went through her, from the crown of her head to the soles of her feet. Everything inside of her told her to run, but her body remained, unmoving, captivated by the lith's aura of power.

The voice that had spoken continued—the lith's voice, Salmaara knew. *"The empress has decreed that no buildings shall stand on this land, and this people has disobeyed. But the empress is benevolent. Yield to us willingly, and it and its kindred shall live. Here there shall be mines and quarries that require service. Come, and live. Flee, and die.*"

At the conclusion of the lith's address, the spell that had hung over the plaza broke. Many remained kneeling on the ground, while others scattered. Someone shouted, and then Relaro shoved Salmaara aside. The physician had a long knife in his hand when he charged the lith, followed by several others, each armed with similar implements. She didn't get to see what happened next.

Illun had leaped to his feet beside Salmaara. "We have no time to lose!" he said, strained. Snatching one of her hands, he dragged her away, toward the plaza's edge. "Go into the woods. Hide yourself. Bury yourself if you have to. Keep your mind quiet. These creatures'll hear you if you don't guard your thoughts."

"But he said if we come—"

"It's a lie," he cut her off, and she swallowed her rising panic as she caught his. "What he has offered is a brutish life of servitude beneath merciless masters. Also ..."

People fled in every direction.

She hurried after her father. "Also, what?"

"I hate to think ... what they would do to you ... if they discover who you are."

A chorus of chilling screams sounded in the distance behind them, and Salmaara whipped around as the twilit sky filled with an intense orange glow. Smoke coiled from the buildings on the northern rim of the city.

"What? Who am I, Father?"

She could sense over a thousand soldiers approaching from every direction. Never had she known it so clearly. It felt like stinging smacks on the cheek. Something was different about many of them than the people she had grown up with. Part of the ring had reached the north and east sides of the city, pushing people southward where more waited.

We're surrounded. We have nowhere to run.

Illun snatched Hend's arm as the young man approached them. "You get her to safety, boy."

Hend nodded and extended his hand.

Salmaara simply looked at it until Illun, still with a death-grip on her arm, put her hand in Hend's, who pulled her forward, away from Illun. She looked back, but Illun was already sprinting from the other side of the plaza. Toward home.

The potter's daughter twisted her arm from Hend's grip. He tried to snatch her again, but she was faster.

"Hey!" he called after her.

Ducking through the oncoming masses, she quickly lost Hend. She darted through the growing panic, after Illun. *He will run straight into them. I cannot let him die like this.*

She sprinted up the dirt road outside the city, past the field of wild-flowers bathed in silvery light. Her blue house rose on the horizon. There, she saw her father run up the stairs and into the building. Steel gray clouds rolled toward her, masking the moon and stars as they came.

Salmaara reached the house and burst inside where she saw the narrow cellar door stood open. She clambered down the stairs, her lungs burning.

We can't possibly escape them now, Father. Why are you running? And, who am I? Salmaara wondered, her heart pounding in her ears.

In the library, Illun had grasped the corners of the blue rug in the center of the floor. There was a metal door underneath. He seized a ring and yanked it upward. The trap door groaned open, and Salmaara saw a stone vault inside, certainly large enough to hide in. *If we go in there, we'll suffocate.*

As he began to throw the books inside, Salmaara joined him, taking an armful from the nearest shelf and tossing them in.

Illun's face darkened, but he didn't stop loading the books inside. "Salmaara, why are you here?"

She added another armful to the vault. "They're approaching here fast. You have to get out. These aren't worth your life."

"Yes, they are. I swore to protect them with it, and the invaders will burn this place."

Breathlessly, they worked to place all the books into the vault.

With her last armful, Salmaara paused before setting them in place. "Father, who am I?"

"Not now, Maara—"

Salmaara ground her teeth and took a shaky breath before repeating, "Father, who am I?"

"Put them in. There's no time!" Illun snapped.

Throwing her armful in far harder than she should have—the books were treasures, leather-bound, with silk pages, metal leaf, and colored inks in many, not to mention their content and age—she shouted, "For once, just answer me!"

Illun slammed the vault's lid and threw the rug back in place. "When you are safe."

The potter snatched her arm, dragging her up the stairs. At the top, she wrested her arm from his grip.

As she glanced into the kitchen, she spotted a pair of llama eyes peering at them through the window. "What about—"

"We can't afford to bring it. It's old, anyway," he said as he ran toward the front of the house.

But I can't just leave it. Salmaara freed her arm from his grasp and, snatching a knife from the counter, leaned out the window and cut the beast's tether in a single swipe. Then she waved the beast away. "Go! Get out of here!" Her heart hammered. Sweat ran down her face and throat.

Illun waited for her beside the door. "Let's go!"

They ran outside, toward the thick woods behind the house.

A column of armored figures emerged from the black woods in front of them.

Thunder boomed in the distance. Dry lightning flashed above.

Another group of armored figures came from behind. Although she couldn't see them, she knew there were at least forty. They threw torches in front of the house as they came.

Illun shook his head as the dark figures closed in around them, trying to cut them off and turn them toward the burning house.

A tear slipped down Salmaara's cheek.

"We'll run. Run as fast and hard as you can for as long as you can. You'll have a chance of losing them in the woods," he murmured breathlessly into her ear. "Ready?"

She nodded, her heart hammering so hard that she feared it would burst from her chest.

Illun launched forward, and Salmaara went after him.

They darted between the converging lines of invaders in full sprint. Salmaara tripped over herself but still managed to keep pace with her frantic father as they hauled toward the dark cedars illuminated by their burning house. She didn't look back to see if anyone pursued.

Illun panted out, "I will draw ... them away. You'll run, Maara. Run for your life! Hide. And don't look for me no matter what."

"But, Father!" she whispered.

"Run away from me, or you'll be sorry," he said as they broke through the first line of trees.

Salmaara plunged forward through the spiny boughs, too terrified to cry anymore. This wood had been her playground since she and her father had come to Bhevir, and she knew it well, its established paths and the secret paths she had made for herself.

The brush tore at the exposed parts of her feet in her sandals, and she slapped at branches when they scratched at her face or tangled in her hair. The farther she went, the more the clay-like sense of her father receded from her awareness. She could not recall a time when that feeling that was him hadn't been strong, simply there, a part of her. Its fading heightened her panic. *I should go back!*

She stumbled twice when her stinging feet caught on rocks and branches but kept on, desperately wanting to but not daring to look back for Illun. The sense of him vanished as she passed her reading pond, which still glowed in the light of suspended water bugs. They lost their appeal in her haste and terror. Her chest ached. She had never run so hard in her life.

Disconcerted by the loss of the connection to her father, feeling like a child who had lost hold of a beloved parent's hand in a crowded place, she looked over her shoulder as she passed the water.

A root caught one of her feet and ensnared her toes. Her ankle twisted with a searing *pop*. The forest floor of leaves and shrubs yawned open to receive her as she fell. And she kept falling, swallowed by a narrow but deep shaft.

Salmaara struck the bottom on her side. Pain exploded in one of her legs. She bit her hand to silence the shriek that would have surely betrayed her location, and blood welled around her teeth. The fire from her injured leg burned consuming and bright.

Debris rained down on her until she lay buried. She couldn't see anything, just dark earth. Held down by the heavy blanket of soil, Salmaara thought she heard a distant cry.

Then she lost consciousness.

CHAPTER SIX

BHEVIR,
SOUTHERN YENDU

Salmaara peeled heavy lids from sticky eyes. A sprinkle of rain had dampened the dirt that lay over her. She shivered. It was still dark, but she could see the distant sky. It glowed soft lavender, like it always did at dawn.

Every limb throbbed in pain from the fall, but none more than her leg. She coughed and lifted a heavy arm from beneath the soil, brushing the filth from her face. Then she sat up and rubbed her neck, squinting up at the smooth sides of the shaft, which were three times deeper than she was tall.

She saw a long root hung from the pit's side and heaved herself to her feet, leaning all of her weight on her good leg. She couldn't put any on the other. She brushed herself off with an aching arm. Straining, Salmaara reached for the root.

As she pulled, the thin root slid free, and she toppled back into the mud as loose silt rained on her face.

She wondered if she would die there, alone in the pit, in that surreal nightmare, knowing her beloved home gone, and separated from her father and friends. She worried for them, wishing she could see them alive and well. *I have to find them. First, I have to get out of this hole. But, how?* Perhaps she would have had a chance of escaping if she had wings.

An animal snort sounded from above.

She wiped the clods from her face and looked back up, and recognized the sinister llama face glowering down at her. Its tan head blocked the little sunlight that had reached her a moment earlier as it munched on a mouthful of bush.

She flinched. "Don't you jump on me," she told it warily.

She felt a strange relief at seeing it alive. Something familiar was still as it should be.

The shaggy creature knelt upon knobby knees, dropping a long rope into the pit.

Despite the agony in her leg, Salmaara managed a smile and shook her head. "You foolish beast, are you here to help me?" she asked it as she took hold of the severed tether.

The llama demonstrated an immense strength that belied its decrepit state as it scrambled backward, and lifted her free of the deep shaft.

She rolled over as the beast made its way back to her side. Salmaara lay by its feet, gasping. *My leg must be broken, I'm not going to be able to walk.*

"Thank you," she said.

The llama's cloven feet swam in and out of focus. She waited for it to bite or stomp on her. It did neither.

"I need to find Father and see if he is all right," she said, her voice a hoarse rasp.

The llama ducked its face level with hers and bowed its legs beneath it.

She dug her hand into the dirt and tugged herself forward. She wrapped an arm around the beast's patchy back, which was now very near the ground, and pulled herself aboard.

It stood, its twig legs shaking for a moment before its knees locked into place.

She thought the beast might collapse or buck her off. When it didn't, she let out a long sigh of relief.

It leaned down and took a wad of bush in its maw. It wasn't going anywhere.

Salmaara calmed her heart and listened. Silence. *Perhaps the soldiers have gone.*

Scooting forward, she took hold of the rope and gave it a short, sharp tug.

The llama's head snapped up, and it brayed in protest, but it started forward through the thick forest as the suns rose higher. Its legs wobbled with each step, and the creature snorted with apparent displeasure, yet it didn't try to throw her off.

Even in the sanctuary of the forest, Salmaara could smell and see smoke. It hung thick in the air between tree trunks, obscuring everything. She buried her face in the llama's putrid pelt, worried she would faint if she breathed any more of it.

When she looked back up, she saw the ruin of the place that she had called home through the trees.

The windows gaped like screaming mouths, their panes of colored glass no more. Scorched, blue shingles littered the ground around the half-collapsed building, and Salmaara could see a faint orange glow from within where the fire still smoldered.

Her chest tightened, pressing upon her heart. Heat filled her cheeks, and a small sob burst free into the fleece upon which she lay. She squeezed her eyes tightly shut, unwilling to believe this could have happened. *I shouldn't have left Father, no matter what he said.*

She looked at the remains of the back of the house. Only black ashes remained, never again to be a sanctuary or bid a fond greeting or farewell as another day began or concluded.

She clutched at the llama's woolen coat, sobbing wretchedly.

The llama jerked back into motion, stepping over a toppled section of the white fence.

When she looked up, she spotted Illun's crumpled form sprawled on the stone step leading into the one-time kitchen.

"Father!" she croaked then urged the llama forward with a feeble slap of her hands on its sides.

It approached the fallen potter warily, where she rolled from the strangely helpful beast. When she hit the ground, the pain in her leg flared, all the way up to her throat. She tried to stifle a cry, but a moan escaped.

After a moment's recovery, she rolled onto her stomach and dragged herself to Illun's side. Her gut twisted, and her vision blurred again as she took him in.

A long rope was cinched around his bloody throat, its free end nailed to the side of the ruined house like a tether. His breaths came in short gasps. Too much blood bathed his torso to discern where it had all come from. Several slashes covered his face, as well.

"F-Father?" She rested a hand on one of his shoulders.

"Maara. No. What are you doing here? You have ... to run ..." he croaked, opening his eyes halfway.

"What have they done to you?"

"What pleases their kind."

"I will find help," she whispered. She rested her hand on his chest pulled and it away immediately. It was soaked with warm blood.

"It's too late for that. Leave me, or they'll come for you."

Her lips trembled. "Tell me how I can save you! Please don't go." She had to force the words out of her constricting throat.

She took a handful of his shirt, gripping it hard. Tears moistened her eyes, but she didn't let them fall. She didn't want him to see her panic, her rising anguish. *I was insane to think that I could ever leave him for a family I don't know!*

Illun smiled the best he was able through bleeding lips. "I'm sorry." His voice was barely audible.

"No!" She tore a strip from her tunic, and wadded it up, pressing it on one of the wounds on his chest.

"Don't worry about me, Maara. You were always meant for something more than this … Something greater."

"Father—"

"I have to tell you … Please.

"The day I pulled you from the river, I had fallen into despair. I missed my family. My wife, Tessa, my three sons, my little girl …" He coughed, and blood trickled down his chin.

Tears filled Salmaara's eyes anew.

"Mauvias took them. Burned Tess with the house. Left my children's mangled bodies in the yard where they had been playing. I'd gone hunting for my son's birthday supper. It was a surprise for him.

"They took my whole world. I'd never hear Tess's violin or hold her to my heart. Never see the children grow or hear them laugh or cry again. It hurt, Maara.

"I lived on. Empty, purposeless. My life as I knew it had to end. In my hopelessness, I forgot that I still had the most sacred gift we are given—life. And, as long as there is life, there is hope." He shuddered as he struggled for another breath.

Salmaara added another strip to the first, trying to enlarge the wad. It seemed to do nothing.

"I went down to the river and tied stones to my arms, my legs.

Around my neck. As I moved to cast myself into the swift current, I spotted a ribbon of auburn coming toward me. Your little face surfaced and, although you weren't all conscious, you reached out for me. Your strength was nearly gone.

"I pulled the stones free and swam out to you. They sank to the bottom of the river without me.

"You told me where you came from. They looked for you tirelessly—your real family—but I couldn't give you up. I loved you too much already. So, I brought you here, away from them and their troubles, away from the world. You are more a part of their quarrels than you know—the people in the books.

"Forgive my cowardice if you can," he murmured faintly, his blue eyes dimming.

"I forgive you, Father," she whispered. "Please... tell me who they are..."

"Your mother is ... Queen Kusae Zamazcus, who fights the empress," he gasped softly.

"Sweet Maara ... dark days will come, but no matter what happens, even if you lose all possessions and fellowship, you can always be grateful for one thing: treasure the gift of the life that is in you and ... live. Choose hope. Choose life.

"Tess ...?" Illun's voice faded and died. His eyes stared lifelessly into hers, and the little smile that had always masked his pain was gone.

She sank her forehead onto his shoulder and sagged against him as all her strength left her. Salmaara would never see him form a masterpiece from a wad of earth or be lifted by his quirky smile again. She would never bound home or into the shop to his warm embrace. Strangers had broken him, and she couldn't do anything about it. *Because I let him go. Because I left him.*

She heaved a sob into his bloodied chest. "Come back," she whispered. "Please come back. I'll help you. You'll get better."

An unspoken male voice penetrated her thoughts with a sensation like the blade of an axe pressing against her skin. She recognized it and the sensation that belonged with it as the one belonging to the lith who had interrupted the wedding and decreed their doom.

"I knew it wouldn't be able to resist returning to his side. Prey."

She shivered violently and turned her head to see a cadaverous face with gray skin bent near her own. Amber eyes streaked with ember-like veins of red bored into hers.

"A worthy hunt. But, in the end, it was so easily lured. I am disappointed. But, being a creature of mercy as I am, I shall give Prey another chance. It is such a pretty one and shall make a fine pet. Come with me," he said, extending a sinewy hand.

"I can't walk," she said numbly, still clinging to Illun's body with one hand gripping the saturated wad of fabric with which she had tried to staunch the bleeding.

The lith narrowed its eyes. *"Then I shall carry Prey."*

Her heart fluttered in fear as the mouthless man gathered her into powerful arms as though she were featherlight.

Salmaara's hands, slick with blood, could not hold onto her father as the lith tore her from him.

Her captor glided through the rubble and toward the broken fence, where a party of twenty lithian soldiers, arrayed in black leather armor, waited. The llama had vanished.

Although her leg seared and throbbed, the ache of her heart made it seem a paltry thing. She shut her eyes tightly and did not look back.

CHAPTER SEVEN

PLAINS,
SOUTHERN YENDU

B hevir still smoldered on the horizon as darkness fell. Salmaara's mouthless captor left his army behind to continue their destruction and took only a small contingent with him.

Despite the pain in her leg and the hot tears that had obscured her surroundings, the potter's daughter had tried to wriggle free of her captor as he had walked away from her ruined home and her father's lifeless body, but he had squeezed her in such a way that she thought she would break in two should she so much as take another breath.

She knew that the cacophony of screams and destruction, and the stench of smoke on the evening wind as she had been carried thence would be fixed in her memory forever.

So it was that she hung limply over the monster's shoulder as he oversaw a party of fifteen or so men and women, mostly of his own race, minus three or four of Salmaara's own, erect a camp well outside of Bhevir.

The potter's daughter couldn't help but wonder why the commander had not even stayed to occupy or at least ensure the city's destruction. *And ... why me? Why aren't I dead? Dead like father. Oh, father ...*

A sob welled up in her but, to her relief, did not escape. Still, it lingered in her chest, pressing outward like a caged thing.

The lith who carried her entered a black, octagonal tent once it had been erected and furnished. Simple rugs favoring greens and blue lay over the ground, and a writing desk and metal chair stood to one side. Opposite the desk, two pallets, one on a frame and one on the ground, had blankets that had obviously been hastily thrown over them. Trunks of varying sizes took up the remaining space around the tent's perimeter.

Salmaara's captor set her on the ground-pallet, sitting with her back against the bed beside it. He took her chin in a cool, grey hand and stared at her with amber eyes flecked with red.

One tear slipped free, and then another. Instinctively, she tried to pull away, but her captor forced her to look back at him with an effortless jerk.

As more tears tracked down her face, she ground her teeth, furious that she couldn't seem to stop them. Her heart was a stone in her chest, heavy and crushing. *I shouldn't have left him ... Why did I leave him? What if I hadn't?*

Again, she felt the sensation, like the cool blade of an axe against her throat, the feeling that she now knew belonged to the creature holding her face.

"*I have sent for things to wash and to feed my Prey,*" he purred, his silky voice sounding only in the confines of Salmaara's mind.

A convulsive shiver shook Salmaara's body, raising gooseflesh as it went.

The brown feathers growing from the lith's scalp quivered in a gesture that struck her as agitation. "*I will have nothing of mine looking so unkempt.*"

At last, he let her chin go, and Salmaara, desperate to look anywhere but at his mouthless face, looked down at herself. It was a mistake. Illun's blood. So much blood! It had come from everywhere—she couldn't find its source or stop it. It had dried down her front, on her hands, on her arms, dark and crusty.

She slowly lifted her hands to touch her tunic, dazed. The wet rattling sounds he had made as he struggled for his final breaths, the salty, metallic smell, and the warm stickiness welling up between her fingers as she had tried to stem the flow—it all returned to her in a vivid flash. She wanted to scream, or sob, or ... or anything!

Even with the lith watching, she wanted to strip the fouled garments from herself and run, run, run away. She wanted to go home—she'd pretend it was still there. She would go home, and her father would be there, concerned that she had been out so late. Supper would even be ready. No, he wasn't even hurt. It had only been a dream that she'd had after staying up too late reading, and she had dozed off in the woods. He would forgive her for always asking about the family that wasn't right there in front of her, who truly loved her. She would ask his forgiveness for thinking that she would leave him to find her real family, and she would be content to live that life until her time under the suns came to an end. She would never ask about the outside world or anything so troubling again.

Instead, she just stared at her father's blood with misty eyes from which no tears now fell and, with gore-caked fingers, slowly tried to rub the stuff from the back of one of her hands.

Grey ones took both of hers, and the lith shook his head. "*Prey must not tax itself overmuch. It is weary and injured,*" he purred.

Behind him, another of his kind entered, one with darker grey skin and grey head feathers. He carried a basin and cloth. Offering a neat bow to the lith facing Salmaara, he set his burden beside her captor then left.

"*Now, while I clean it, Prey will tell me who its family is.*" He took the cloth in hand, submerged it in the water, wrung it out, and delicately began wiping Salmaara's hands.

She tried to take the rag from him, for she had not been bathed by another since the day she had turned seven, but the lith swatted her hand away and continued his task.

Suffering the humiliation, Salmaara tried to answer his query, her voice coming out as a hoarse croak. "My family is dead." Saying it seemed to make it even more real than all the blood, smoke, or anything else had. Her throat tightened until she thought she would suffocate.

"*Surely Prey would never lie to me,*" said the lith, increasing the pressure of his scrubbing until it stung.

Salmaara clenched her teeth, taking a shallow breath against the pain.

Her captor paused, rinsed the rag, which turned the basin crimson, and moved on to her face—jaw, cheeks, nose, then forehead—scrubbing with a sickening tenderness.

She wanted to snatch the rag away and fling it in his mocking face, but the only thing she thrust at him was, "*You* killed him! *You* killed my family! Why didn't you kill me? Why didn't you kill me, too?" She wanted to cry again so badly, but no tears came, only a strangling lump in her throat and a crushing pain in her chest. She gasped.

The creature before her didn't deign to answer. He simply forced her arms up, stripped her ruined tunic and underclothing from her, and tossed them aside.

Realizing what had happened, Salmaara crossed her arms protectively over her bosom and pulled her knees to her chest. Only one leg bent as she thought it would, while the other blazed in protest when she tried to move it.

Unfazed, the lith set the rag back in the fouled water and unhooked a length of rope from his belt.

Realizing what he might do with the rope, she tried to dodge to the side, but too late. The grey-skinned monster had leaned forward and pinched her broken leg.

Pain blossomed like fire, and Salmaara heard someone scream. Then she fell down into a dark abyss.

She didn't know how long she stayed in the dark, but when she regained her senses, she lay on her side, clean, and dressed in a warm tunic not unlike the one she had been wearing and tight pants that reached to her ankles. She feared to learn where the clothes might have come from, whose they might have been. Her captor had arranged her on her pallet and covered her with the blanket.

Although clean, she felt filthy. She wished it were possible to take her own skin off, just to be rid of the sensation of her father's murderer having touched her all over. He had clearly not violated her in the way that she had feared he might, but he had bathed her thoroughly—she could feel that. His ropes bound her wrists securely, and he had splinted her leg. She realized the last with a start.

What sort of tormentor splints a broken leg? she wondered hazily.

Wasn't he going to torture me for information? Father told me that they can't find out ...

The realization descended upon her like every stone in the world in a great tumble. *Who I am. I am the daughter of Queen Kusae Zamazcus, who fights the Empress Velanoma. Empress Velanoma who ordered the destruction of my home, my friends, my father ...*

Sudden horror blossomed in her bosom, and she cracked one eye open. She located her captor at his desk across the tent, attending paperwork of some sort.

Can he hear my thoughts? How do I not think my own thoughts?

She closed her eyes tightly and focused on breathing in and out, in and out. *Think nothing. Think nothing. I'm ... thinking that I should think nothing.*

When no retribution for her thoughts came, she risked peering through slit lids once more. The lith gave no indication that he could hear her or cared that she existed at the moment. She sighed.

The sensation that was him was absent. *Maybe that means he can't hear me right now ...*

With the thought came the dreaded feeling— cold, like an ax blade at her throat.

He flourished his pen and set it down. "*Prey is awake, at last. It must be hungry. I shall feed it now. It will eat, yes?*"

The lith rose from the metal chair and stooped to gather a lidded pot, which he carried to her side. He kneeled beside her and rested an arm under her back, propping her up. The stench of him—leather, oils, and something decidedly like the huge snake that had lived under the baker's shop for many years—filled her until she wanted to vomit.

He sat with her back to his chest and positioned the pot so that it rested between both sets of their legs. Unable to move, due to her injured leg and tied hands, she sat there and helplessly watched as the lith removed the lid from the pot.

Some manner of spiced stew of a dark orange color filled it, and a deep spoon lay inside. Her captor filled the spoon then raised it to her mouth. Chunks of a transparent substance wobbled in it.

She kept her lips pressed tightly together. Even the smell of the stuff made her nose burn.

"*Come now, Prey,*" the lith's voice purred in her mind. "*It will weaken if it does not eat. This will be good for Prey's body.*"

He tapped the spoon's edge against her lips lightly, playfully, like a mother chiding a picky child.

Not wanting to find out what the consequence of resistance would be this time, Salmaara yielded, taking a little slurp. The soup was as spicy as it smelled, and more. The transparent chunks were not quite solid and turned to tiny lumps of mush on her tongue.

In silence, focusing on not coughing with each bite and swallowing, she suffered being fed like a helpless infant, with her perfectly capable hands tied in her lap.

When she had finished the pot, the creature of Vias the Destroyer's making set it aside but did not move. To Salmaara's horror, he fished a fancy brush full of sharp teeth from somewhere and proceeded to pull it through her snarled hair. The feeling rising in her made her think of the llama that had haunted her backyard for her growing years. *Perhaps it was right to attack us.*

Her captor brushed her hair to silk, braided it, and bound it. She hoped then, in vain, that he was done with her for the night, that he would leave her to her suffering in solitude.

He pulled away from her and crossed the tent, where he rummaged about in a chest sitting by his desk for several moments. Then he returned with a small bowl with a wad of cloth and flask in it.

Salmaara had remained sitting up when he had pulled away from her and met his gaze when he returned.

He cocked his feathered head to one side, his eyes crinkling at the corners. If he had possessed a mouth, she supposed he might have been smiling.

He stood thus for many beats of Salmaara's aching heart, examining her as though she were a particularly prized possession that he had finished polishing. *That's just it,* she realized. *That's what I am to him—a prize of battle. A thing. An "it," as he has been calling me.*

Once he had finished admiring her, he sat at her side and revealed the purpose of the items he had fetched. He mixed a white substance from the pouch with a viscous fluid from the flask in the bowl. Then he soaked the resulting mixture into the cloth. Holding it up to her face, he cocked a brow. *"Prey will not bite while I clean its teeth. Let me see."*

With a quiet moan of despair that she could not contain, Salmaara tilted her head back and pulled back her lips so that he could rub the cloth over her teeth and gums until she was sure they were cleaner than they had ever been in her life.

CHAPTER EIGHT

FRINGE TOWN,
NORTHERN YENDU

During the ensuing weeks, Salmaara saw nothing. The lith had blindfolded her the morning after they had broken camp outside of Bhevir. At night, she curled in the back of a wagon on a thin blanket. During the day, she flopped back and forth on her captor's shoulder or rode the back of some huge beast that stank of reptile and jostled her with its long steps. She didn't know what would become of her and had begun to understand what Grey Face—what she had decided to call her lithian captor—might have meant by "pet" the day he had captured her.

Salmaara lay on something soft with wrists bound and her leg in a splint. Her mind teemed with fearful speculation. Most of all, she feared that Illun might have been right—that they knew who she was, despite Grey Face's repeated attempts to get her to confess. She couldn't think of any other reason they would take her and guard her so carefully. And she couldn't hear signs of other prisoners. She was alone.

Although Salmaara had survived when her father had not, she questioned which was more merciful. From what she understood, liths had been created to torture or assassinate enemies of their goddess, Vias the Destroyer.

She would have to wait for her leg to heal before attempting any sort of escape. She tried to put weight on it one night, but the pain was still too intense. *When I can walk again …*

Salmaara had no idea where she would go when she escaped. Her heart paused, constricting. Her father was dead, her house stood corpse-like, in ruin, and Bhevir shared its fate.

Did anyone escape Bhevir? If they did, I can't guess where they have gone. Her thoughts shifted. *What about my mother? Even if I can find her, will she want me?* Salmaara had little notion of where she was or where her captors intended to take her.

She grieved for her father, for her life. When it hurt too much, she focused only on breathing.

She wondered what was real, what the world could be. She thought of the stories she had read, thought of the troop of liths around her.

Can this horror be some sort of dream inspired by one of my father's books? Tomorrow, when I open my eyes, I'll skip to the shop to scrub the windows and dust the vases. But not before hugging the llama.

Sometimes it seemed only moments ago that she and her father sat at the table in the safety of their home, gazing upon the old drawing of her would-be assassin, wondering what it all could mean.

She wrapped her arms around herself, stifling a cursed sob. *"Prey is awake,"* Gray Face's silken voice whispered in her mind, jarring her from her thoughts.

Salmaara shivered from top to bottom. She would never get used to having another's voice in her head. Whenever he spoke, she still felt an axe blade resting on her throat, though when she brushed at it with her fingers, nothing was there. She so wished she could simply brush him away.

Opening her eyes slowly, she squinted at her captor's silhouette as he took the blindfold from her eyes. She lay on a mattress stuffed with straw, on a stone floor. Several windows lined the square room.

A woman clutching a filthy boy huddled in the corner by the door. A neat slash spanned her starved face horizontally across her eyes. An identical mark rendered the boy, who looked barely old enough to walk, blind as well.

"What happened to them?"

Gray Face gathered Salmaara from the floor and made for the door, ignoring her question. The woman started and scrambled to open it, bowing. The mouthless creature took no notice of her as he stepped outside.

"Those creatures the empress allows to live here cannot see what is forbidden unless they have sworn the oath, the oath that makes them Forbidden Guard, and that oath is costly. For Prey's pretty eyes, I make exception, for it shall not pass this way again.

"They are fools, all. They have forgotten the mighty she who raised the empress they now deem so holy." He narrowed his eyes. *What more can be expected of such inferior creatures?"*

It had bucketed rain for days, but as she looked at the sky, numberless stars filled the firmament. The crescent moon glowed brightest of all.

Forbidden guard of many races filled the paved street and dilapidated houses surrounding them. A few of the sad buildings had pitched roofs, but most were flat and tiled. Several women, blinded by slashes across their eyes, offered water from jars to a group of men clad in black leather armor, each with the outline of a green octagon emblazoned on the back that contained a single calligraphic character that Salmaara didn't recognize.

One of the Guard guffawed and snatched the nearest woman, swatting the water from her hands. The jug shattered on stone as the man threw her to the ground.

The other men followed suit, felling the other two as they tried to run.

Salmaara could no longer see them through the surging mass of bodies, while four male liths stood watching in silence.

"Where are we?" she asked, her voice quaking. Her heart pounded, and her gut twisted as the women's cries faded into the distance. She wanted to go to them, help them any way she could. Meanwhile, her captor seemed not to notice any of it.

"*In Northern Yendu, Prey, near the Forbidden City of the Blue King.*"

Salmaara gasped quietly. "Kalitoomba?"

"*So it used to be. Prey is overly educated to know such a name.*" The lith's eyes glinted in the starlight. "*If Prey looks there, it can see the ruins.*"

Salmaara craned to see in the direction that Gray Face had indicated. He had almost reached the edge of the little settlement, where a bridge spanned the wide river just ahead.

He walked over the bridge and a short way up a grassy incline that shimmered blue in the moonlight. He paused at its brink.

Salmaara lifted her eyes to the hills before her and beheld the corpse of a city illuminated in silver. It was difficult to discern more of the city's details in the soft light, but its size was unmistakable. It went on forever.

From what she knew, it must have once spread well into the valley surrounding her, though there was little evidence of it now. Most of the city covered the rolling hills before it fell from sight on the other side of the massive humps of earth.

According to the books, the broken glass towers that dotted the hills must have once been double or triple their current height. Holes pocked the massive city wall. Part of it caved in as Salmaara watched.

Kalitoomba had enjoyed a warless existence for millennia. Not a society without crime, surely, but most enjoyed widespread harmony after King Yulari incarcerated his wife, Vias the Destroyer. The people had been able to build and develop freely.

It had taken seven thousand years to build, and now it crumbled slowly, abandoned, forbidden.

"It's beautiful, even in death," she said softly.

"*Indeed. It was splendid in life. I knew it well, for I worked in the city for a time.*"

Salmaara's eyes widened. "You were alive then? How long ago was that?" she breathed out, her eyes still on the crumbling edifices.

"*Over a century, Prey. Lives have shortened since that time, certainly. And they shall shorten further. Some peoples lived more than a millennium in that time. Some of us live nearly as long still. But only for now.*

"*The gods have left us. Living near them made us greater, expanded our lives. Many of us find our own children live the smallest fraction of what we have and what we will if we were given the gift.*"

Salmaara's heart sank. *The gift of long life. If what my books said is true, then Empress Velanoma is responsible for our decline. She threw down the Blue King and took the world for herself. Look what she has done with it— blinding people because they live within sight of her enemy's city. Certainly a cruel way to make people forget what came before.*

As she pondered, Salmaara remembered an ancient phrase from her readings that had always vexed her. According to the books, it was an awesome power, but nothing she read specified for what it was used. She had always wondered. *Perhaps he knows.*

"Did they lose Xin'Dai, as well?" A strange, warm sweetness thrummed through her when she spoke the term, like honey in tea.

"*Xin'Dai? Where does Prey learn such dangerous language? Xin'Dai is the power of the Destroyer's creations. It gives me and all my people voice and more abilities for the elect.*" His eerie amber eyes bored into her. "

Has Prey seen enough?"

She nodded reluctantly. "Where are we going after this?" She tore her eyes from his to stare at her hands.

"*To Günhai, Prey.*"

"My name is Salmaara, not Prey, Gray Face." She glared at her hands, balling them into fists. Looking back up, she set her jaw. "Is Günhai a lovely place?"

"*Prey is not so educated as I originally assessed. Of course it is.*" He scrunched his eyes to slits, as though he might laugh. "*I am called Yezhr, Prey, and I, as its master, and as the city's superintendent, must wish you beforehand, a most pleasant life within Günhai's cheery walls.*"

As she gazed into his alien eyes, she had a sinking feeling that this Günhai was not as he suggested.

CHAPTER NINE

GÜNHAI,
MAUVIAS

G ünhai City crouched in the mouth of the Nva Pass, the only break in the jagged T'Skel Mountains that separated Mauvias, the northernmost nation, from the rest of the world.

Northward, to the east and west across vast expanses of arid wilderness, lay the cities Tzu Tihas, Capital of Mauvias, and Kaskahai, city built into an ancient volcano on the western plains. Legend had it that the soul of Vias the Destroyer Goddess was still imprisoned in Kaskahai seven millennia after her defeat.

Immediately south of Günhai was the Trelta, a thick, poisoned forest, said to be cursed by one of the four creators, the Green God Esthadya Lordian. The labyrinth of bleached white trunks and the toxic yellow haze that hung over it ran south until the trees thickened and became the temperate rainforest that covered the nation of Arvitra. It had once been the empire's goal to make Arvitra capital of the world. Those lands were under the rule of Queen Kusae.

Günhai's expansive collection of buildings was uniformly cubical and squat. Squared stone corridors linked all structures, which were built close together and formed a vortex that increased in density and height from the outside in. A mammoth cube jutted from the city's center, toward the sky.

The city had once been a pale gray, but millennia of ashy staining from Mauvias' cursed air had turned everything black as a starless night.

Most striking about Günhai was that even from the distant road that led to its gates, an endless cacophony of shrieks, cries, and wails could be heard.

Within the city buildings, all was dim and hot. Disembodied screams echoed through labyrinthine corridors. Sometimes the cries dimmed, at other times they rose in intensity, but they never ceased. All time in the Prison City was one eternal span in the dark, occupied only by the incessant entreaties of those condemned to the hands of the talented masters there.

Gjordkra stood in the governor's office within the center cube of the indoor city beside an ancient stone desk, more aptly described as an altar for how its master used it. A mutilated half of a body lay on it. The head hung over the side nearest to her. It had long ringlets, so might have been a woman…

She didn't examine it too closely.

There would always be another in its place. She would have to deal with it later anyway. Governor Jhaill Opthonne never cleaned up after himself. He made her do it.

The past few weeks had been a nice reprieve from the usual, with the young men and women her master had worked on and then sent back to the rebels, alive. While her master was truly expert with blades, it was the mind, heart, and very soul that he most loved to dissect and dismember. Even though she didn't know much about the rebel queen and her people, she did feel a little sorry for the people those men and women would return to. There wouldn't be anything left of who they once were, that was just how it was after Jhaill was done with you.

Gjordkra was short for a seventeen-year-old, standing well under six feet. Her seven-foot lithian master dwarfed her.

Her skin was fair beneath the ash and blood that discolored it. She had matted black and purple hair that reached to her middle. Her masters saw fit to hack it shorter only when it threatened to choke her. She kept her gaunt features carefully neutral, for with every passing year, her thin frame became less and less resilient to Jhaill's experiments. Thick lashes framed bitter, violet eyes.

She'd been stolen from her home when she was three years old, a home of which she had no memory. She didn't even know what her name had been. Jhaill had bestowed the cumbersome name "Gjordkra" on her sometime after her arrival, an old name that meant "mischief." It was the only name she knew.

The corpse's freshly spilled blood plumed from the floor in a rosy cloud as Mauvias' cursed air steadily sucked it up. It misted her face with its tangy stench. She stepped back, out of the cloud, absently brushing at her cheeks. Such things no longer bothered her. No fluid survived the unquenchable thirst bestowed on Mauvias by its goddess. The blood vanished.

Her attention returned to the mouthless man who knelt before her. "*And so it is with the utmost humility and sincerity,*" Governor Jhaill Opthonne of Günhai paused, his telepathic voice reverberating in her head. All gifted with mind powers had their own signature. Jhaill's felt like thin wire constricting around her head.

He took one of her slender hands in both of his, blood caked them, "*...that I command you to be my wife,*" he purred.

Jhaill cocked his black-feathered head to the side. He was bald on top, and the mangy assortment of feathers that still sprouted from his skull formed an upside-down crown. Scars scored his body where he regularly cut away pieces to satisfy a long-standing habit of brewing potions. Two ghastly scars stood out on his back from where his wings had been removed at birth, as was custom among liths. He possessed scarlet eyes, like twin embers.

"Your wife? What is a wife?" Gjordkra asked. She fought the urge to take a cautionary step backward as so to place herself out of his reach. Unfortunately, to do so would please him and give him cause to break her hand, which he still held. She remained, but tensed, and wondered why he was kneeling.

His slick voice enveloped her mind. "*A wife will be called governess and bear my heirs. A wife cannot be touched by any other man. Wife is a southern notion, which the empress has suggested we adopt.*"

Mirth hung on every word. Why did he find this so amusing? She yanked her hand free of his and shook her head slowly.

"You're as foul a fiend as any indecent Mauviasen woman could desire for herself, Jhaill Opthonne," she said. Her voice trembled. If she played along, he might let her be.

"*Then we have an accord?*" His scarlet eyes grinned with savage delight.

If she defied him, she'd wind up among the remains on the altar. He had cut what resistance she had out of her long ago. She had decided to live.

She closed her eyes against the sight of him and imagined a weathered face surrounded by vibrant black plants that shimmered green, blue, and red where the brightest sunslight touched their leaves. Gjordkra didn't know who the old woman in her vision was but liked to think she had been part of her life before Gjordkra was abducted and given to Jhaill. She envisioned the old woman's leathery brown skin, twinkling eyes, and coarse silver hair filled with clods of the fertile soil the old woman loved. Gjordkra loved it, too.

Jhaill's chill voice broke into her thoughts. *"Where are you going, my Mischief?"*

Her eyes snapped open as one of his arms caught her around the waist. She had been walking unconsciously toward the door.

Gjordkra's breath caught. She focused on regaining it to quell the shiver that threatened to quake her body. A reaction of that sort would only amuse him. It was what he wanted.

Jhaill rested his sharp face in her black mane. Someone cleared his throat in the dark hall just outside the open door. Jhaill's scarlet eyes narrowed with displeasure as he looked up. She exhaled quietly.

"G-Governor Opthonne," Governor Ghu of Tzu Tihas said in a tremulous voice. He stood in the doorway.

Ghu was a dwarf of a man, barely five feet. His ashy flesh matched his glazed, orange eyes. Patchy wisps of brown hair poked from the thick bandages wound around his pasty scalp. He wore a translucent black robe that tied on his shoulders, much like the one that Jhaill wore—robes of a Mauviasen official. An olive-green robe that reached to Gjordkra's knees adorned her body, its color and style an indicator of her status as Jhaill's property.

Everyone except Ghu in Mauviasen government knew that Prince Soar, Ghu's master, planned on killing the little Governor eventually. Gjordkra pitied him. If his wounds from the latest clash with his ruthless prince were not trying, he was in a chronic state of near fatal anxiety about something else.

Jhaill pulled Gjordkra into his side with his arm around her torso. His fingers pried slowly into her ribs.

"To what do we owe this visit?" he said coolly, extending his telepathic

voice to Ghu. He didn't bother to sever his connection with Gjordkra.

"You seem busy, G-governor," Ghu said. He folded his arms and smiled nervously at Gjordkra.

Jhaill probed deeper between Gjordkra's ribs. She grunted as a sickening pop sounded within her.

"Please, do come in, excuse my fiancée. Tell what you have come to say."

The lithian governor shoved Gjordkra directly out from his side. She toppled over a stone chest near the desk.

She lay scrunched up and clutched her ribs, which now seared where his fingers had pulled one away from its proper location. Just another skilled dislocation, one out of thousands. Her eyes watered.

If she'd had the strength to pull herself up in a dignified manner, she would have. And better yet, left the room. Now would be a good time to escape and get some sleep. She couldn't recall the last time she'd had any. Also, Jhaill would have her clean up the desk soon if she lingered too long.

Gjordkra turned her misty eyes back to the governors who conversed in terse tones. She cradled her ribs.

"She was taken. Some are c-convinced that Vadik Asenar is the perpetrator," Ghu was saying.

Jhaill stiffened.

"Vadik Asenar? The Prince of Kaskahai is dead, is he not? I attended the hanging of the remains myself." Jhaill attempted to mask his fear with a mocking tone, but Gjordkra could feel and see it, for she knew her master well.

As she understood it, Prince Soar of Tzu Tihas was the last of the Mauviasen princes, and since all had been assimilated into the great empire, even his influence was much diminished.

Who is this man who frightens my master, who lives to terrorize anything that breathes?

"The f-facts surrounding the prince's death are now under c-considerable scrutiny. The timing was perfect. His t-treacherous daughter had just committed her sin. He must have known there was no h-hope for her—or him, by association. And so he faked his d-death, went into hiding, and waited. We cannot guess his m-motives for what he has done," Ghu said animatedly.

Jhaill's scarlet eyes narrowed. *"Has she placed a bounty on his head?"*

"Y-yes, a high one. He owes the empress information and the creature he stole." Ghu paused and cast a glance back at Gjordkra. Jhaill followed his gaze, his own lingering upon her with gruesome pleasure for several moments. They looked away from her.

"H-he is a dangerous opponent. I know of few others who could snatch what was most staunchly g-guarded from the empress's bosom and escape with such a bang. He hasn't lost his touch," Ghu stuttered with a slight upward curve of his lips. "He wounded many on his way out, my p-prince included."

Gjordkra knew that all of Ghu's problems would disappear if Prince Soar did. That must be the source of the glee she could see building in his features.

"You're saying that he infiltrated Tzu Tihas and then Fortress T'Vulus alone, for the second time in his life, and stole the little oddity? Then escaped?"

"In short, y-yes."

"Destroyer damn him."

"My message is one of c-caution. If you hear anything, r-report. He's been moved to priority one on the f-fugitive list. She wants him a-alive if possible, and the dragon p-princess, too," Ghu said.

"A condition I do not feel inclined to pander to given past grievances perpetrated by the party concerned. Has she found the emperor, yet?"

Ghu shrugged. "He slipped her a-again."

Silence fell. Sethmar Danvi, former Emperor of Mauvias, had been the top fugitive since the empire's break with Queen Kusae. Gjordkra loved to hear about him and how he could thwart the omnipotent empress, how he always disappeared into nothing and caused trouble when the tyrant had her fist around him.

"I've heard that you p-plan to wed this creature. That… southern custom," Ghu said uncomfortably after a moment. He waved a hand as if to swat the unpleasant word from the air. Both of them turned to eye Gjordkra again.

Still clutching her throbbing ribs, she pretended to be unconscious. She had hoped they might take their discussion elsewhere so she wouldn't attract their attention when she got up.

"*It shall be the grandest event Günhai has ever seen,*" Jhaill said.

"That's saying n-nothing. Why're you even b-bothering with the tedious southern ritual?"

"*Why not? To be in good graces with her majesty is cause enough. Of course, Gjordkra's stunning lineage, from both sides, cannot be ignored. She shall produce a fine heir to my seat.*" Gjordkra could feel Jhaill's malevolent gaze as he spoke.

Her mouth cracked open in the dark. She didn't know Jhaill knew where she came from. Inquiring would mean staying. Worse, it would authorize him to play with her as payment for such an indulgence of her fancy. Jhaill never rendered any service without a price—he was of Shazrah blood.

"*Scurry off, find food, and rest,*" he told her. "*I shall require you later.*"

She didn't know how many of her thoughts her lithian Master of Torture heard. He rarely acted on them. He seemed to save them up for those dreadful occasions when he used her secrets against her. Occasions that involved sharp implements and being hung at any angle or strapped to whatever he fancied.

Gjordkra staggered to her feet. A reprieve of this nature was rare. She stumbled from the room with a hand on her side. She felt the familiar withdrawal of Jhaill's mind from her own as she fled from his presence, the only breath of free air she ever got.

CHAPTER TEN

TRELTA FOREST,
ARVITRA

Salmaara slept fitfully. Her stomach roiled with gelatinous hydration powder. Water did not exist in Mauvias, her captor Yezhr had said, unless you were the absurdly rich and innovative Prince of Tzu Tihas. Any open water would be sucked up into the cursed air in moments, so it was hydration powder or nothing.

Since the powder made her ill, she had decided to try nothing, but quickly became thirsty enough to put the wretched stuff in her mouth when it was offered. The fine powder turned to thick sludge by the time it reached her stomach. It served all of water's purposes, and most important of all, Yezhr instructed, it kept Mauvias's toxins at bay and those were not few or to be underestimated. Without the magenta powder she would die quickly and painfully, but she still found herself longing for the feel of liquid in her mouth. Yezhr said the sickness would pass.

She lay on a soft pallet, panting, with her head turned to the side. She had thrown up the powder again. Yezhr and his silent group of followers, only about twenty strong by Salmaara's estimate, camped among a cluster of massive boulders, each the size and height of a single-story house. The stones blocked all wind and sound, but Salmaara could smell something bitter in the air.

Yezhr took great pains to ensure her comfort. He loomed over her with a tattered rag in his slender hand. He wiped fresh vomit from the corners of her mouth with an expression of mock tenderness.

Everything about him deeply unsettled her... his wraithlike movements, his telepathic voice, and especially his wide eyes. All traits common to the race the Destroyer had created to be her assassins and promote chaos so long ago.

Yezhr gazed down at her, his head cocked to the side, apparently admiring his handiwork.

Salmaara decided this was what it felt like to be a pet.

She found herself thinking of the nameless llama. *Did our denial of its intelligence, our care-taking, however well-intentioned, make it feel like this? Trapped, degraded? Is that what drove the poor creature over the edge, to sulking, slinking, and frenzied assault?*

When Yezhr walked away, she gazed into the night sky with dry eyes. The tears stopped after the first week, and the only feeling that remained of her father and home was a dull ache deep in her chest, and guilt that never left her in peace. She tried to remember Illun's face, or even the scent of clay, but couldn't...not while in thrall of this eternal nightmare. She tried to think of things to be thankful for, as her father had always told her to do when she thought the world was being unfair, but could think of nothing. Salmaara remembered Illun's last words to her, to be grateful for her life, but in her captivity, she could only feel the bitter sting of loss.

Salmaara's leg was healing, but Yezhr insisted on carrying her everywhere with perverse pleasure. He said he wouldn't want her taxing herself overmuch. He took over every mundane task for her, even those she could do without his assistance no matter how hard she tried to resist.

The potter's daughter hadn't previously considered grooming something precious. Yezhr tied her hands behind her back with silken rope and proceeded to feed her, bathe her, brush her hair, and clean her teeth. With the lith's every unwelcome touch, when his voice, thick with mock patience, reverberated in her mind as though it belonged to her, a primal scream swelled inside of Salmaara.

It built up a little more daily, filling her chest, pressing upon her vitals until she felt she could no longer breathe. Somehow she kept the scream within, but knew it wouldn't be long before it escaped. But she couldn't protest.

Every time his voice violated her mind, she wondered if what her father had said was true, that the lith could entertain himself with her thoughts. She worried about it constantly, but thus far, Yezhr gave no sign that he could.

She was losing herself, forgetting the potter's daughter, the girl who loved to sneak into her wooded sanctuary to bury herself in her wondrous books. That was another life. She was becoming a desperate animal—a creature called Prey. A creature that wanted nothing more than to vanish into a deep crevice, safe from Yezhr's touch forever. Or claw his eyes out. And a creature with small chance of escape until her leg healed completely.

Yezhr returned to her side.

"*Now, Prey, I have ensured it is ready for my home, which it too shall adopt until sweet death carries it hence. Its leg is still damaged, regrettably, but this shall soon pass, I sense.*"

She nodded hastily, not knowing how else to respond. Anger began to build from the aching place in her chest, but she kept it in check. She squeezed her eyes shut.

"*No, no, Prey must not sleep, I want it awake when we arrive. We leave now.*"

Salmaara opened her eyes. "We do?"

"*Yes, Prey,*" he replied. Yezhr gathered her into his arms once more. Her bound limbs hung immobile and flopped as he strode along. She stared ahead.

"*We shall be in Günhai this afternoon,*" Yezhr said. He strode onto a bluff overlooking an emaciated forest wreathed in a dense yellow haze. Its many bereaved trees, bleached white, reached for the sky like jagged teeth covered in acrid breath.

The air in front of the forest looked strange, thick, like an undulating bubble. Threads of water flowed toward it from the ground, from the trees, from the sky. As the threads arrived, the ominous bubble assimilated them, but it didn't seem to grow. "What is that?" Salmaara croaked.

"*The Destroyer's Lands—Mauvias, Prey.*"

Salmaara gasped, her eyes widened. "We're going to Vias's lands, as in the Destroyer Goddess's?"

A sound like snickering vibrated unpleasantly in her mind. "*Where did Prey suppose we were going?*"

She said nothing and turned to stare at the streams of moisture being sucked into the bubble. *Vias's lands. The Destroyer. The goddess responsible for the ruin of worlds. I've got to get away.*

"*Prey will wear this,*" Yezhr said. He tied a heavy cloth over the lower half of her face.

"*Now we go,*" he said. They stepped into the bubble, the lithian troop close behind.

The air tore every bead of moisture from her skin, from her hair, from her clothes. A faint mist in her shape hovered for a moment in the thick air, then vanished. She squeezed her eyes shut in attempt to moisten them, and they stayed closed.

Soon, the rhythmic motion of Yezhr's steps pushed her into sleep.

Salmaara realized her nakedness with horror. She wondered if she could cover herself with a shred of the black nothing that engulfed her. She groped around herself, her limbs numb with cold. She felt empty, alone.

Heart pounding, she staggered forward. A host of voices sounded in her ears, all speaking tongues she did not know. Fingers brushed her leg. The burn started on the surface, penetrated her skin, spread from her thigh until it consumed her. She gasped, afraid, and broke into a sprint. She stumbled and pitched forward onto her knees. Her open palm fell upon a smooth object. It ignited with silvery light. Salmaara took it in both hands and lifted it from the darkness.

She gazed at it, into it. Swirling constellations surrounded numberless worlds. Suns and moons, dark and light. Her heart sped at the vastness of it.

I want to be part of it, *she thought.* I am needed. So desperately needed.

Something moved in front of her. She looked up. A young man stepped into the light of the orb. She had never seen someone so beautiful. Darkness draped much of his form, but she could see fair skin like white alabaster, covering warrior's muscles. Silken black hair reached to the nape of his neck, and the shadow of a beard colored his chiseled jaw. He wore a quizzical smile as he examined the orb in her hands. His eyes were a dazzling swirl of red, blue, violet, and silver, like the night sky at winter festival. Gazing into their depths made Salmaara's heart pound. In them, she saw raw power, and a vast sadness. Sadness unlike any she had ever seen, not even on her father's face.

Something deep within her stirred. I know him, *she thought.* Why is he so sad? *Aloud she said,* "What is wrong?"

He was so intent on the orb in his hands that he didn't seem to see or hear her. He turned away abruptly, and strode back into the dark. "Wait!"

She took a step forward, and fell.

Her eyes snapped open, dry. She sucked in a mouthful of empty air. Yezhr looked down at her as she did so, his brow quizzical. She coughed, tried to wet her mouth, but couldn't. *Who was that?*

Salmaara twisted to gaze ahead and beheld a maze of square edifices that spanned the entirety of a narrow pass, blocking the way forward. A scream echoed through the pass, then another. More followed, shrieks, cries, howls. They blended together into a discordant symphony. She shivered as she discerned the source.

The sound was coming from the city.

CHAPTER ELEVEN

GÜNHAI,
MAUVIAS

"**W**elcome to *Günhai, Prey*," Yezhr said with chilly delight as they entered the prison city beneath a cracked gateway of rudely piled stones. The gates themselves were of the same bland stone, stained black.

Black flags hung to either side of the gates. A solitary emerald octagon covered the center of each, with a vertical slash sundering the octagon in two, and a coil of fire surrounded the octagon. She knew the flag— its name was *Maliem Esculis*, the Conqueror, ensign of the Destroyer.

Salmaara squeezed her eyes shut against the screams that grew in volume as they entered the vast courtyard leading into the labyrinth of buildings that comprised the city. She turned her head, but the shrieks and moans seemed to come from every direction at once.

A male lith approached, accompanied by a second man of Salmaara's own race, who was short and trailing a small stream of slowly disappearing sweat. She felt her heart rise somewhat at the sight of him. Having been among liths for the majority of her journey, she had seen few sulmai.

"*You've returned at last, Yezhr,*" the former said coolly within the minds of all present. His scarlet eyes flicked down to Salmaara, still held in Yezhr's arms.

She stared up at him. She had never seen such a face.

Several drops of blood rose from his black-stained cheeks then disappeared as they drifted into the air. His head was tall and narrow, and his cheekbones jutted, accenting his lack of a mouth. Thin feathers, black as pitch, barely covered his balding head, while haughty brows hovered over scarlet eyes.

"*I see you brought a prize,*" the lith said, not removing his nauseating gaze from Salmaara's face.

She met his gaze and held it, hoping her face showed none of the fear she felt.

Gooseflesh spread down her arms. She could sense his malevolence and a profound darkness around him. She didn't know how, but she knew it had to do with countless lives he had cut short.

When the scarlet-eyed lith cocked his head and looked back to Yezhr when he spoke, Salmaara released a long breath. *And I thought that Yezhr was bad. I am in the Destroyer's lands now, among her people,* Salmaara thought to herself, although she struggled to believe it.

It had been over a month since Yezhr had dragged her away from Bhevir, yet she still often held out hope that she was dreaming. *I'll wake up, Father will be down at his wheel, and then I'll ...* She cut the thoughts off as her heart constricted painfully and shoved the memories of her lost life away to a place deep within herself where they couldn't hurt her.

"*Indeed, I have, my governor Jhaill. It gave me a good hunt,*" Yezhr was saying, clearly pleased with himself. He looked down at her as though Salmaara were a felled doe. "*I request your permission to house my Prey with your Gjordkra.*"

"*Granted. Did word of our engagement reach you in your southern escapades?*"

Yezhr remained silent for several moments. "*No. Certainly not. What sort of engagement?*" His brown head -feathers rose slightly.

The sulmai man smirked from behind the lithian governor while tugging at his pudgy fingers, twisting them nervously. "They shall even have a w-wedding," he said.

"*A wedding?*" Yezhr cocked his head slowly, his amber eyes intent.

"*A legally binding ceremony accompanied by grand partying. Surely, having travelled in the south, you are familiar with the terms* husband *and* wife? *Gjordkra shall become my wife and governess of Günhai and shall bear my heir,*" Scarlet Eyes explained.

"*I know what a wedding is, Jhaill. Will such a thing not provoke the Shazrah?*" Yezhr asked.

Jhaill laughed, a short sound cold as winter's heart. "*Of course it will. They just don't understand my aim yet.*"

"*Perhaps you would do well to explain it to them.*" Yezhr's grip on Salmaara firmed.

"*With pleasure, but later.*"

Yezhr relaxed and shifted Salmaara. "*I beg your pardon governors, but I would like to put my Prey where it belongs and attend to my duties that have no doubt piled up in my absence.*"

"I, too, m-must take my leave," the jittery man said, his glazed eyes falling on Salmaara, who loosened her clutch on her captor.

The two liths inclined their heads then turned their backs as the little man hurried to a metallic carriage near the gates, drawn by two winged men, and entered it. Turning away from Yezhr and Salmaara, the lithian governor reentered the shrieking edifice ahead.

"*Inside we go,*" Yezhr said as he moved to follow.

The stuffy chamber made her sweat. Not little droplets, not even large ones as though she had run for miles. It saturated her. She was certain she was leaving a wet trail behind her, except she could feel and smell it around her in a cloud. The air was sucking it up. She would be a dehydrated husk if it continued.

She could not see anything beyond the faint outline of her hands in front of her as she crawled along the stone floor, away from where Yezhr had laid her. Salmaara could feel no grooves or variation in elevation.

She continued forward, her gut contracting at the constant shrieking that surrounded her, each sounding nearer and nearer, more pleading, more desperate, and more despairing. Her ears rang with them. She wondered how long it would be before the ghastly cries shattered her ears.

She strained to see her way in vain. *How can I stop sweating?*

She could not tell how large the room was— it seemed eternal. *What am I going to do? I am so far from home—not that home exists anymore— and a prisoner of Mauvias, at its mercy and that of its creatures.*

For the thousandth time since her capture, Salmaara wondered, *Am I really doomed to be a pet for the rest of my life? A slave who serves no purpose other than to busy her master's hands when he grows bored?* The anger and panic at the notion rose until she was breathing hard.

She shook herself. *I'll escape. I'm not meant to die here. Father died for me. I won't waste his sacrifice, no matter what.*

Setting her jaw, she continued forward, wondering if there was anything in the room. Even bashing into a wall would be a welcome encounter, but the interminable floor merely continued.

She could sense someone just ahead, and then one of her quaking hands fell on something soft.

Rough fingers snatched her wrist and wrenched her hand violently around.

Salmaara fell onto her back, stunned.

Red light within a lantern sputtered to life immediately beside her, illuminating the fierce face of the girl who bent over her.

"Who are you?" the gaunt woman demanded tersely. Her violet eyes flashed, and tangled black curls framed her hard face.

"S-Salmaara!" the potter's daughter blurted. A tear slipped down her face to mingle with the sweat then disappeared into the cursed air. "Friends call me Maara," she added in a small voice.

"Are those tears? You won't last long here shedding those," the girl said severely.

Salmaara said nothing and pried her wrist from her attacker's grasp.

"My name is Gjordkra. Who put you in here?"

"Yezhr," Salmaara replied and flinched as another ear-splitting wail sounded from somewhere nearby.

"You'll get used to that," Gjordkra said. She turned to rummage through a wadded blanket then turned back to Salmaara, extending something that might have once been bread.

"It sounds as though the very walls are screaming," said the potter's daughter, accepting the foodstuff.

"You know stone, right?" Salmaara's new companion looked around them, at the stone comprising the floors, walls, and ceiling, before returning her gaze to the red-haired girl. The crimson light of her lantern danced in her violet eyes.

Günhai's newest prisoner shook her head in answer.

"It records and holds memories. Sometimes it just lets the memories back out, so ... the walls probably do scream," Gjordkra said as though

Salmaara was silly for not knowing something so basic.

Then she shifted the conversation away from their surroundings. "You shouldn't have to worry too much, I think. Yezhr likes to collect them, show them off. He's not as bad as Jhaill. Did you come from the south?" She bit into a second piece of "bread" with a crackling crunch that was nearly drowned out by another high-pitched wail.

"Yes," Salmaara said slowly.

The food seemed to writhe in her mouth. The flavor reminded her of a fungus that she had once sampled in the woods behind her house but considerably spicier. It was also salty, with a little tang.

Salmaara recognized the taste of blood. She choked and spat it out. Her comrade, however, didn't appear to notice.

"Even better. He must think you're worth something," she said then downed the bread effortlessly as Salmaara swallowed a gag.

Gjordkra gestured toward the pathetic excuse for foodstuff. "You'll get used to that, too, I guess," she said with a shrug.

She tossed a small pouch to Salmaara, who recognized the hydration powder. Although she knew it wouldn't quench her thirst, Salmaara downed it eagerly.

Gjordkra settled into a cross-legged position. "So, where are you from, Salmaara?"

The potter's daughter sighed. "Bhevir, in Southern Yendu."

"How old are you?"

"Sixteen. I'll be seventeen later this year." Salmaara looked at her empty pouch.

"You're lucky. If you're eighteen, there's no limit to what they do with you. They think that contact—you know, that way—with any younger female will curse them somehow. This land was founded by a woman ... don't know if it means anything. You'd think they'd be more respectful either way," Gjordkra said.

"I … I'd think so, too," Salmaara said.

"You? Where are you from?" Salmaara asked before deciding to choke down some spicy bread.

"I was taken from my home before I can recall. So, no idea. I was a present from the empress to Governor Jhaill Opthonne or something. He's in charge. If you can avoid him, you should. He's the foulest slime in this stinkhole. I belong to him. We're due to be married sometime soon, for my eighteenth birthday. He just learned what marriage is, a southern notion that the empress condones. So, I guess that will make me Governess of Günhai. Not saying much, you know," she said, her eyes narrowed to slits.

The lith's demonic face, still fresh in her memory, swam into Salmaara's mind—his black feathers and smoldering scarlet eyes. Yezhr had referred to him as governor.

"I'm sorry, Gjordkra," said Salmaara.

"Why?" Gjordkra asked, tearing another chunk free from the bread and crunched on it. The sound reminded Salmaara of the resonance of splintering bone.

"Because … well, it sounds unspeakably horrid. We'll just escape. Between the two of us, we should be able to get out of here," Salmaara said, staring into the dark, toward where she thought the ceiling must be. *It's up there somewhere.*

Gjordkra snorted. "Get your head out of the clouds, they'll choke you. You seriously don't think I've tried? Do you want me to show you what it looks like when you try to escape?" She lifted her ratty shirt to expose one of her sides.

Salmaara craned to see. She stared at the inflamed skin, the endless myriad of scars that covered the girl's side. It looked as if a toddler had scribbled a nonsensical creation into Gjordkra's flesh, heedless that room ran out long ago.

Salmaara gasped and tried to tear her eyes from the maimed flesh but couldn't.

Gjordkra covered her ruined body once more. "You see?"

"So, you stopped trying?"

"Oh, and you wouldn't? A girl who cried when I touched her wrist?" Gjordkra raised a brow quizzically, folded her arms, and cocked her head.

"I lost everything. They killed my father, burned my house, and wouldn't let me do anything because my leg is broken. Not even clean my own teeth. I have nothing to lose. But, I will not live out my life in this dark place."

Gjordkra scooted closer to Salmaara. "Accept your lot. People who come here never leave—not in one piece anyway. Might as well serve your master. They might let you live longer if you do."

"That doesn't sound like living to me." A shriek punctuated the statement.

Her bad leg twitched with a cramp, and she gritted her teeth.

Gjordkra took another overly large bite of bread. "Just reality."

"I won't accept it," Salmaara declared.

Gjordkra frowned and shook her head once but said nothing.

"I won't let them win. I won't forget the people they killed and will kill. Besides, you can't fail until you stop trying, and I don't intend to," Salmaara said quietly through cracked lips.

"You really won't last here. They haven't even started on you and you're already delusional."

"I'm going to get out of here," Salmaara said without conviction.

"In several pieces. I've heard it all before. There are so many that have gone before you with the same stupid notion. They're dead. Hundreds.

Thousands maybe. That's just who my master alone has done away with. You do know when they aren't here, they keep track of your signature, right? If you think the wrong thoughts, it gets their attention. If you're in the wrong place, they know." Gjordkra rested her chin in her hands.

"Signature …?"

"Yeah. Wait. Don't tell me you don't know what a signature is?"

Salmaara's ears heated. "Sorry, no."

"It's the feeling your soul gives off. Everyone's is different … Jhaill's kind of feels like thin wire wrapped around your head. Yezhr's—"

"Reminds me of the blade of an axe against my throat," Salmaara finished for her.

The feelings associated with others that she had sensed since she could recall were what Gjordkra had named signatures. Illun's signature, which she had been aware of each day they had lived together up until the moment he had died, had been soft yet cool, like the silky clay he molded for his trade. Rianne's had always made Salmaara think of the gentle wingbeats of a small bird, flitting here and there. As she considered the matter, she realized that she had known the signatures belonging to most of the folk in Bhevir.

The potter's daughter swallowed and wrung her hands. *I cannot bear to think of them now …*

"Yeah. If you want immediate death, carry on, delusional girl. Or accept that you're here now. There are few who win the curse of long life from our masters. Those people, such as myself, live carefully. Before I speak a word, or even think, I have considered what might happen. I understand what makes me valuable. It's my master's right to carve me into a feast if he feels like it. That's why I'm still alive and other girls lie in rotting pieces. You're another cute little thing with crazy ideas." She rested a hand on one of Salmaara's shoulders. "I don't want to have to clean you up off the floor." Gjordkra took a long breath. "So, for your own good, think about why Yezhr would want you."

Salmaara remained silent. Then she said, "I don't wish to talk about it. I'm going to sleep." She lay down and closed her eyes.

Gjordkra snorted. "Good luck."

Salmaara heard her move away on the hard floor, and then the dim lantern light that shone through her eyelids extinguished.

As Salmaara lay there, Gjordkra's words taunted her. *"Accept your lot. People who come here never leave—not in one piece anyway. Might as well serve your master. They might let you live longer if you do."*

What am I going to do? "Reality," she said. This is reality. My father is dead, Bhevir is gone and, with it, everyone and everything I ever loved. I lost my freedom, am subject to a master who calls me "it" and "Prey." Perhaps she is right. Perhaps I should accept my lot. Maybe I will get used to this life in the dark where every day is likely to be the last.

She curled up, knees to her chest, around the growing ache in her heart as despair took hold. *Why did this have to happen?*

As she thought to surrender to her sorrow, the deep, booming voice she had always imagined belonged to King Yulari as she read her father's books sounded in her mind: *Times of sore hardship come to all. Do not be discouraged; be believing, be happy, for these times will not last forever. They shall be but a small moment, and if you but endure, there is nothing you cannot overcome.*

On the heels of those words, came some of the last that Illun had imparted to her, spoken in his gentle voice. *"Where there is life, there is hope."*

Salmaara opened her eyes. *There is life. I will face this. I can endure. I won't be here forever, for I will find a way out.*

CHAPTER TWELVE

GÜNHAI,
MAUVIAS

No dawn of any sort came, for in Günhai, there were no dawns, nor was there dusk, day, or night, just an indefinite stretch of time in its lightproof halls. Salmaara suspected that days had passed since she arrived but couldn't be sure.

A rough hand grasped one of Salmaara's shoulders and shook it firmly. She gasped and sat up. The muscles in her back cramping, she doubled over and muffled a moan with her hand.

"It's me," Gjordkra said wearily. "My master wants us. I guess you won't be avoiding him after all."

Salmaara rubbed her eyes, which crusted them with more filth than had already clotted her lashes upon waking. She swiped at them again with no more success. Turning her sleeve inside out, she removed enough dirt to see.

"Which way do we go?"

Gjordkra was already gone.

Salmaara swiveled to her knees. She bit her lip and pressed on her toes, causing a faint ache to swell up her leg. She thrust herself to her feet from her palms, tested her weight on her bad leg, and found that she could walk. So, she hobbled toward the crimson-lit doorframe and into the hallway, where she saw Gjordkra stood a short ways ahead, lit by a dim, red lantern that hung on the wall.

Like the outside of Günhai, its corridors were squat and square. They constricted in on those who dared traverse them, as if slowly digesting them. Squinting lanterns lined the halls on both sides, shedding faint, ruddy light. They didn't reveal the source of the chronic shrieking.

Salmaara limped behind the future governess. "What do they do here? Why does the screaming never stop?"

Gjordkra did not turn or slow her pace. "Interrogation. Mutilation. Every sort of torture one could think of," she said with a shrug.

Salmaara shivered. "Don't they ever run out of people to torture?"

"Why would they? Is the world short on them?" Gjordkra asked.

She led Salmaara up a narrow passage that reeked of blood, toward a door that stood open, a rutilant glow emanating from within.

The two girls entered, Salmaara staying behind Gjordkra.

"*Here you are at last.*"

Salmaara did not need to look around Gjordkra to know the speaker was Governor Opthonne. She wouldn't forget that voice any time soon. Besides, she recognized the sensation of the lith's signature, which felt as though a thin wire wrapped around her head, squeezing. Once, she might have rested her hands on her head to feel where she thought something touched her, but weeks of traveling with Yezhr had taught her that there would be nothing there.

Gjordkra bowed and stepped to the side. "Yes."

Jhaill Opthonne's scarlet eyes shifted to Salmaara. "*She is in need of proper clothing, she must be uncomfortable. Fetch her some,*"

he commanded, his black head feathers twitching at each inflection.

Salmaara had been uncomfortable with Yezhr during their travels, but he was nothing compared to Jhaill. The nausea she had felt when she first saw him returned in a flood.

The hairs on her neck and arms prickled. The sensation reminded her of the time that she had been out in the woods and a thirsty wolf had shambled out to her pond. Fortunately, she had been in the middle of the water on her twig raft, but she had seen the wild hunger in its yellow eyes. It was a predator, and she knew it. She felt no different under the governor's gaze.

Jhaill looked down at her, his intense scarlet eyes boring into her, his face smeared with dried bloodstains.

With her eyes, Salmaara traced the sheer robes that hung from his thin frame, and then she looked to her own clothing—her comfortable tunic and riding pants that Yezhr had dressed her in over a month ago.

Her clothes were too warm, but she didn't want to let them go. They were the last tie to the life she had known.

Accept your lot. People who come here never leave—not in one piece anyway. Might as well serve your master. They might let you live longer if you do.

Salmaara still couldn't get Gjordkra's cynical voice out of her thoughts. Jhaill's voice replaced it.

"Yezhr tells me he collected you from a hidden city in Southern Yendu."

He sat on a three-legged stool formed of something black with patches of cold white. The shape of the legs made Salmaara think the seat might have been made of bone.

"And being of one of the heathen cultures, I assume you know how the bride of a wedding is supposed to behave and appear, do you not?" His voice rang forcefully in her mind, and his scarlet gaze made her feel small and powerless.

She began to wonder if Gjordkra had been right, perhaps her hopes for escape were a delusional spell. *How can I possibly get away from such creatures?*

She started. Can he hear my thoughts? *Yezhr never gave any indication that he could if I didn't direct them at him ... But ... do they listen, and then only react if I do something wrong? Do they use my signature to keep track of where I am, like Gjordkra said?* The idea chilled her from top to bottom.

"I ... do," Salmaara replied haltingly.

A cloud of red ascended from somewhere behind him then vanished. Salmaara began to breathe through her mouth to avoid the stench.

"My servants will supply whatever you demand." His eyes sparkled with perverse mirth. *"I want my bride to be perfect. You have a month to accomplish this. Then the wedding will take place."*

"Do you know how the groom ought to look?" Salmaara muttered in disgust before she had thought it through and blanched.

She braced herself, and when no blow came, she looked back to the governor.

His eyes narrowed, and he looked slightly unsettled. That couldn't be, though. It must have been the lack of light, or her own exhaustion. Then the uncertain expression wiped from his blood-smeared face as soon as she had noticed it.

"Such a funny creature you are. Perhaps I shall have you later if Yezhr is willing," he said as he watched her. Cold, calculating, predatory.

Salmaara felt that her modest clothes did not cover enough as she squirmed beneath his gaze.

She took a steadying breath. Her leg ached. It should have been better by now. *Why does it still hurt so much?*

When Gjordkra returned, carrying a bundle of sheer, olive green fabrics, Salmaara broke eye contact with the governor.

Gjordkra offered her the robe. "Here you go."

"*Take those clothes off,*" Jhaill demanded, his scarlet eyes tracing Salmaara's body.

Salmaara didn't move.

"*Now. Off with them. I don't want to see them again.*"

Salmaara, her cheeks aflame and heart in her throat, removed her garments and let them drop to the gory floor. She crouched over, attempting to conceal herself as she felt his gaze caress her.

She slipped quickly into the sheer dress robe, swallowed, and managed to meet the lith's gaze once more. A tear escaped and drifted into the air, vanishing.

"*Take her down to the dungeons, Gjordkra. Her work awaits her down there,*" Jhaill said.

"As my master commands," Gjordkra said. She then bent down and snatched Salmaara's old clothes from the floor. She flipped her ratted hair out of her face with a toss of her head as she straightened, took hold of Salmaara's forearm, and whisked her from the chamber and down the passage beyond.

Salmaara swallowed her tears and twisted her arm from the other's grip.

How will I explain our wedding rituals, meant to be happy and beautiful, to that monster and his minions? To him and his city, with its incessant shrieking and bloodshed?

She realized she would have to watch Gjordkra with great care if she wanted to survive. She resolved to act as the future governess did, observe and mimic her as well as she was able.

Salmaara needed Gjordkra. *She has survived. And she seems to be the only person who doesn't have foul intentions in this place. How do I win her respect? Her friendship? Nothing here is like home.*

Gjordkra reached the top of a staircase that stretched down into darkness.

She said I need to discover why they should keep me ... The first thing that Yezhr asked me was to which family I belong. Does he know, or not? He also seemed to think my knowledge was valuable somehow. He was surprised I knew about Kalitoomba. And now, the governor thinks I know something important about weddings. I hope it's enough to keep me alive until we can escape.

She folded her hands in front of her and set her jaw as she and the violet-eyed girl descended the winding stairway into the bowels of Günhai.

CHAPTER THIRTEEN

GÜNHAI,
MAUVIAS

Günhai's dungeons lay deep beneath the city. A plethora of cramped stairways led from the dark cubes and tunnels above into darker catacombs below.

Salmaara and Gjordkra continued down the stairs from the governor's cube. The volume of the screams intensified the deeper they delved until Salmaara's body seemed to shake with them.

Dim red lanterns shed ominous light on the steep staircase, only wide enough for the two, shoulder to shoulder. They descended for what seemed like hours, and Salmaara slowed.

Gjordkra tugged on one of her arms. "Hurry up. You don't keep them waiting, even if they don't know you're coming," she hissed.

Not having realized she had stopped completely, Salmaara started forward again, pulling her arm from Gjordkra's grip.

Why does she keep grabbing me and pulling me along like a lost child? I've had more than enough of being carried, coddled, and led.

They descended the last few stairs and onto the stone floor at the bottom. The screams that had enveloped them during their descent quieted. For the first time since she had arrived, Salmaara heard nothing from below.

A short hall stretched ahead and turned. Salmaara walked along behind Gjordkra, determined not to limp or fall behind. They rounded the bend at the end of the hall and entered another corridor, to which Salmaara could see no end. It shot ahead in the dark in an erratic zigzag. More of the city's red lanterns lined the walls.

The hall would have been silent if not for the muffled cries coming from above.

Despite the dungeon's placement deep underground, it was no less hot than the land above. Doors, most of them closed, lined both sides of the hall as they wound through it. A yell sounded from the first open door they passed, halfway down the hall, shattering the brief quiet. Salmaara backed away from it, bumping into the opposite wall, heart pounding.

She stared into the room, where a man lay on the ground, sobbing, his head beneath a metal device with a crank on it that enclosed the top of his head. A shadowy figure turned the crank, putting more pressure on his head with each turn. The man tried to cry out again, but only a groan escaped. Then a gut-wrenching crack sounded.

Salmaara gasped and turned away as two round objects sprang from the man's compressed head.

His eyes.

Bile rose in her mouth as she scrambled after Gjordkra's shadow up ahead, away from the man and his tormentor.

The man's weak sobs followed her down the hall for several steps then ceased. She bowed her head. Despite her attempt to stow them, several tears escaped from her eyes, only making it a short way before the air snatched them and devoured them.

How can people do things like this to one another?

She bit her lip to suppress a sob. She could see Illun's bloody body in the light of the morning suns, but she couldn't remember his face. She could only remember what they had done to him, what they did to the man down the hall. *If only I could have helped them, could have stopped it.*

Gjordkra halted in front of a stone door at the hall's terminus and turned to Salmaara. "Better collect yourself before we go in there," she said sternly, "because I am going elsewhere."

"Do you have to?" Salmaara wished she had bitten her tongue. She didn't want Gjordkra to know how scared she was.

Gjordkra sighed and placed her hands on her hips. "It's not my decision to make."

Salmaara fought the urge to step back.

Clearing her throat, Gjordkra said, "You will be going in. My master commanded me to show you to her, and so I will. I would rather you not earn both of us a night under the lash or the knives."

"*H-her?*" Salmaara swallowed thickly and brushed at her eyes as though it would soothe her aching heart.

Gjordkra placed a hand on the door and gave it a shove. "Come on."

Bright red light washed over them from within, and Salmaara had to shield her face with a hand, blinking until her eyes adjusted. Smoke hung heavy in the air from fires set in several braziers around the austere chamber, which was much smaller than the governor's office upstairs.

Salmaara gasped as the bright light drew her attention to the room's main feature: a half-naked man, hung spread-eagle by chains attached to the ceiling and floor, his dark-haired head bowed to his chest, obscuring his face. A rapidly disappearing crimson cloud of blood hung around him. As the blood thinned, Salmaara could see the silver of his insides, some of which dangled from a massive incision that spanned from his chest to his navel and brushed the floor.

As a sensation like an itch touched Salmaara's mind from behind the man, a lithian woman stepped around the mutilated man and into the light. Blood evaporated from her face and arms as she gripped a long knife. Much of her imposing musculature showed under a sheer midriff and tight leather trousers. She had blonde head-feathers and coral pink eyes.

"*You are the one the superintendent brought,*" she said in her inaudible, silky voice.

She ignored Gjordkra, as the older girl bowed and exited. The door grated closed behind her.

Salmaara remained, staring at the lithian woman who came closer until she stood between Salmaara and the hanging man. "*I am Pezra, Dungeon Mistress of Günhai. I had not received word you were coming. Who sent you?*"

Can't she hear my thoughts? She knows who I am just by looking at me. She should know who sent me.

As the woman waited for her answer, Salmaara cleared her throat and managed to speak. "The governor."

"*Ah! About the wedding. Good. I was beginning to think I would have to ask the general,*" she said, indicating the man behind her.

She stepped back and trailed a finger over his cheek in mock affection. One of the man's feet twitched, and he moaned softly.

Salmaara stared, revulsion twisting her stomach.

"*He is still alive … but I fear he has nothing more to say.*" Pezra turned from her disemboweled victim and back to Salmaara.

Salmaara tried to keep her gaze on the dungeon mistress but could not ignore the suffering man as the air sucked more blood from his ruined body, greedily drinking it, even as she watched.

He sighed his final breath so softly that Salmaara barely heard it. But heard it, she did.

Paying her deceased prisoner no notice, Pezra asked, "*Tell me; what do I need to gather for the governor's ... wedding?*" She said the word as though it were an irksome fly buzzing around her head.

"Y-you need a dress for the bride—a white dress—and a feathered veil for her head, and a train for the dress. The bride chooses the color of the train and asks someone to be her train-bearer. The train-bearer makes it and carries it," Salmaara answered.

The lithian woman nodded then waited for Salmaara to continue.

"And wine for the party—"

"*Wine? What is that?*" Pezra folded her arms.

"It's a drink," Salmaara replied.

Pezra stared blankly.

How do I explain what a drink is? Salmaara wondered. *How do I explain any of this to these barbarians? If I have to do this for a month, I shall go mad.*

"A drink is a liquid you—"

Pezra stiffened and wrinkled her nose. "*A liquid? How ... vulgar.*"

Before Salmaara could ask how a liquid was vulgar, the door opened behind her, drawing Pezra's attention away.

Yezhr stepped in, the light from the braziers playing on his amber eyes as he stepped up behind Salmaara and took her shoulders in his hands. When Salmaara tensed, he caressed her shoulders.

"*Apparently, no one has informed you, Dungeon Mistress, that my Prey can write. Perhaps you should have it form a list and question it later, as you see fit. I must feed it and clean it. It is in dreadful repair,*" Yezhr said, stroking her hair with an open palm.

Hatred swelled within Salmaara, but she focused on the moment, on survival.

Pezra's lithian eyes widened. "*She can write?*" At that, she turned and disappeared into the shadows behind the dead man then returned with a leather-bound book. She opened it and held it out to Salmaara, along with a stick that Salmaara supposed was charcoal.

Salmaara accepted the proffered items and wrote: *For a Wedding.*

The liths stared at her as she wrote, hovering over her like vultures. She hunched her shoulders, afraid they would descend on her before she finished.

She scrawled everything she could think of that she had seen at the weddings in Bhevir and returned the book to Pezra's waiting hands.

The dungeon mistress glanced over the list and nodded. *"I will set about obtaining these things. I shall require her to verify that they are satisfactory once I acquire them,"* she said, bowing to the superintendent.

Yezhr nodded, took Salmaara's hand, and escorted her from the dungeons.

He led Salmaara through the maze of corridors to his office. The square room was in a complex adjacent to the governor's central cube. Red lamps hung from the walls, a worn, stone desk occupied the room's center, and a dilapidated cabinet stood against the wall beside the desk. Shadowy implements of steel and leather hung on hooks beside the cabinet, and a door behind the desk led into the superintendent's sleeping quarters.

Yezhr released Salmaara's hand and pointed at the desk. She sat on it as Yezhr swept past her to the cabinet and opened it.

Red light shimmered on the sides of sleek black cubes in a myriad of sizes that occupied the upper shelves. They were too many to count. Yezhr paid them no notice, however, as he selected a hairbrush with steel teeth from a lower shelf. He then turned back to her and cocked his head.

"What are those?" Salmaara indicated the cubes.

"They are the governor's stores, which he has entrusted to me. Perhaps Prey has not heard, but Governor Opthonne is most gifted with the brewing of potions. He is Kaskahai, one of the Shazrah. Prey certainly does not want to ever taste one, no," Yezhr said as he arrived before her.

He extracted an ash-stained rope from his pocket and bound her wrists with mock tenderness. Then he set the brush against her scalp and forced the metal teeth through a snarl.

Salmaara's eyes watered for a moment before the air took the extra moisture. She longed to pull away, snatch the wretched brush, and throw it in his face. Instead, she fixed her gaze on the shimmering cubes of potions in the open cupboard.

If those are as nasty as he said, perhaps I could use one on him while he sleeps and escape. I will get out, and I'll take Gjordkra with me, she thought.

"Perhaps, since Prey is curious, I will allow it to view the governor's inter-rogations," Yezhr said. *"His work is an unparalleled art, envied far and wide. He is Master of Torture here."*

The vision of the men in the dungeon returned. One lying on the floor, his skull slowly squeezed until his eyes popped out. The other hanging from the dungeon mistress's ceiling, still alive, although his guts dangled in plain view. Both had died in this vile place, without dignity, without mercy.

Salmaara shuddered to think what Gjordkra's scarlet-eyed master might do to his victims. She had seen Gjordkra's disfiguration, and that was enough. She did not want to know, let alone see what that vilest of creatures did in the darkness that covered his city.

"Prey is speechless?"

"No, I don't want to see," she whispered.

Yezhr stopped brushing and set the implement aside. A small mist rose from its bristles.

Salmaara rested a hand on her stinging scalp and pulled it away wet. The air dried it after a moment.

Yezhr observed her upset with brows furrowed in mock compassion. He opened a pouch that lay beside her and scooped a handful of hydration powder from it. He massaged it into her scalp in silence, alleviating the sting the brush had caused. He then propped her mouth open and poured more of the magenta powder into it.

Salmaara swallowed then closed her eyes.

"*Does Prey want sleep?*" Yezhr asked, stroking one of her cheeks.

She kept her eyes closed and nodded.

Before he could pick her up, she flopped over sideways and curled up on his desktop.

"*Poor Prey needs a blanket,*" Yezhr said.

When Salmaara heard the superintendent's bedroom door open, she risked a glance at him from over one of her shoulders. He had disappeared into the chamber beyond.

She sprang to her feet and reached the open cabinet in three steps. She selected a potion small enough to hide in a dark fold of her translucent clothes and tucked it away. Scrambling back onto the desktop, she clutched her new treasure, hoping that her signature wouldn't give away the fact that she had moved off the desk and back again.

When the lith didn't immediately return, she let out a breath that she hadn't noticed she had been holding.

For the first time in weeks, Salmaara smiled.

CHAPTER FOURTEEN

GÜNHAI,
MAUVIAS

S almaara woke in the chamber she shared with Gjordkra. The vio-let-eyed girl squatted nearby, watching Salmaara as she chewed on a scrap of Günhai's foul bread, illuminated by a lantern.

Salmaara lurched up and felt her robe for the pilfered brew. She sighed with relief when she felt the hard lump where she had left it.

Gjordkra raised a brow.

"How long have I been here?" Salmaara breathed.

"Not long. Couple of minutes maybe," Gjordkra said.

Salmaara settled back down and slipped the stolen cube from her clothes. "We're going to escape tonight."

Gjordkra rolled her eyes, stuffed the last bit of bread into her mouth, chewed, and swallowed. "You're on to that again? Already?"

Salmaara hoisted the black cube into view. "I'll use this on Yezhr so he won't know we've left for a while."

Gjordkra plucked the cube from Salmaara's hand, tossed it into the air, and then caught it. Salmaara tried to take it back, but Gjordkra kept it from her reach.

The future governess stood and paced in the lantern light. "All right, delusional girl"—she pursed her lips—"you're going to hit Yezhr with this—under the assumption he doesn't know what you're planning from your thoughts beforehand—hope that it does something useful, and run for it? Where? No one escapes Günhai alive. Even if you manage, by some freak chance, to get outside the city walls, how are you going to evade those who will come after you? Say Yezhr survives. He's the best tracker in the world. He'll find you, no matter where you hide. If you kill him? He's the closest thing my master has to a friend. Jhaill'll come after you then. He takes things like that pretty personally. You don't want him after you— trust me."

Salmaara scrambled to her feet and recovered the cube from Gjordkra's hand.

Gjordkra froze.

Salmaara lifted her chin. "It'll work. Yezhr has never reacted to my thoughts and thinks I'm a docile pet besides. I just have to surprise him with this to make sure he—"

Gjordkra snorted. "What are you going to do? Pour it up his nose?" She folded her arms tightly across her chest.

Salmaara tightened her jaw as she met the older girl's eyes. "Something like that. I've seen what happens to liquids here. Shouldn't be too hard to get him to inhale it while he's sleeping—"

"It won't work. You're going to die. It's been nice knowing you."

"Come with me, Gjordkra. There is so much to see and be out there. You don't have to live at the whims of others, accept the torment, the broken bones—any of it. How you live is up to you."

"Leave me out of this." Gjordkra resumed pacing.

"Gjordkra, in a dark time, a wise king once told his people, *'we can bear difficult things.'* You have done hard things—harder than I can imagine—to survive here for so long. If you can survive here, then you can also escape this place. Yes, it will be hard, but we'll never escape if we don't even try."

Gjordkra snorted and turned away from her companion, saying nothing.

Salmaara clutched the potion in a trembling grip. *This is a chance I just can't not take. I'm going to lose myself if I stay here another minute. I will escape. I'll live. I'll escape for Illun, Rianne, Hend, and everyone. I'll escape for Gjordkra, who has never known kindness or breathed free air. I will. She'll be able to see then how ridiculous and paranoid she's being, how she's just lying down obediently to the monsters that run this place.*

Resting a hand on her companion's shoulder, Salmaara said, "Gjordkra, if you won't come with me, then I will come back for you. I promise."

The other girl pulled away from Salmaara's grip, strode over to her pile of blankets, and sat down.

With a sigh, Salmaara turned and made for the door. As she left the small patch of lantern light, she held her arms in front of her, feeling her way forward.

Gjordkra indicated the wall behind Salmaara. "The door is over there."

Salmaara turned, abashed, and then made her way across the chamber and gripped the stone handle. She had always struggled with a lack of direction and had gotten lost more than a few times on errands around Bhevir. In the few days she had lived in the prison city, she had managed to learn many of the passages in its convoluted spiral, most of which Gjordkra had taught her, but it had been difficult. Tonight would test those teachings.

Salmaara opened the door—it was unlocked, as always, for their captors assumed that she and Gjordkra knew their places.

In the corridor outside, Salmaara squinted. Nothing beyond darkness and cries filled it. She tried to swallow, but her mouth was dry.

When no one came for her to stop her, she clutched the potion and made her way toward the tunnel that connected Governor Opthonne's cube to the one adjacent, where Yezhr kept his office. *What did she mean "something useful?" It must do something awful. It's got to. Also … I need to stop thinking about it, just in case.* Salmaara emptied her mind.

Red light spilled into the hall from Yezhr's open office door. She pressed her back against the wall and sidled toward it. Reaching the doorframe, she peeked in.

Yezhr was pacing in his bedroom, with his eyes fixed on a stained bit of paper. He tapped it with a finger with every step.

Salmaara waited. Then, dropping to her knees, she crawled in, crouching with her back against a thick leg of Yezhr's stone desk. She couldn't hear the superintendent's footfalls but could sense him there. It seemed odd that his mind didn't connect to hers immediately, yet she was grateful.

Yezhr strode back into the office, and Salmaara peered through the opening between desk legs to see his bare feet and translucent robes fluttering around them.

She scanned the office and tried to remember if she could fit in the cabinet. She shook her head and leaned it back.

Movement in the hall caught her eye, making her racing heart leap into her throat. She slunk to a deep shadow behind the door.

Three female liths entered, two of them pregnant, and all three wearing dresses of sheer crimson fabrics that did not well-conceal their curvaceous bodies. They possessed dark head-feathers and glittering eyes.

Yezhr looked from his paper and froze mid-step. He narrowed his amber eyes and made his way to the women.

Salmaara let out a long breath after Yezhr passed her.

One of the women wrinkled her nose and shook her head. Another pointed to the woman in the center, the only one who was not with child.

Yezhr squared his shoulders and struck her across the face. She staggered back and fell into the hall outside.

The woman who had pointed at her tried to raise her arms but was too slow. Yezhr's strong hand met her face, as well. Blood sprayed from her nose when it snapped, but she did not lose her footing. She clutched her womb, with sullen eyes on the superintendent.

The third woman looked at the other two imperiously, with her delicate hands upon her full belly.

Yezhr faced her in silence, and Salmaara cringed, wondering what they had done.

She tore her eyes from them and crawled around the office's perimeter, toward the bedroom door. Once there, she glanced over her shoulder at the four liths by the door and, certain they were still engaged with each other, scrambled into the bedroom and under the bed, the only article of furniture in the austere chamber except for a leather chest.

When the office door slammed, her breath caught. The red lights in the office behind her extinguished, and four pairs of slender feet entered the bedchamber. She relaxed when no one stooped to look under the bed.

Then the stone frame groaned overhead as the party mounted it. She hadn't considered that Yezhr might not sleep alone. She folded her arms and rested her chin on them.

If they keep track of me through my signature all the time, why don't they know I'm here? What if I didn't need to come here at all? A rebellious hope rose in her heart, a hope that she was safe from the violation of her mind that she had feared since her capture. That hope faded, though, turning to panic. Now she was stuck under Yezhr's bed with four liths overhead.

She waited beneath the bed until her eyelids began to droop.

As sleep descended, the lamps in the bedroom went out.

Later, Salmaara's eyes snapped open, and she strained her ears. For the first time in her life, Salmaara consciously sought for signatures and sensed all four of the liths', each one distinct from the others. She kept herself apart from them, not touching them. From that awareness, however, she could have known that the liths lay still, likely sleeping, if she was fortunate.

She dragged herself forward on her stomach, trying to see in the impenetrable dark, and paused as she was about to poke her head from under the bed. She listened.

Nothing, just the barest whisper of steady breathing.

Holding her breath, she edged from the cover of the bed, half expecting to be snatched from above. When no grasping hands came, she rose to her knees and proceeded.

She crawled through the office doorframe and exhaled. Running a hand along the wall to find her way without bumping the desk, she continued around the edge of the room until her searching hand fell on the latch set into the stone door. She turned her head again, looking back toward the bedchamber, but nothing seemed to have changed.

Sucking in a shaky breath, she twisted the latch. The door groaned quietly as it swung toward her. She slipped through.

Red light from the hall washed over her, and she raised a hand to shield her eyes. As she turned to close the door, a slender hand darted through the crack, snatched her shoulder, and jerked her around. Salmaara gasped.

Yezhr's amber eyes bored into hers.

One of the women peered over his shoulder, her cheek swollen and blackened, and her eyes glazed.

Yezhr connected to Salmaara's mind, his signature like the sharp blade of an axe, resting against tender flesh. "*What is Prey doing out of its bed?*"

Salmaara acted before terror could set in. She snapped the top off the cubical potion jar and hurled it in his face. Yellow liquid splashed over his sharp nose.

Staggering back, Yezhr fumbled for the container as it fell.

The air drew the potion from the receptacle and into the superintendent's face. His eyes widened in alarm for a short moment as he realized what he held. He exhaled sharply from his nose twice with his head bowed then collapsed onto the woman behind him, motionless.

Salmaara jolted forward, sprinting through the long corridors, heart in her throat. She stumbled once, but thrust her arms out, clawing at the air, and managed to keep her feet. Trying to keep her head, she ran to one of the narrow passages that Gjordkra had showed her just the day previous and slipped into it. The other girl had promised that it was a good route between the governor's and superintendent's offices and the room where the liths kept the girls, because most people didn't know it was there. Gjordkra had also advised her that sticking to low-traffic areas was a good way to keep out from underfoot of the prison city's nasty denizens. Not keeping out from underfoot meant beatings or worse for people like Salmaara and her, Gjordkra had promised.

The potter's daughter paused to catch her breath and orient herself. Certain that this was the passage she had meant to enter—barely wide enough for one person to squeeze through—she trotted forward, straining to hear any sign of alarm or pursuit. Hearing none, she sped up.

The long and blessedly lonely passage terminated in a large chamber attached to many different corridors. That chamber swarmed with liths and a handful people of Salmaara's own kind—sulmai. Since most of the excited population consisted of liths, an unnatural quiet hung over them, despite the energetic manner in which they darted to and fro. Most were armed with spear, sword, or kamas.

A shriek echoed up Salmaara's passage, seemingly right on top of her, and she flinched but managed to stay where she was, and not sprint out into the gathering ahead. Most of the assembled in the chamber made for the passage that Salmaara knew would lead to Yezhr's study, while others split from that column and disappeared into the blackness of other tunnels.

They must know, she realized. *Even if whatever I threw at Yezhr incapacitated him, one of his mistresses could have raised a telepathic alarm. Stupid!*

Where a moment earlier a shriek had come from behind, now came shuffling footsteps and the clink of weapons brushing against the narrow corridor's walls.

Swallowing, Salmaara forced herself back into motion and into that large chamber. She kept to the shadows against the walls with her sight set on the passage that she had decided to take next, forcing herself not to sprint in order to avoid attention or colliding with something or someone.

As she wound through Günhai's twisting hallways, Salmaara became more and more aware of the signatures that filled the place. They numbered so many that she could not count them all while she darted along from shadow to shadow, passage to passage. How many people were trapped here, suffering in this evil place, made her heart ache. *What can I do for them if I can't get free myself?*

She rounded a corner and, sensing the sudden arrival of a pair of signatures, had to scramble atop a crate, with knees tucked to her chest to not only avoid being seen but also keep from being knocked over by the bulky liths that appeared a moment later.

Curious, she touched the pair's signatures and felt that she had connected to them somehow. The low voice of one sounded in her mind.

"*... the one called Prey. It must be heading for the gates. Has to be stopped at all costs and brought back to the superintendent.*"

"*She will not get far. We have already arranged to cut her off there.*"

What if I could know where they all are, if they know where I am, and where they think I'm going?

Salmaara reached out to all those signatures that she had felt just moments earlier and connected to them all. It was at once thrilling and utterly overwhelming.

Crouching in the shadows atop the crate, the thoughts and emotions of Günhai's denizens engulfed her in a waves. A dizzying array of pain and pleasure, terror and rage, loathing and admiration tossed her in their currents until she thought she would drown.

Panting, she leaned back against the wall. She had lost the connections and, in their place, a deep, throbbing ache had started behind her eyes. Blinking it away, she waited for the liths to retreat before she scrambled from her shadowy perch and fled onward.

Sweat rose around her in a small cloud by the time she had conquered much of the indoor city's spiral. Despite several wrong turns along the way, she recognized the stretch ahead—Yezhr had brought her there the day they had arrived.

Salmaara took several shuddering breaths, her heart pounding in her ears. *I'm almost out. There's only one real way out of here—the gate. But I can't go there. I know that ...*

She set her jaw and wiped a quaking hand across her brow, although it was dry. Several pairs of doors opened to the world beyond from the building that Salmaara had reached, and she chose the set of side doors farthest from the central ones through which most entered and exited the shrieking halls to make her exit, for it was there that she sensed she would have the best chance of avoiding all of the signatures she could sense around the main gates.

Staring at the doors, she tried to feel the signatures outside more clearly, to see how many awaited her outside and where. At the attempt, a blinding pain shot from her eyes to the base of her skull. Even so, she glimpsed that a sizable force had amassed outside the main doors, blocking the way to the main gates on the other side of the building from where she planned to exit. She could still make it to the wall—the way was open. It required all her strength to keep her feet, but keep them, she did.

Straightening, she cracked one door open, preparing for what might await her on the other side. No one threw the doors open and snatched her or waited to apprehend her there. Instead, a courtyard of stone stretched out before her until it ran into the city wall. Stairs led from the doors to the courtyard floor.

She could see the masses that spanned the space between the main doors and the gate, and the forms of armored guards up and down the crenellated bulwarks, some twenty feet up, and others on the ground.

She squeezed from the doors and scrambled over the railing to her right to hide in the shadow of the building. Even though still thick, the air that filled her lungs felt fresh compared to the stifling rooms inside the prison city.

Ash concealed the stars overhead, but she knew they were there. She had feared never seeing the moon and stars or the suns again. Wind brushed her cheeks, and she detected the faint scent of sulfur.

She returned her gaze to Günhai's fortifications. The only way out that she could see would be over the wall, between groups of guards.

Salmaara slipped from the dark beside the stairs, wary of the milling soldiers over by the gates. She fixed her gaze on a trio of armored liths that strode away from her, along the base of the outer wall. Behind them would be the perfect opportunity. They showed no sign of altering their course.

She paused in the wall's shadow, keeping her attention on the three retreating backs. Then Salmaara looked up. Darkness covered the ancient wall.

She ran her hands over its pocked surface in search of a hold, and ash rained down on her with every futile brush of her hands. With her groping fingers, she found a protuberance a short ways up, which she grabbed. She heaved herself onto the wall, climbing upward. She hung for a long moment before she found another hold.

The air took her sweat as soon as it formed, and her mouth was so dry that she feared she would choke. Still, she forced herself up, arms and legs burning, gritting her teeth. *I won't be a helpless pet any longer!*

The guttering light of the guards' torches on her stretch of wall retreated from where she clung to the ancient stone, to either end of their stretch of rampart. She scrambled up faster, determined to be up and over before those lights returned.

Reaching the edge between battlements, Salmaara raised herself up and peeked between them. The rampart lay in darkness. Nothing moved.

Heart leaping into her throat, the potter's daughter clambered onto the dark walkway, stumbling forward from sheer momentum, and fell to her knees.

A red lantern ignited in front of her, illuminating a lone figure comfortably seated on a merlon opposite where she had come up, one leg folded over the other.

Salmaara screamed.

Governor Opthonne's scarlet eyes sparkled in the lantern light. *"It is good of you to join me, Prey. I thought you might not come after all, considering how many times you got lost on the way."*

Salmaara's face grew hot, and she willed the tears that had flooded her eyes not to fall.

When she tried to stand, Jhaill easily stepped on one of her hands and went from sitting to crouching in front of her in a fluid movement. The potter's daughter ground her teeth, not wanting to give him the satisfaction of a second cry.

The stink of the lith overwhelmed anything else, a mixture of the metallic scent of blood, leather, urine and, she realized, something rotten.

He smells like death, she thought, revolted.

Memories of her father's final moments threatened to surface, but she crushed them back down.

Grunting in fury, she tried to reclaim her hand, but the governor only exerted more pressure. Any more, and he would likely break all the bones in her hand, she decided, and so she held still.

"The superintendent sent me. He requires your presence, and it will not do to keep your master waiting. Naughty pets who keep their masters waiting have painful lessons to learn," he purred.

Salmaara snatched his ankle with her free hand, trying to get him to relieve the crushing pain on the other.

Where the knife came from, Salmaara never saw. She barely saw it even as the lith slashed the back of her hand with it, but the hot pain of the cut made her release his leg.

"How?" she demanded, ashamed when the air pulled the first of her tears from her cheeks and droplets of blood from her hand.

Jhaill cocked his head.

"How did you know where I was going?"

The lith leveled his stare with hers and procured a small bottle from a pocket in his robe. He unscrewed the cap. *"Perhaps if you don't wish to be caught, you should not share your thoughts for all to hear."*

As Salmaara tried to understand how she might have done that, the lith lifted the lid free, and a pink mist came up into her face. It stung her nose and made her choke, but before she could worry overmuch about what it might contain, darkness took her.

CHAPTER FIFTEEN

GÜNHAI,
MAUVIAS

Salmaara's hands prickled with fire, her back throbbed, and her entire body felt as if she had taken that long fall into the pit in Bhevir again, making her wonder if she was not a single, blackened bruise. Her lungs rattled with each breath and, though her eyes were open, she couldn't see anything but red and black shadows drifting in and out of focus. She blinked. *What was in that bottle?*

A hand was waved back and forth just above her nose. As it came into focus, so did the screams and the dark.

She lay on a ratty mess of coarse cloth, with a red lantern beside her. The sour stench of bile filled the chamber.

A weary servant of her own race knelt over her. Tattered scraps of cloth barely covered the woman's cadaverous form. Black underlined her dark eyes, and limp, brown hair hung around a sallow, starved face. The woman looked as though she might die any moment.

"Awake," she mumbled, heaving to her feet, legs quaking as though they wouldn't hold her, disappearing into the dark beyond the lantern's reach. A moment later, she stumbled back into view just ahead of Pezra.

The dungeon mistress shoved the woman out of her way, and the poor wretch collapsed and vomited.

Salmaara tried to reach for her but found her arm too heavy. "She needs help. What's wrong with—"

Pezra's itchy signature filled Salmaara's awareness. "*She is southern,*" she said, as if it should have been obvious.

Salmaara's heart sank as she remembered that the air in Mauvias poisoned those not of the Destroyer's people. *Why aren't I sicker?*

As the lith hauled Salmaara to her feet, the girl's back and ribs felt aflame, and her legs stung as though she was sitting too close to a fire. She cried out and nearly fell, but Pezra caught her, slinging her over a shoulder and leaving the chamber and the dying southerner behind.

As Pezra weaved through the long corridors for a small eternity, Salmaara watched her tears drift away from her face to become nothing. Although she tried, she could not make them stop.

She wished the dungeon mistress would stop jostling her. The pain flared with each brisk step, and Salmaara had to bite her lip to silence the gasps that would otherwise have streamed from her throat like the tears from her eyes.

Pezra rounded a final bend and approached a familiar door. Yezhr's office.

Salmaara tried to resist, but her feeble movement caused Pezra to tighten her grip as the blond-feathered lith stepped into the doorframe.

Jhaill Opthonne stood beside Yezhr's desk with his gore-stained arms folded. His scarlet eyes shifted to Salmaara as Pezra entered, and they shone with vast amusement. Yezhr sat at the desk, hunched over, with his head in his hands. The superintendent's three mistresses cowered in the doorway behind him, brows furrowed.

Yezhr looked up. Yellow pus crusted his amber eyes, and a heavy bandage wrapped around one of his forearms. He narrowed his eyes and clenched his hands into fists when he saw Salmaara.

The governor continued to regard her with what Salmaara would have thought was a smile, if the lith had a mouth.

The feeling of thin wire wrapped around her head. *"I trust you will now see to your business, Superintendent?"*

Yezhr stood abruptly, his chair clattering to the floor. He pointed to the bare wall opposite the one that sported the cabinet, and Pezra strode over and set Salmaara on her feet. Her knees buckled, but the dungeon mistress did not release her hold.

"Turn her around and bind her hands," Yezhr growled.

Goose bumps spread over Salmaara's entire body as Pezra flipped her so that her back faced the superintendent. The dungeon mistress then locked Salmaara's wrists into manacles attached to the wall.

Salmaara tried to keep her feet but could not, so the weight of her useless body pulled on her arms. Tears flooded her face again as she strained her neck to see over her shoulder.

Jhaill and Pezra exited via the main door, and the three women edged back inside the bedchamber, closing the door. Yezhr didn't approach, though. He faced the wall with the cabinet, his back to her.

"Prey has not learned its place. I am master, and Prey is my property. It must learn to do as I direct it, for I know what is best for it, and it knows nothing. It should rejoice that I have chosen to be its master, that I will provide it, low and filthy though it is, a purpose for its meager life." He scanned the leather and steel implements hanging on the wall beside the cabinet, fingering several before selecting one.

Salmaara could barely see him through the haze of tears. She tried to stand on her toes to relieve her numb arms, but fire still spread up both of her legs, so she sank back down.

"*Now Prey will learn its place. I am its master. It will not forget this again.*" Yezhr wrenched her translucent robe up and shoved it over her head, so that it only covered her shackled arms.

Salmaara didn't see the first lash coming before knotted leather strips bit into the bare flesh of her back, more shocking than the pain of having her hand stepped on and the other one cut. More painful even than the poison that made her feel like she had fallen from somewhere high.

She screamed.

Yezhr struck her again, and Salmaara shrieked as she tried to get away. However, the manacles only bit into her wrists, holding her in place.

He waited.

Let me die. Oh, please, let me die …

Father, where are you? It hurts so badly.

No, he cannot come.

Yezhr raised the whip. "*I am Prey's master. It will accept my will and let go its foolish and ignorant ways. I am Prey's master!*"

Salmaara nodded. *Anything, anything to end the pain …*

The whip tore into her back a third time.

Salmaara sagged. Bright spots covered her vision as she sobbed softly.

Yezhr tilted her face so that she looked into his. "*Does Prey wish to rest?*" he purred, all traces of his wrath vanished, his amber eyes shimmering.

"Y-yes," Salmaara croaked out.

"*Yes?*"

"Yes!" she whispered fiercely.

Yezhr cocked his head and raised the whip again.

Salmaara tried to look at him but couldn't move her head as he threw another blow. Her body quaked, and she could feel the hot cloud of blood as it flowed from and hung above her broken flesh.

"*I am Prey's master. And, as its master, I asked if Prey wishes to rest?*" He turned the leather whip over in his hands.

Salmaara groaned. "Y-yes, master."

"*Very good, Prey. Do not forget it.*" He tossed the whip onto the stone desk behind him. It landed with a *slap* that made Salmaara flinch. Yezhr unlocked her hands and caught her when she crumpled.

She couldn't think of anything but pain. Fire seemed to consume every inch of her. She had never known such agony.

She stared above as Yezhr carried her from his office, returning Salmaara to the dark chamber that she shared with Gjordkra. He laid her on her ratty blanket and ignored her gasp.

She tried to roll off her bleeding back but could not move. Her blood stuck the blanket to her back, despite the air's continuing efforts to take all her life force from her.

Salmaara tried to nod, but her head didn't move. "Yes," she whispered through cracked lips.

Yezhr raised an eyebrow.

Salmaara curled, expecting another blow. "Yes, master."

When the door closed behind Yezhr, shutting out the ruddy light of the hallway, Gjordkra lit a lantern where she sat in the corner of the room and made her way over to Salmaara. Crimson streams still drifted up around Salmaara's body from her wounds.

Gjordkra sighed loudly. "Roll over. I'd better fix you up before you bleed to death."

Salmaara looked up into Gjordkra's annoyed yet concerned face, and her fear and pain melted away for a moment. She smiled as she did what she had been asked.

Her companion eased Salmaara's arms from the sleeves of her robe, carefully peeling it from her back and down to her waist.

"What are you smiling about? You just received what will be your first scars, if you don't bleed out, like I said."

Salmaara heard her companion tear one of the blankets. The room still swayed, and the pain made her entire body shudder.

"I just realized something. My father always said it was important to name things I am grateful for, especially in times of hardship. I tried to after Yezhr first captured me, but I couldn't. Just now, in the most pain I've ever been in in my life, I finally see something to be thankful for." Salmaara shakily turned her head so that she could see Gjordkra.

The other girl had a clear jar of yellow paste in her hands, which she opened. Coating her hands in the gelatinous stuff, she rubbed it onto Salmaara's torn and burning flesh. Salmaara shivered under the cold balm as Gjordkra continued to apply it ruthlessly.

"Yeah? What?"

Wincing under her companion's ministrations, Salmaara replied, "You."

Gjordkra snorted and laid a segment of torn blanket on Salmaara's back, applying pressure to the wounds. "You're crazy."

"No, really. You … you didn't have to help me. You could have let me lie here and die, but you didn't. My father's final words to me were to treasure my life and to live. You valued my life more than I did just now and, for that, I will be forever grateful to you."

Gjordkra said nothing in return but added another piece of blanket to Salmaara's back.

CHAPTER SIXTEEN

GÜNHAI,
MAUVIAS

S ince her new companion had saved her from bleeding her life away,
and Salmaara's declaration of gratitude three days previous, it seemed
to Salmaara that Gjordkra was avoiding her as much as she could. Unfortunately, Yezhr had done the opposite.

He had given his Prey little time alone, and for those stretches, he had
her tied up, bound hand and foot in heavy chains. When he did not
have her tied to the wall or floor, he fastened a golden chain to a match-
ing collar, which he had affixed around her neck, and walked her around
with him like a sheep to market.

The previous day, Salmaara had suffered another beating for forgetting to name him her master. She could still feel the sting of where his
whip had fallen across her shoulders and the swelling on one cheek from
where he had applied a powerful hand.

That morning, when she had awoken, her lithian master had removed
her of her translucent olive robe in favor of another of the same color,
which had no sleeves and had been cut short to bare her legs from the
mid-thigh. She wondered if the revealing clothing, too, was a punish-

ment for her assault on him.

Yezhr strode ahead of her, leading her along by that infernal gold chain. Ruby light from the lanterns on the walls played on its links like so much blood. Salmaara glared at it, the desperate need to snatch it away from the lith and get it around his neck rising in her until she had raised her arms up. However, the pain in her shoulders and back prevented her from going much further.

As though he could sense her enmity, Yezhr's signature touched her mind and connected, like the blade of an axe against her collared throat. *"I have a task for Prey. If it does well, I will allow it to eat its supper with its own hands."*

Had she not just endured three days of the lith forcing food into her mouth as though she were an infant while her hands and feet were chained, the offer would not have been so enticing. She had never thought that feeding herself had mattered before. Or bathing. Or brushing her hair or teeth. Those were just things that she used to do to take care of herself, to live.

He'll let me feed myself if I just cooperate ... Oh, how it all mattered now, more than anything else she could think of.

Except for escaping all this. Life doesn't always have to be this way, a hopeful voice whispered in the back of her mind.

To Yezhr, Salmaara offered what she hoped was an attentive expression and nodded. Her throat was raw from crying over her torn shoulders the previous night, and she didn't want the superintendent to hear how much he had hurt her by speaking without need. She was certain that her eyes, puffy and bloodshot, had done enough in that regard already.

Rage swelled against the limits of the cage that she kept it in deep inside herself. She hated what Yezhr had done, was doing, and would do to her. But, at present, she hated herself mostly. *I deserve this pain.*

She hated how easily she had decided to leave Gjordkra behind. The other girl had done nothing but help her since she had arrived, and when the moment came, Salmaara had left her. Yes, she had promised to return, but how hard would she have tried? Would she have stayed away like a coward? *Like the coward I am?*

If I were her, I would keep my distance, too. I'm an ungrateful, useless traitor. I left father, too. And all the others.

She hated that she had believed she had a chance. She hated that she might have to obey Gjordkra's counsel and accept her lot. Try though she might, she still couldn't imagine living out her days in this evil place as its vile superintendent's submissive pet. *Maybe I am crazy, just as she says.*

Something snapped across one of her arms, and Salmaara bit her lip to silence a gasp more of alarm than pain. She looked down to see a thin line of blood rising into the air from a slender cut where Yezhr had struck her with a thong. She hadn't noticed when he had stopped walking.

His chestnut head-feathers quivered. *"It is most disrespectful to ignore your master when he is speaking, particularly since I intend to reward Prey should it comply. Can it not even listen? Perhaps I should return it to its room, or my desk, to help it reflect on the error of its ways."*

"I am sorry," she rasped. "Master," she added quickly, wincing at herself more than him when he shifted the thong in his hand.

Disgust at her fear of his lash rose in her like a foul stench.

"Prey is forgiven." The lith hooked the leather strip back onto the belt under his robe. *"I shall repeat what I told Prey before, while its mind was wandering. The governor has need of one of the rooms, but there are things to be cleaned out. I told him that my Prey would do well for the task. The governor has offered to send his Gjordkra to assist it and ensure it does the work properly. Now, we go."* He tugged on her chain as he started forward once more, leading her through a passageway that Salmaara knew led

into the next building in the prison city's vast spiral.

They passed red lamp after red lamp until Yezhr apparently reached their destination and opened a door. The lith stepped inside, and Salmaara, on the other end of the golden chain, followed.

"*Now, Prey must promise to behave, and then I will remove its chain. Yes?*"

"Yes ... master," Salmaara nearly groaned the title.

He offered a curt nod, unhooked the chain from her collar, and took his leave.

Thankfully, his unsettling connection to her mind went with him. Or, at least she thought. Even after so long, she still couldn't be certain how much of her thoughts or feelings her captor was privy to. She hoped it was as little as she thought, based on how he rarely reacted to anything she didn't want him to hear. That, and Jhaill's words up on the wall still haunted her—that she had shared her thoughts with everyone so that he knew where to wait for her.

I know so little of these things ...

Massaging her neck around the collar, Salmaara surveyed the room. Four large lanterns that were set in the middle of its stone floor lit most of the small chamber. A large basket woven of something that Salmaara thought looked like wire stood to one side of the lantern circle, while another item of the same material, but more like a blanket with handles, lay on the other. Sharp implements stained with dark blotches, interspersed with coils of chains, littered the floor. In one corner, two large mounds lay just out of the light, and a foul, sickly-sweet aroma permeated the whole room so thickly that it made her want to choke. She couldn't begin to guess what might produce a smell like that and didn't want to find out.

Even though she desperately wanted to turn and leave it all behind, Salmaara wanted more to feed herself dinner. *Just pick them up. Don't think about what they are, what's on them. It won't be that hard ...*

"You going to just stand there, or what?" Gjordkra wandered out of a deep shadow at the room's perimeter, dragging a length of chain with links thicker than her scarred arms behind her.

The other girl had been attired the same way as Salmaara—in a short, sleeveless, olive robe. The color, Salmaara had come to realize, denoted their status as property, letting others know on sight.

She stared at the grizzly patchwork of scars on Gjordkra's arms and legs for a moment. Then, when the other girl's brows lowered, she looked away. She couldn't help wondering if she would look the same one day.

No, it can't be. Yezhr is very purposeful with his punishments. Just enough to let the lesson sink in. Those marks were made by someone who couldn't stop because they were enjoying it so much ...

The thought utterly sickened her, as did the image of Governor Opthonne's cruel face that quickly followed. She shuddered.

"No! No, Yezhr brought me to help."

"Oh. Well, just put all this stuff in the basket. Then help me get the other things out to the grave."

Salmaara took a halting step toward the litter of knives, and then knelt down to start her work. Her blood chilled as she asked, "*The grave?*"

Gjordkra shrugged. "Where all the city's rubbish goes. It's out in the middle of the spiral. I'll show you."

Salmaara took the nearest knife by its leather-wrapped handle, held carefully between two fingers and, against her better judgment, fixed her gaze on it. Something flaked off of it as she looked. Something with several hairs attached to it. She quickly tossed it into the basket, resisting the urge to gag.

She made quick work of the remaining instruments, only looking at them enough to avoid cutting herself as she deposited them in the basket. Gjordkra also added things—chains, long knives, stones with things carved on them.

"Gjordkra?"

"Huh?"

"I'm sorry."

The other girl dropped a saw into the basket. "For what?"

"For making a run for it and just leaving you. I shouldn't have left you. That was wrong. And selfish."

Gjordkra scoffed. "I remember choosing to stay, crazy girl."

"I can tell you're upset with me, and I'm saying that I'm sorry."

Salmaara added the final blade to the basket then stood, wishing there was some way to wash her hands that didn't involve wiping them on her clothes. Since there wasn't, she did.

Gjordkra said nothing in lieu of her statement. The silence stretched between them until it became a painful pressure.

Salmaara tried to sound as nonchalant as possible when she asked, "What's next?"

Her companion indicated the corner where two mounds lay in shadow. "Stuff to go out," she said, a peculiar flatness coloring her tone.

Despite it, Salmaara sensed a tendril of emotion. She's trying to cover fear. *She's ... afraid?*

Salmaara slowly crossed the room to the heaps, wondering what could unsettle her seasoned companion.

Behind her, Gjordkra picked up one of the lanterns and brought it over. "Anyway, I'm not mad at you. There's nothing to be sorry for. Yet."

As Salmaara opened her mouth to reply, the red light illuminated the mounds. The potter's daughter bit back a cry and shied away.

They were corpses, the source of the thick, disgusting smell filling the room. Salmaara covered her nose and mouth with a hand.

Both corpses had marbled, greenish-black skin, similar to the olive slave's robes adorning their wasted frames. One had been a man and lay stiffly on his side. The other, whom Salmaara barely recognized as the woman who had tended to her after Governor Opthonne had poisoned her on the wall, lay curled up like a babe. Thankfully, they bore no cuts or signs that they had been the victims of the blades that Salmaara had just picked up.

"These … people … are considered *rubbish?*"

Gjordkra nodded. "Yeah. To our masters, anyway. This is what I meant when I said I didn't want to clean you up. I mean, at least these two are in one piece. Could be worse. Much worse."

Salmaara stared at them, blinking back tears. They had lived and died horribly.

"Do you know what their names were? Where they came from?"

"No." Gjordkra fidgeted with the lantern handle. "It's better that way, you know."

"Is it?" Salmaara's voice came out as a bare whisper. "How can you say that?"

"Whatever. Come on. Let's get them out. Get it over with." Gjordkra pointed to the metal-woven item with handles that Salmaara now realized was a litter.

Salmaara swallowed the growing lump in her throat and fetched the litter, laying it out beside the woman. Then Gjordkra moved so that she stood between the bodies, grasped the woman's thin shoulder, and pushed, rolling her onto the carrier. The body was so stiff that not a limb moved.

Salmaara gripped the two handles on her side and set her jaw. In silence, the other girl took the handles on her side. Together, they dragged the body from the chamber and into the corridor outside.

The potter's daughter let the other prisoner lead, and she wound them and their grim charge through several more hallways until, at last, they came to a door outlined with a dull light. Not red light, but sunslight.

Salmaara's heart rose a little at the sight of it. She hadn't seen natural light since her failed escape attempt.

Gjordkra released her half of the litter and shouldered the door open, leaning on it until a sharp click sounded, and then it relented.

Wind licked at Salmaara's face, but instead of bringing relief from Günhai's stagnant interior, it brought a great and terrible stink.

Salmaara had dealt with refuse heaps and pits aplenty back home, but never had she smelled something so foul. Even the reek of the woman's body seemed to disappear into the stench of unnumbered rotting bodies that no doubt filled the "grave" before them.

Gagging, Salmaara dragged her charge outside with Gjordkra. Around them, the cubical buildings walled the filthy expanse in a circle. A vast pit yawned blackly in its center. And how deep it must go, Salmaara could not bear to imagine.

The girls dragged the litter to the pit's edge then lifted it by the top until the stiff remains of the woman tumbled from it and into darkness. Having completed the task, the girls stood side by side, still holding the litter and gazing into the abyss at their feet.

"Is this going to be you and me someday?" Salmaara didn't realize that she had spoken the question aloud until Gjordkra answered it.

"Probably." She folded her arms against herself as though chilled in the hot wind.

Salmaara understood the gesture and, unable to help herself, mirrored it.

"It doesn't have to be. It won't be," Salmaara said, her own denial sounding false even in her own ears. "We will find a way. Otherwise, who will there be to remember that poor woman?"

"Aren't you forgetting something?"

"What?"

"There's still one more. You going to remember him, too?"

"Who else will?" Salmaara took the litter back up and made for the door, trailing it behind her.

Gjordkra came after her, shutting them both back inside the shrieking dark to repeat the harrowing process. By time they were done, no amount of wiping seemed to get Salmaara's hands clean.

CHAPTER SEVENTEEN

GÜNHAI,
MAUVIAS

"*Prey has done well. It shall eat its supper with its own hands this night,*" Yezhr said as he led Salmaara into his office. The gold chain linked the two of them once more, and when the superintendent reached his desk, he fastened his end to a ring set into its stone surface. It allowed Salmaara a little room to move about, but no more than a step or two in any direction.

She leaned against one side of the desk. "Thank you, master," she said, supposing that he expected gratitude for his supposed "kindness."

"*Yes, very good. Prey is improving.*" Yezhr cocked his head, his amber eyes shimmering with pride.

"Master, may I ask you something?"

Yezhr seated himself at his desk. "*It seems that Prey already has. It may ask another question if it must.*"

"When I die or … someone kills me, I suppose, will I go into the grave?"

The door that Salmaara knew led into the lith's bedroom opened behind him, and one of his three mistresses, the only one not with child, entered. She wore a translucent robe of crimson and bore a platter of what appeared to be fresh fruit and some manner of spiced meat.

Since she had been taken into Yezhr's custody, Salmaara had not seen fare so fine. Her mouth watered and, before she could stop herself, she leaned forward a little.

Yezhr's eerie rustle of a laugh sounded in her mind. *"Prey is a sulmai creature and so, yes, it would find its end in the grave, where such things belong."*

Curiosity overrode the sickening feeling that accompanied his confirmation. She shoved the memories of the day aside to ask, "What about liths? When you die, Yezhr, what will they do with you?"

The superintendent's brown head-feathers quivered with displeasure. *"Prey is a most forward and ill-mannered creature too often, but I shall tell it. There is no harm."*

Still at Yezhr's side, his mate started unbuckling the bracers that he wore at his wrists.

Salmaara could sense the woman's signature now. The feeling of her was delicate, soft, like a feather brushing her cheek. Its gentleness surprised Salmaara as she had never encountered a lith with a pleasant signature before.

Because she was so focused on that signature, she noticed another, one that she already knew. Thin, constricting, like a wire wrapped around her head.

Revulsion and disgust rose in her as she sought its source. She found that Governor Opthonne's mind, along with the rest of him, was standing in a deep shadow against the wall by the door, watching her.

She swallowed and gripped the edge of the desk, not daring to look over her shoulder to confirm what she felt.

"Does Prey not wish to feed itself? I am certain that I or Rimse could aid it should it be necessary." Yezhr indicated the lavish platter.

Heat flooded Salmaara's cheeks, and she shook her head. "No! No, I didn't know that this was for me. Thank you, master."

Stupid. How is he supposed to eat any of this with no mouth? Come to think of it, I've never seen him eat … Perhaps he avoids doing it in front of me?

The potter's daughter took hold of the platter and pulled it closer. First, she selected a sweet-smelling strip of orange fruit. She took a bite, and it flooded her mouth with juice. She had to stifle a moan. She hadn't had anything resembling liquid since she and her captor had passed through the cursed barrier that separated this land from the others.

"*When liths die, Prey, it is a significant occasion, as we are a long-lived people. Most of us will end in the Destroyer's city of Kaskahai, our bones added to the houses of our families, if they served them and our goddess well. Prey asks what they will do with me? It is an interesting question, one I had never considered. I suppose they would burn away my body and lay my skeleton whole, Prey, upon the first step of our Lady Destroyer's throne, that I might be avenged.*"

As she ate the flavorful feast, Salmaara scrambled to recall what she had read of the City of Kaskahai. Her father's books had little to say of Mauvias or anything or anyone within it, but one could not tell the story of the War for the World without mentioning Vias's city, built inside a volcano, where King Yulari and two other of the creators had imprisoned Vias the Destroyer's soul seven millennia ago.

"Why—"

"*Prey has asked many questions,*" Yezhr cut her off. "*I now have one of my own.*"

Salmaara closed her mouth and reached for a strip of spiced meat. She popped it in, chewed, and waited.

"*Who are Prey's family? To whom does Salmaara belong?*"

His use of her name was as shocking as the question. It had been one of the first questions that he had ever asked her. "I told you, master. My family is dead. You killed him to trap me."

"He was not Prey's blood. Surely, it knows this. Tell me its family name, and I shall reward it. Perhaps with a bed and allow it to have more time to itself. Perhaps I shall even allow it to name its own reward, provided it is prudent in its demands."

He doesn't know who I am. She had thought it was so, but to have it confirmed after all this time made her weak with relief.

I'm Salmaara, daughter of Queen Kusae Zamazcus. That makes me ... Salmaara Zamazcus. Not Salmaara Sultos anymore. That life is gone. I'm Salmaara Zamazcus, and I belong to my mother, who fights the empire. Her thoughts shifted. *If I tell him, I could ask for anything. To groom myself, feed myself, maybe ask that Gjordkra and I be allowed outside for a walk each day ...*

The moment she thought it, a deep sense of wrongness settled on her heart. No, she would not tell him, no matter what he offered.

Why does he want to know? There must be something about me that made him capture me. I may be a pet and a trophy, but also a curiosity. He didn't like my answer the first time, so he's asking again.

She remembered that Governor Opthonne was spying on this exchange and easily located his wire-like signature, still over by the door. He had not moved. *They all want to know.*

"Sultos is the only name I know." Salmaara hoped that the lie came out as smoothly as she intended.

She picked up and ate another piece of meat. Where a moment ago, the food had tasted delicious, it now seemed like ash in her mouth. It had all been just to get her to talk. She wanted to take the platter and throw it in Yezhr's smug face.

"Surely, Prey would not lie to its master?"

Salmaara's heart sped, and she swallowed the last bite slowly as she shook her head. "No, of course not, master."

"*Very good, Prey. If it is done supping, Dungeon Mistress Pezra has need of its services. Something to do with ribbons, I understand.*"

"I am done, master."

Yezhr rose and unhooked her chain from his desktop, taking it in one of his sinewy, grey hands. "*Come along, Prey. There is still much to do.*"

CHAPTER EIGHTEEN

GÜNHAI,
MAUVIAS

Gaudy crimson and pink ribbons swathed Günhai's walls and corridors in swags and badly tied bows. Bouquets of twigs gathered
from the edge of the poisoned Trelta forest hung in the ribbons and on
doors and tables. Stained chairs had been scrounged from the prison
city's chambers wherever they could be found and were arranged around
tables set in the city's only outdoor venue. The courtyard had been selected for the event because none of the halls within the shrieking edifices could contain all of the invited guests. The wedding would take place
very soon—one hour, two at the most.

Chipped, stone goblets sat on the tables. The most novel items were
tightly sealed boxes of wine that formed a grandiose stack against one
of the courtyard's austere walls. They had been imported from Southern
Yendu at Salmaara's recommendation. Most of the prison city's denizens
averted their gazes and gave the boxes a wide berth, as though poison
filled them instead of sweet wine, all excepting Yezhr and Governor
Opthonne, who seemed vastly amused by the wine's presence. Even the
servants who had unloaded and stacked them winced at touching the

boxes containing the sloshy substance. When she had asked Yezhr the why of all of it, he had told her that liquid was a southern thing; a lowly thing, a filthy thing, suited only to the children of the Blue King.

Yezhr had hovered over Salmaara relentlessly during the previous month with an exasperating pride for her knowledge of wedding rituals. She had done as the governor and Yezhr had commanded her: she had shared every needed detail involved in a "proper" wedding, but she knew the lith watched her overmuch because he thought she would try to escape again.

It had been a week since he had made her wear the collar and chain. Just that new measure of freedom made her yearn to escape anew, but her limp and the scars on her back—Gjordkra had been right—reminded her to obey.

Until today, at least. We will all be out here in the courtyard, with the gates in sight. They have obtained the double order of wine I recommended and, clearly, this will be their first experience with liquid refreshment. Not to mention this is strong liquid refreshment. If I'm fortunate, it will present an opportunity for Gjordkra and me to slip away should they spill it or get drunk on it ...

Salmaara became more and more certain as time passed that Gjordkra hated her after all. The bride-to-be continued to avoid her at every turn and spoke little with her when they were together. Trapped in this dark place, the potter's daughter had hoped that she might find a friend in the other girl, and that she in turn might be a friend to her. Instead, Gjordkra left Salmaara with no one save the liths to talk to, which made her miss her father and everyone in Bhevir so much that she feared she might give up the fight to survive and, more importantly, to escape.

Whenever she thought of them, she took those thoughts and feelings and buried them deep inside herself, imagining sealing them in an iron box. She could not think of them for long and still find the will live in the barbaric prison city. But live, she would.

Gjordkra refused to speak to her even though they still shared sleeping quarters. Whenever Salmaara tried to force conversation, the other girl turned a steely, violet gaze on her that felt like a dagger twisting in Salmaara's heart. She had clearly wronged the girl in some deep way, but Salmaara could not fathom what she had done. She had only tried to do what Gjordkra had suggested.

The girl openly loathed Salmaara's cooperation with their masters and disapproved of everything Salmaara did and said. She sometimes had the feeling that the governor's bride-to-be wanted Salmaara to act up until her master would tolerate it no more and do away with her.

There's no sense in getting myself killed before trying another plan. Besides, Yezhr shadows my every step, and getting flogged again is not going to aid my escape. She thought of the thin scars that now crisscrossed her back with a shudder.

Perhaps if I can get Gjordkra out of this place, things will be different.

The potter's daughter found herself away from the liths for the first time in what seemed an eternity. She wandered between the tables in the gloomy courtyard, straightening chairs for lack of anything better to do.

Yezhr slipped from the building across the courtyard. He straightened when he spotted her and made for her immediately.

"Good evening, Prey. It is required in the chambers of the future governess." He took her hands in one of his own, which were clean in comparison to some she had become acquainted with. Still, she shivered as his rough skin enclosed hers and he pulled her into the nearest building.

The lith led her into the dark chambers that she shared with Gjordkra.

As they entered, Gjordkra kicked a lithian woman in the knees, which sent her sprawling across the slick floor into Salmaara's legs.

Salmaara offered her hand to the woman, who glared spitefully at it, stood, and fled the room.

Yezhr's eerie chuckle echoed in Salmaara's head as he placed his dim lantern in her hand and retreated.

Salmaara turned her gaze to Gjordkra, who stood tall and dignified in a white dress, off the shoulders with a swooping neckline. Obtaining the fabric had been quite a chore and keeping it white another entirely.

Gjordkra had her gloved hands clenched into fists at her sides as she faced a full-length mirror smeared with grime. Every time Salmaara saw it, she wished she had the means to clean it.

"So, they send *you*?" Gjordkra muttered stiffly.

"Yes. The wedding is very soon. You just need to put the train and the veil on," Salmaara said warily, remaining in the doorway and folding her arms.

"You do it," Gjordkra said, avoiding Salmaara's gaze. "I wouldn't know how."

Salmaara gathered the blood-red train she had made for the bride from a nearby table and draped the white-feather veil over one arm. She then buttoned the train in place and lifted the veil.

"You wear it on your head, like this," she said with a little smile, hoping to cheer the future governess a bit as she set it in place over Gjordkra's face.

"Is this really how they look?" Gjordkra asked suddenly, taking the hem of the veil in her fingers.

"Who?"

"The brides of the south."

"Yes," Salmaara replied, "and you look prettier than any bride I've ever seen, even a girl I knew from Bhevir. I wish your groom were equally handsome."

Oh, Rianne. I miss you.

Gjordkra snorted and rolled her eyes with a contemptuous smile, but Salmaara could feel her sorrow.

"We're ready," Salmaara said. She then embraced the gloomy girl, which Gjordkra permitted but did not reciprocate. She hung rigidly in Salmaara's arms until the potter's daughter released her.

"I suppose we should be going outside soon. You walk behind me, you said?"

"Yes, and don't forget your, um, bouquet." Salmaara offered a bundle of withered Trelta twigs.

Gjordkra accepted them with scarred hands, sighing softly.

As Salmaara opened the door, Pezra stepped into the room. The dungeon mistress wore a short, leather dress with pants underneath. She connected to the girls. "*You must wait.*"

An hour later, Pezra escorted them into the dark hallway. Salmaara wondered if it was her misperception or if the screams had quieted somewhat.

As they reached one of the doors to the courtyard, a racket sounded from outside. Voices rose, chairs and tables rattled and shook. It sounded as if the place was being torn apart.

"What's happening?" Salmaara asked, pressing an eye to the crack in the stone door.

"Oh, move!" Gjordkra said as she brushed her aside, opened the door further, and peered cautiously outside.

Pezra stood to one side, watching them expressionlessly.

"People are arriving for the wedding," she muttered bitterly. "Quite a few, too. My master does have high standing with the rulers of the empire, after all."

"The rulers of the empire?" Salmaara's voice shook.

"Let's go. Pick up my train," Gjordkra told Salmaara, glowering over her shoulder at the red train that collected ash and dried blood as it trailed in her wake.

"Got it!" Salmaara said quickly as she scrambled to obey. She flushed, worried that she had displeased the bride further.

The stone doors groaned open as Gjordkra leaned on them. She glided into the sacrilegiously adorned courtyard with Salmaara behind her with train in hand.

Liths and other Mauviasen peoples, whom Salmaara did not recognize, as well as other sulmai, filled the seats. Gnome servants darted among them, setting tables and dispensing goblets. All the voices combined created a hiss in the courtyard. None spared the bride or Salmaara any notice as the former stomped toward them from the side door.

Gjordkra's mood visibly darkened as she progressed nearer her doom. Her shoulders hunched and her hands clenched. She would surely break her bouquet if she squeezed any harder.

It made Salmaara wish that she could do something that moment, stop this horrid thing from happening to this girl who had already endured so much.

I will be here. She won't face it alone, at least.

All conversation stopped, and Salmaara froze in her march, unable to resist staring. Gjordkra, not wishing to do the same, continued forward, causing a grinding tear to sound as her train, still clutched in Salmaara's hands, remained stationary. Gjordkra fell on her backside, with half the train still attached.

Pezra had disappeared into the crowd.

Salmaara gasped and helped Gjordkra back to her feet. Fumbling to re-button the train, she craned to see the procession entering the open gates before them through the crowd ahead. All present stood in reverence. Salmaara's lips parted in awe.

Lithian men and women, clad in suits of armor, comprised of a coat of many squares inlaid with black gems set in silver and laced together with silver thread worn over a knee-length robe of deep crimson, marched beneath Günhai's open portcullis inside the gates in rows four long and three deep. Each held an ornately decorated spear and wore a black, rounded helmet topped by a streaming tail of hair dyed the same red as their robes. Several carried poles with the black banner of Maliem Esculis attached, while others carried black flags decorated with a ruby sword and a crown of rubies floating around its hilt, all over a large calligraphic character that Salmaara didn't recognize.

Although impressive, it had not been the guard that had snatched Salmaara's attention from the task she had been about, but the woman in their midst.

A palpable aura of command radiated from the woman as she leaned on an elegant staff of black metal with a ghostly flame burning at its top. She limped slightly, but with grace, back straight. She glided across the courtyard, clad in a fabulous satin gown of black and silver that floated around her body like a cloud of ashes. Flesh the color of fine porcelain stood out from her filthy surroundings. Her crimson hair gathered in an intricate bun atop her head, and a crown of spherical rubies hung suspended in the air around her brow. A broadsword rode on her back, mostly hidden by a black scabbard with silver embroidery. It was half the woman's height of seven and a half feet.

As she made her way across the courtyard, Salmaara saw the reason for the woman's limp. She was missing a portion of the left half of her midsection.

Salmaara stared, wondering how she could be alive. *How can she stand, let alone walk?*

Even though the throng stood between Salmaara and the woman, their eyes met. The woman's crimson eyes with their vertical pupils froze Salmaara's heart.

Gjordkra looked over her shoulder and glared when Salmaara didn't start walking again immediately. "Destroyer! What are you playing at?" the bride demanded under her breath as she straightened her torn gown with as much poise as possible.

"Who is she?" Salmaara asked, still dazed, looking after the retreating woman in fascination, her heart still racing.

"The Empress Velanoma, obviously." Gjordkra turned her head to look after the empress, as well.

Salmaara swallowed. *Legendary Empress Velanoma, chosen of the Destroyer who, it was said, threw down the Blue King Yulari, one of the four creators. The empress.*

The empress seated herself at the table in front of the stand. Her guards and subjects maintained a careful distance.

"Let's just get this thing over with," Gjordkra muttered as Jhaill stepped up onto the stone platform. He wore a white robe, lightly stained with crimson from merely touching his body.

The empress regarded the Master of Torture with her lips set in a firm line, as though tolerating the antics of a silly child.

Salmaara followed Gjordkra from the crowd and up the gray-carpeted aisle that clove the courtyard in two, loyally carrying the train, determined not to cause any further mishap.

The attention of all bore down on them as they approached, Gjordkra walking erect and Salmaara her silent shadow.

What if Yezhr decides to wed me? Salmaara thought, disgust twisting her belly. She wondered if she would be able to walk down this mocking aisle with her head held high.

Salmaara waited at the bottom of the platform's stairs as Gjordkra joined the governor of Günhai on his perch. Gjordkra stood as far from him as she was allowed.

Salmaara sat on the ground, leaning back on her hands. A new signature, like rough rope, pushed at her mind. She turned from the couple on the stand to see the empress sitting behind her, her cool gaze resting on the governor and Gjordkra.

It was her. I know it was her.

Only one person was missing—the person meant to officiate the ceremony.

Governor Opthonne said they had procured someone.

The crowd held its breath with her.

Salmaara turned to see if anyone was coming.

The empress's eye twitched as the elected individual, so short that Salmaara barely saw him, sauntered into view. As he passed Salmaara, he stepped over her hand and stole a glance at its owner. Cold, beady eyes looked through her.

Salmaara's heart froze and, before she was able to restrain herself, she gasped quietly.

It's him.

The gnome climbed irreverently onto the platform. He bowed mockingly to the governor and future governess, so low that his nose and gut touched the ground, then remained for several moments.

"Carry on," the empress said.

He straightened. "As my empress commands."

Salmaara recovered herself, surprise turning into a swelling rage.

He tried to kill me, and he doesn't even recognize me. Who is he? I can't let him leave until he answers my questions. Yezhr won't allow him to hurt his pet.

"We convene here, on this ashen day, in this gruesome city of Günhai, to bind in miserable matrimony before the great Destroyer Vias, Governor Jhaill Opthonne and Gjordkra," the gnome said in a drawn-out way, as though the notion would put him to sleep at any moment.

As Salmaara sat on the stone ground and watched him, she thought she felt the empress bristle behind her. She turned to look at Velanoma's face, but she appeared calm, no irritation evident in her exquisite features.

Salmaara turned back to the impudent gnome. *Why do all these people tolerate him? He's so small and powerless compared to them.*

"Do you, Jhaill Opthonne, swear to torment and dishonor Gjordkra as your wife so long as you live?"

Salmaara blanched. *Why is he doing the ceremony? He has it all wrong! And everyone is going along with it. Maybe they don't know any better.*

She couldn't bring herself to interrupt, not in front of all these people, especially with the empress present. She wished to remain as far from the woman's notice as possible.

Jhaill nodded curtly in reply to the gnome's query.

"And you, Gjordkra, do you swear to be tormented and dishonored by Jhaill Opthonne, your husband, so long as you shall live?"

"I guess so," she said.

"Well then, by the authority given me by her majesty, Empress Velanoma Privii Zamazcus, I pronounce you husband and wife. You may now *kiss* the bride," the gnome said, stretching his arms overhead as Jhaill leaned forward and pressed his mouth-less face against Gjordkra's full lips.

The governess cried out in alarm and staggered backward. She would have fallen from the platform had the governor not caught her and pulled her sharply against him. He stared into her revolted eyes with his own, which filled with dark mirth.

The Mauviasen stood and applauded, assuming that moment to be the correct one.

The governor then led his wife from the platform by the hand, victorious. Gjordkra stared ahead, stunned, and allowed him to show her off to his comrades.

Salmaara tore her eyes from them.

The gnome, he's gone! She frantically searched for a sign of him. *He could not have escaped already. Surely, he held some amount of authority if the empress had allowed him to do the honors … or dishonors, as the case may be …*

He had vanished.

"Master!" she called out in distress and looked for Yezhr.

The brown-feathered superintendent made his way to her curiously. "*Prey?*" He stood before her, waiting, indulging.

"Who is the gnome who did the ceremony and where has he gone?" She took one of the lith's filthy hands in hers, hoping it would hold his attention.

"*No one of great import, a favored servant of the empress's guard, I believe. As to his whereabouts, he is back to his work, no doubt.*"

Salmaara pouted. "Surely, he's someone."

"*Why does Prey vex itself over him?*" Yezhr purred in amusement.

"I'm not. He's a repugnant little brute," she said, releasing Yezhr's hand. "I just wanted to know why he was chosen to do the ceremony. Usually, the person who does the ceremony is someone of authority or importance."

Yezhr cocked his head. "*The governor's sense of humor is an acquired taste.*" He gazed into the throng, his brows lowering.

Salmaara looked to see what he scrutinized with such concern. On the opposite side of the courtyard, some of Günhai's masters labored to open the wine caskets. The containers were black and cubical, much like the buildings of the city, but with silver faucets. Numerous glass bottles stood near them, awaiting contents. Salmaara had suggested the bottles.

Those who had managed to activate a faucet stared as the liquid gushed out while others jumped back with revolted expressions, as though the wine might burn them. Meanwhile, several gnome servants tried to catch the wine in their hands to prevent it from spilling further. It sprang back up in a burgundy mist.

The wine-cloud became so dense that it was difficult to see the confused shadows within it. Some of the Mauviasen fell to the ground as they inhaled the mist, while others reeled, wonder in their eyes.

They scattered as best they could as the empress gracefully slid through the center of the pandemonium. Salmaara was so preoccupied by the display that she hadn't seen her approach.

Velanoma filled a bottle from one of the gushing faucets. She twisted the nozzle sharply, which stemmed the flow from the barrel, and glanced at several of her subjects, who swiftly mimicked her. The chaotic scene ended, and the cloud began to dissipate.

Content that the situation was under control, the empress glided to where Salmaara stood beside her master.

Salmaara's heart pounded as she met the Empress of Mauvias's chilly stare.

Yezhr bowed neatly, and Salmaara mimicked him.

"Yezhr," Velanoma said with a small incline of her head. "And ...?" Her chilly gaze shifted to Salmaara.

"*My new pet, Prey,*" he said proudly. "*I caught it in Southern Yendu.*"

"What ill has Hazc done her? She seemed displeased at the mere sight of him."

Salmaara's stomach plummeted to the hot stones of the courtyard floor. *She noticed my upset. Can she see my thoughts?*

"*She was inquiring about him just now, Empress.*"

Velanoma folded her slender hands in front of her. Her thin pupils searched Salmaara's face with displeasure. "Why do you withhold yourself from me, girl? Where have you learned such a skill?"

Salmaara waited for Yezhr to answer for her. He didn't. Instead, his amber eyes bored into her, as well.

She stared at her feet, unable to face either one.

Yezhr cocked his head as he always did when surprised or curious, respectfully silent as the empress examined his auburn-haired possession.

"Your mind, it is closed to me," Velanoma said evenly.

Salmaara looked back to the empress's face as relief surged through her, dispelling her accumulated fear.

My thoughts are safe.

"I … I don't know." She shrank beneath the empress's titanic gaze.

As Velanoma shifted it back to Yezhr, the superintendent shrugged. Salmaara could tell he was conversing with the empress. He did not extend his mental voice to his "pet."

She clenched her jaw, wishing to hear what he said. Then a faint murmur sounded in her mind. She knew it was Yezhr, but he seemed far away. She focused on the feeling he always gave her—sharp, like an axe. *What is he saying?*

"*… none of us can. It nearly escaped me, Empress, because I could not hear it, could not locate its mind. The governor also attempted to penetrate in vain. We two, and Pezra, can speak to it, but no further. Even then, it is difficult. None of my men could speak to Prey—they tried.*

"*A connection of any sort requires great exertion. It is not aware, I do not think. It has a natural barrier of sorts. I believe it has a Ka'Bahk, but it is perplexing that its signature is never invisible, as I am certain your*

Majesty observed. But it is unlike any I have ever seen. I cannot seem to learn it, cannot find it unless it is in sight. What difference is in it, I intend to discover."

"*See that you do, Superintendent,*" the empress's voice sounded. "*Silent ones are dangerous ones.*"

"*Yes, Majesty.*"

"See that you behave yourself," the empress said aloud before turning and gliding into the merriment that had arisen in the wake of the wine distribution.

Salmaara stared after her, her mouth hanging open dumbly. *How did I do that?*

"*The empress cannot hear my pet!*" Yezhr said to Salmaara with eerie joy once Velanoma was out of sight, his eyes scrunched. Then he took one of her hands and dragged her across the courtyard to the wine dispensers.

"*Prey deserves a treat.*" He filled a glass bottle then extended it to her.

She took it carefully and sniffed it. The pungent smell made her nostrils tingle. It was already evaporating from the bottle due to exposure. She had thought to try some at Rianne's wedding, but Illun had never let her near such beverages before.

Yezhr stared intently, waiting.

Salmaara nodded nervously, wondering if declining the drink meant a dreadful consequence.

Her euphoria dimmed. Just because they couldn't hear her thoughts didn't mean they couldn't hurt her. She remembered the whip too well.

She took a dainty sip then gasped as her throat seared and eyes streamed.

Before she managed a second sip, Yezhr's face blurred and shifted. She fell backward and felt her head impact the ground before all awareness forsook her.

CHAPTER NINETEEN

GÜNHAI,
MAUVIAS

"**W**ake up," a distant voice commanded wryly.

As Salmaara fought to open her heavy eyelids, a stinging smack swiped across her face. She gasped, and her eyes snapped open. Gjordkra's face fizzled slowly into focus.

"Gjordkra—"

"Quiet. I've been trying to wake you for too long," the newly anointed governess of Günhai said.

Is she hiding a grin? Salmaara thought she saw one.

"You are a gem."

"Why?" Salmaara sat up slowly, rubbing her head. She looked around the dark entry chamber where she must have been dragged while unconscious. *Now she's going to compliment me?*

A loud silence enveloped the prison city's walls.

"The wine you suggested they import for the wedding"—Gjordkra's usually sullen face broke into a grin at last, unable to hide it any longer—"has wiped out the entire city. Everyone who matters, anyway. They're all asleep."

Salmaara's eyes went wide. "So, you and I are escaping. Right now."

Gjordkra laughed for the first time since Salmaara had met her, in a short burst. Then her smile faded. "We can try."

Gjordkra pulled Salmaara to her feet. The latter swayed.

"I know the way south, and you know the rest," Gjordkra said. "I have supplies." She handed a small bundle with a strap to Salmaara.

Salmaara nodded. "Let's go before they start waking up!" Her heart soared.

How did this work out? Perhaps because they, and likely their ancestors, as well, have never had it before, so it has a stronger effect than it should. Either way ...

They moved quickly down the corridor, around one corner, and faced the outer doors that most days served as the limits of their indoor prison. They shoved them open together.

Outside, Salmaara gaped at the Mauviasen strewn everywhere, lying in inebriated heaps, most in the courtyard while others in front of her on the stairs.

The wedding decorations still hung mockingly from the surrounding walls, peering down upon the snoring masters of Günhai where they sprawled with bottles in their red-stained hands.

The empress and her party were absent from the tangled heap. However, a familiar form sagged against the wall at the top of the stairs in front of her.

Yezhr snored, his brown head feathers concealing his loathsome face. He still clutched an empty bottle.

Her blood boiled at the sight of him. *You are not my master.*

She clenched her hands into fists at her sides, imagining her fingers around his throat. Then he would never be able to torment anyone again ...

Gjordkra, apparently reading her intentions, hissed, "No! You'll—"

A cry sounded from the bowels of the fortress.

Salmaara wrenched her gaze from Yezhr and swallowed. *No ... I couldn't have done it, anyway.*

Salmaara held her breath and held up the hem of her olive-green robe so it wouldn't brush any of them as she and Gjordkra stepped lightly through the maze of limbs, careful not to accidentally disturb the air around any of them. Every painstaking step sent chills up Salmaara's legs.

She eyed the distant city gates as they drew closer, trying not to think too hard on the fact that, if she disturbed any of the feet, hands, fingers, or head feathers in her path, she might remain Yezhr's Prey forever.

Gjordkra stepped in front of Salmaara as they reached the stone gates and took one of its metal handles. Salmaara joined her, and then, together, they pulled the colossal gate inward.

As it grated against the rocky ground, Salmaara winced and Gjordkra stopped, still gripping the metal ring.

They glanced back toward the courtyard, fearful, but none stirred.

Salmaara nodded to her companion, whose violet eyes suddenly widened. Salmaara's heart skipped as Gjordkra's limbs stiffened and her face drained of color.

"Let's go!" Salmaara hissed.

Gjordkra shook her head. "We can't. We have to go back. If we go back now, we'll get off lightly. If not ..."

"Where is this coming from? Gjordkra, open the gate!"

When the other girl didn't move, Salmaara turned and followed her frozen companion's gaze across the courtyard.

Jhaill Opthonne lay near a table beside a capsized chair, his scarlet eyes open and glued to Gjordkra, smoldering and challenging.

Challenging her to continue her escape.

"You really think he's going to let you *get off lightly*? You're mad if you think such a thing. You turned eighteen today, and I haven't forgotten what you told me the day we met. Come on!"

The governess remained still and terrified. Gjordkra played tough, but Salmaara knew her master inspired a crippling fear within her. If Salmaara didn't act now, they would never escape.

Desperate, she cast her eyes about, seeing an empty glass bottle laying at her bare feet.

A surge of mad heat filled her as she lunged for it and gripped it by the neck. Then Salmaara unleashed the primal scream of hatred that had been rising in her over the past month and charged across the courtyard toward the groggy governor of Günhai.

She brought the container down as hard as she could on his balding scalp.

She hardly felt the fountain of his blood or the sting of the bottle cutting her as she hit him again and again, screaming.

A hand snatched her forearm from behind "Stop! Don't kill him!" Gjordkra said tersely, her voice low.

Strangely, none around them had stirred at Salmaara's screams. Jhaill was the only one who had awoken.

Gjordkra pulled Salmaara backward, away from the bloodied governor, who had a large piece of glass embedded in his skull. However, the potter's daughter could still see his nostrils moving with breath.

Salmaara looked down at her bloody hand in alarm. The bottle was gone.

In all her life, she had never committed such an act. Illun had always taught her that violence wasn't the answer and hadn't even let her slaughter food back at home. He had, though, let her clean, pluck, and cook to her heart's content, yet he had rarely let her near knives and other such implements. "A violence-free heart makes for a violence-free home, and a violence-free home makes for a violence-free world," he had liked to say whenever she protested about not going hunting with him or carving up whatever beast they planned to eat for supper. It never made sense that he could and she couldn't, but she had taken his words into her heart. She couldn't recall how many fights she had broken up during her growing years because she had just wanted a "violence-free world."

She stared at the lith's bloody scalp and at her hand. *Who have I become?*

When her shock at what she had just done dimmed, it flared anew as she realized what Gjordkra had said. *Why would she stop me from killing him? I can't ask now. Now we have to run.*

Gjordkra was drifting toward Jhaill, so Salmaara seized her wrist.

Her companion flinched at her touch and stopped her advance back to her master's side. She looked from Salmaara to Jhaill and back again with wild eyes. In them, Salmaara read the other girl's conflict. *She really might stay!*

It was then that Gjordkra yanked her arm back and took a step away from Salmaara, a step back toward Jhaill Opthonne. Gjordkra's slight frame trembled visibly.

Why he hadn't connected to Salmaara's mind, as well, before she had knocked him unconscious, she didn't know—perhaps it had something to do with the wine's effects—but it meant that Salmaara didn't know what he had told Gjordkra, how he might have threatened her.

She's lived here almost her entire life. I've never seen her disobey him or even disagree with him. If he has told her to stay, perhaps she thinks there is no other choice.

Heart pounding in her ears, Salmaara swallowed. "Gjordkra, come with me. Leave this place. Leave him," she pleaded. "He's a monster. He's brought you nothing but isolation and pain."

"You wouldn't understand. You should just go, like you did before."

Salmaara placed her hands on her hips. "Gjordkra, I am not going to leave you here, no matter what."

"He … he does bad things, but not always. He treats me with special food, a game, or conversation sometimes, if I'm good. He can be witty, and charming … And you've hurt him! I can't go." The black-haired bride rubbed the back of one of her scarred hands absently. "He needs me."

Salmaara's heart ached at the other girl's words. "Do you remember what you told me about him the day I arrived?"

Gjordkra stared at the ground.

"You warned me that, if I could stay away from Jhaill, I should, because he is the *foulest slime in this stinkhole*, I believe you said. You had the right of it, and we both know it. There are too many confusing things in this world; don't doubt things that you already know are true."

Salmaara offered her uninjured hand to her companion. "Now is your chance to stay away from him forever. Come with me. Be free."

Gjordkra lifted her gaze from her feet and met Salmaara's. Tears drifted from her cheeks as the air greedily lapped them up. As though her arm weighed more than all the world itself, Gjordkra strained to wrench it up and clasp Salmaara's hand.

Not wasting another second, Salmaara pulled Gjordkra back into action.

Hand in hand, they sprinted to the gate, and then the two of them erupted from Günhai.

"I take back what I said earlier about you being a gem," Gjordkra said sourly when Salmaara finally stopped running. The governess sank down on a rock near where Salmaara already lay panting on the ashy ground.

Throbbing pain filled Salmaara's feet where her shoes had rubbed them raw. She flexed her toes painfully, staring at the sky. Her dry lungs burned, too. Worst of all, though, she could still feel where glass slivers impaled her hand. Idly, she picked at it and pulled two pieces free. Small beads of blood drifted from the broken skin and into the air, where they vanished.

Gjordkra glared at her own feet, which looked as bad as Salmaara's. "Destroyer, I don't know why I thought you'd lead us to freedom, you little maniac. Do you know which way you ran?"

Salmaara shook her head slowly, too exhausted to answer. She continued removing glass shards then tore a strip from her olive robe to bind the hand with.

"West. We needed to go straightway south, and then west from Günhai to get out of this cursed country. You can't just go over the T'Skel anywhere, believe me. They're impassable, except by the Nva Pass, which you conveniently ran away from. I've seen maps of this land, one of my few pleasures. I grabbed some supplies, but there is nothing, *nothing* out here. We are not well enough provisioned to survive the wilderness, and we're weeks away from the nearest city. We have two choices: return to Günhai or keep going west to Kaskahai." Gjordkra paused.

"Kaskahai is the Destroyer's city. Legend has it that her soul is imprisoned there." Salmaara looked at the gray sky.

"Jhaill probably won't follow us there. Of course, if half of what Jhaill says about the Shazrah is true, they'll enslave us, or take our bones, or worse.

"Either way," Gjordkra continued with a scathing glare, "they're going to come after us and will find us. Yezhr is Mauvias's most formidable tracker. Even the empress calls for him when she needs something or someone found. And he'll be upset with you for running off. He'll punish you for your trespass, and then you'll really see how nasty he can be. You thought the flogging was bad? He thinks that's a kindness to naughty pets of his! I can't imagine what more my husband"—she choked on the word—"could do to me that he hasn't already, but he is creative." She folded her arms over her chest, on the verge of tears.

Salmaara couldn't focus on Gjordkra's fury, so she said nothing.

What now? I have to solve this ...

"We won't return to Günhai."

Gjordkra rolled her eyes. "Didn't you understand me? This wilderness claims everything that dares crawl across it. If we don't die of dehydration, hunger, or the bloody toxins in the air—"

"We have to try. Nothing could be worse than returning to Günhai," Salmaara murmured resolutely. "We can make it."

Gjordkra shook her head. "You never listen, crazy girl. Jhaill is full-blooded Kaskahai himself, and he fled the place. He must have been too sweet to live among them."

"We will do what we have to," Salmaara said.

Gjordkra resolutely handed her tattered satchel to Salmaara. "I packed a week of food, but we could make it last longer … maybe. About the same of hydration powder. It was all I could find."

Salmaara sat up and tore a strip of her sheer robe free, using it to bind one of her blistered feet. "We'll make it last. We can't turn back. They won't expect us to go this way. If we go south, we'll be caught soon, just as you said. It will take them time to realize we didn't go south, won't it?"

"I guess so, but that would only be because they will have mistaken us for creatures who care about our survival."

Salmaara nodded and took a small sprinkle of hydration powder. *The T'Skel are lesser on the east and west of Mauvias. If we could get over, we could follow the sea to make south. I'll take the wilderness, even the Destroyer's city or the Destroyer herself—anything but Yezhr.*

"We have a start on them. If they go south, into Arvitra, that would give us a three-, maybe four-day lead at least."

"Yes, but it won't matter how long it takes them. All they'll find are our skeletons. We are going to die."

Salmaara forced herself to stand, shuddering at the prickles that spread from her feet and up her legs like a thousand needles. She then looked down into Gjordkra's sour face, clenching her fists at her sides. "Better than returning to that … that place where they maim you for the joy of it!"

"At least we would be alive," Gjordkra grumbled as she straightened, brushing off her stained wedding gown as though that would clean it. Her filthy hands just added more ash to the graying fabric.

"*Alive*? You call that *living*? Wondering which day will be your last, always subject to the whims of creatures who use you as a pet and plaything?"

Gjordkra shrugged.

Salmaara set her jaw and pointed. "I'm going that way."

Gjordkra raised a brow. "That's north."

Salmaara's stomach sank. She reevaluated and pointed west. "Then I'm going that way!"

"Fine, I'll come. I won't have you walking into a cannibal or selti tribe alone. They rove all over. Lots of them in the north especially." Gjordkra pointed north. "That way, if you care. You are sure our escape route is west, aren't you?"

Salmaara's cheeks burned as she nodded.

"Very well, delusional girl. West we will go."

Salmaara looked west, shielding her eyes from the wind that rolled across the cursed wilderness.

"To freedom … or death."

CHAPTER TWENTY

GÜNHAI,
MAUVIAS

As sunsdown approached, Hazc crouched between two crenella-tions on the prison city's outermost ramparts, observing the pro-ceedings in the courtyard below. The masters of Günhai lay helpless beneath the sway of the Southern Yendu wine, which had had a stron-ger effect than it should have—Hazc had seen to that—and the girls had fled into the wilderness.

To the west, of all directions, he thought with amusement. *There is naught out there but ash and death. Ah, but they will not be alone, and I shall not allow them to perish in any case.*

His attention drifted to Yezhr as the lith finally pulled himself to his feet from where he had fallen at the top of the stairs that led into the indoor city. Gripping the railing with a tremulous hand, the lith swiftly scanned the courtyard and, spotting the governor, made his way to the skewered fool's side.

The superintendent of Günhai kneeled beside him, removed a medici-nal pack from his belt, and then tugged on the chunk of glass imbedded in Jhaill's forehead.

Jhaill thrashed awake and grabbed Yezhr's wrist.

The superintendent pried the fingers away and reached for a pair of tongs hanging at his waist. Gripping the glass with the implement in one hand, and holding Jhaill's shoulder with the other, Yezhr tugged until the glass came free.

Hazc watched distractedly as the superintendent cleaned and stitched the wound. *Well, few deserve such a turn of fate more than Jhaill.*

With every passing moment, more of the drunken Mauviasen roused and the courtyard slowly came back to life, like a beast emerging from hibernation, stretching its stiff limbs and yawning. And staggering.

Hazc looked back toward the gate. *So, Kusae's daughter has returned. She is earlier than anticipated.*

He had not forgotten the feisty five-year-old whom he had set adrift in the river. Auburn hair, golden eyes, and a disposition that had not changed at all in the intervening decade, if the intensity of the stare that she directed at him at the wedding was any indication.

She has not forgotten me, either, it would seem. Although she should have. Me wonders what else she remembers concerning that day …

Jhaill climbed to his feet, making broad motions with his arms and stabbing a finger at the main gates, as though he intended to impale them as he had done to many an unfortunate victim.

A few of the governor's guardsmen, all lithian, also stirred, scrambling to find weapons while others ran inside the city.

Having returned his needle and thread to their pouch, Yezhr stood calmly where he had been kneeling, thumbing the shard of glass he had removed from Jhaill's head.

The livid Governor of Günhai himself stalked impatiently back and forth, kicking a man who still slept as he passed him.

You only care that your bride has escaped. You do not think of Salmaara and do not fear her as you should. Yezhr is not so blind.

Jhaill had always been single-minded to a fault, which might explain why the governor had not noticed the danger posed by the city's newest tenant. And he had not seen the interaction between Velanoma and Salmaara.

Well, he won't be getting what he wants.

All of it aside, Hazc would treasure the memory of Salmaara clubbing Jhaill insensate with that bottle for some time to come. That Gjordkra had chosen to go with the girl pleased him, as well.

He smiled a crooked, little smile. Hazc had offered her the choice when he had allowed Jhaill to wake before the others.

Salmaara was turning out to be worth some attention. Few succeeded in entertaining Hazc, let alone in concerning him. Most disconcerting was that he was still thinking about her when he rarely bothered himself with individuals for long. Most were so insignificant in their struggle to make a mark in the eternal timeline. *But the girl does hold some fascination. I will test her.*

More of the party guests in the courtyard stirred as Jhaill's minions poured from the city and back into the courtyard. Several of them led a pair of charcoal-skinned dragons, one belonging to the governor, the other to the superintendent.

The liths mounted up and made their way to the gates, which Salmaara and Gjordkra had left partially open. Sulmai guards scrambled to push the gates wider open while avoiding being trampled as the governor and his party charged out into the Nva Pass.

Hazc watched them plow southward, toward Sunad, and shook his head. *The girl has bought some time by her intriguing choice of direction, but little else. Does she hope to go to Kaskahai, to take tea with Ra'Zhe and Vias, as well?*

Inwardly cursing the shortness of his gnomey arms and legs, Hazc scaled down the wall to the courtyard floor and merged into the growing bustle of servants who had started taking the decorations and tables down. He crossed the procession carpet as a trio of gnomes began to roll it, then dodged between the legs of two sulmai men as they dragged chairs back toward the doors leading into the indoor city.

He approached the wine boxes and, taking a goblet for himself, sipped it. The smooth, spiced wine of Southern Yendu slid down his throat pleasantly with none of the drastic effects the wedding-attending Mauviasen had suffered.

No one around him seemed to notice that the wine remained in the open basin of the cup as Hazc made his way to the open city gates and into the wilderness of the Destroyer's land beyond.

CHAPTER TWENTY-ONE

WEST WILDERNESS,
MAUVIAS

Despite their best efforts to ration supplies, Gjordkra and Salmaara found themselves out of hydration powder six days' walk out of Günhai.

Ash-blown wilderness surrounded them on all sides, seeming to stretch forever in every direction. Shards of igneous rock and pebbles skittered across the ground beneath the ashy current of filth flowing over it. Massive columns of dirt rose from the ground like trees. The dirt split into branches at the top, reaching toward the suns, which were just visible through the ash cloud above. The dust-trees reached out to gather dirt, ash, and stone. As the tops became too full for the columns to support, each tossed its burdens away in great bursts and sank back into the dreary waste with a lifeless hiss.

Salmaara had wondered what caused them until the previous day when Gjordkra fell and cut her hand. The moment her blood hit the dirt, one of the dust-trees sprang up.

It's that cursed air. It gets so thirsty for moisture out here that not a single drop goes unnoticed or left behind. It even sucks the dirt up to get the last drop.

Thirsty. I cannot think about thirst …

"I'm going to die. There's no food, no powder out here. Thanks for nothing," Gjordkra muttered at the ground as she limped alongside her.

"We'll find something. You are not going to die, nor am I," Salmaara said hoarsely, searching the horizon. Another thing she had learned was to watch for forming dust-trees. They weren't made of just dust but were full of sharp shards of rock and grew to over thirty feet high, and some were as big around as a house. She hated to think what might happen should one fall on them. *Then Gjordkra would be right. All that would remain to be found is our skeletons, if that,* she thought with a shudder.

Salmaara cast her eyes to the left to ensure the black bumps, only a finger high from so far away, were still there. *I have to keep the T'Skel to our left. Then I'll know we're still going west. I'm not getting us lost.* She could see them, although only faintly through the black debris pelting her face.

Salmaara looked back to Gjordkra. The older girl stumbled forward, eyes fixed on her feet, holding her blackened wedding dress away from the ground. Gjordkra's small frame had carried too little on it when they had left the prison city. *And now … I don't think she heard me. She's not going to last much longer if I don't do something.*

"Gjordkra?" Salmaara said loudly. "Have you heard of Castle Errasitka?"

Gjordkra shook her head without taking her eyes from the ashy ground.

Salmaara looked away from her to watch for growing trees again. "It's where King Yulari Digarious Lordian, ruler of the world—which is called Inaria—and one of the four creators, lived. A place of astounding beauty, with white towers and windows of countless colors, yet darkened, haunted by the king's tragic past."

Gjordkra looked up, her glazed violet eyes losing some of the hopeless look that had been growing there. "Yulari Lordian? That sounds maybe familiar."

"Yulari Lordian, the Blue King, Lord of Sorrows!" Salmaara said softly.

"Oh, him. The enemy of Mauvias."

"Not enemy. He was sad his wife's people and his could never be one. The war he fought strove to unite the lands, but the Mauviasen wouldn't have it. Their goddess wanted destruction and chaos, and so did they."

"Looks like we got it."

"Yes," Salmaara said sadly. "Imagine what it would be like if the empire was no more, if we could return to Kalitoomba. If we could read a book in the open or go to a school. We could have schools. We could live lives free of fear, free to be whatever we wanted. We wouldn't be subject to a vicious empress who serves a Destroyer Goddess.

"Yulari once said that '*what is past, cannot be relived, or restarted, but anyone can begin today and realize a new ending.*' I think we are responsible to fight such tyranny and help create a better world."

Gjordkra raised a brow. "Where do you get such crazy ideas? As if anyone could ever harm the empress, or even threaten the Destroyer. Those others they say are gods? They're dead. The Destroyer is supreme, Greatest of the Four Creators. And it's been a hundred years, right? I don't think things will change any time soon."

"Yulari Lordian is not dead, he just vanished. Things that vanish can reappear, especially when the vanished is the god who created most of this world and loved it more than anything. I know he'll return, and when he does, all of this will end! All people will be free," Salmaara said passionately, surprising even herself.

Gjordkra froze mid-stride, eyes going round. "You're a lunatic and a heretic. Good thing you never mouthed off like this in Günhai. We would have had a heretic's execution rather than a wedding. How do you know all this? No one knows so much who didn't live over a century ago. All that about the heathen king not hating Mauvias? Madness! You said you're sixteen."

"I am. I just read a considerable amount."

"You read? You read what?"

"Books."

"Those are illegal. Illegal because they make people crazy, obviously. How did I get stuck with you? You make me lose all sense. And now I'm going to die."

Salmaara sighed. *Well, I distracted her for a few minutes at least.*

"Gjordkra, don't you think it's odd to revere someone who condones the things the governor did to you? The Destroyer made him and his race. Jhaill stole you from your home, tortured you, and derives pleasure from misery and suffering ..." Her words trailed off.

"And made me his bloody wife. And I wouldn't say people revere her ... I would say *fear*. It would be stupid not to. It's kept me alive. You could do with a little yourself—fear, I mean. Lady Destroyer, the goddess, handpicked the empress to rule the world, an empress who can't be killed. You saw Empress Velanoma at the wedding, right? I seem to remember some dress-ruining thanks to that."

"She was missing half her middle ..."

"Yeah, she is. She can't be killed. People have tried and failed. Powerful people. Those who want stay alive have wised up and stopped trying."

A gust of wind moaned across the plain, and two nearby dust-trees fell, scattering debris.

Gjordkra took a resigned breath. "But you're not most, are you? You'd actually try."

Salmaara's heart sped at the memory of the empress's cold gaze.

Setting her jaw, she looked ahead. "If it comes to it."

Gjordkra threw her hands up. "Why don't you ever give up? You're always going on as if you know what's going to happen. You know we'll make it. You know the heathen king will return. We are in the middle of the wilderness with no end in sight, starving, and you're going on about how we're going to live."

"I just know in my heart that things will work out, because I believe the things that happen to us are for a greater purpose. My father's last words to me were to choose hope and choose life. I do choose hope, and I choose to live. I don't see any reason to stop fighting until the moment I drop dead. Do you?"

Gjordkra shook her head and muttered under her breath, turning away.

The wind quieted for a moment, and a muffled clacking sounded from somewhere across the plain. It grew louder and louder until a carriage materialized a short run from their position, just squeezing between two dust-trees as they toppled.

As it barreled toward them, Salmaara dropped to her knees, trying to disappear beneath the flowing ash cloud that obscured the ground. Gjordkra followed quickly.

As the coach drew nearer, Salmaara could make out its details. Iron composed it, and two men with black flesh, ribbed wings, and long tails drew it. Nothing covered their powerful bodies, save scraps of rags tied around their loins. The doors on both sides of the coach hung open and flapped wildly with every bump the vehicle encountered.

Salmaara's heart leaped. She couldn't sense anyone inside. *Empty ... It must be empty!*

Gjordkra leaped to her feet, waving her arms as the coach neared. "Stop!" The winged men didn't slow.

Salmaara leaned over, snatched a fist-sized rock, and hurled it as far as she could. The stone thumped to the ground just short of the men.

Salmaara ran toward them, yelling and throwing more rocks. Still, the men did not slow. She ran as hard as she could, her heart sinking as the gap between the men and her widened, but she kept running.

When a massive dust-tree suddenly appeared through the haze directly in the creatures' path, hurling rock and dirt, the men finally stopped, shielding their faces.

Heart pounding, Salmaara took another stone in hand and threw it into the thinning "trunk" of the dust-tree as hard as she could. It collapsed, debris falling in a ring around the men and the carriage. Her stone then bounced, coming to rest at one of the creatures' feet.

Both cast their yellow eyes about in alarm until they locked on Salmaara. Then they relaxed, and one rolled his shoulders while the other shot her a sideways glance.

They ignored her when she reached their side.

"What are they?" Salmaara asked, looking at the men.

Gjordkra stepped up beside her. "What? Selti?"

"Selti … they seem to be waiting for us," Salmaara murmured as she approached one of the doors.

The carriage stood empty. A single bench faced the front where a green-tinted window allowed the only view out. A dark stain covered much of the bench and floor. Looking up, she could see more spattered on the front glass. Blood. None of it was wet, of course.

Stepping back from the carriage, she looked for Gjordkra. "Gjordkra, what do you suppose—"

Gjordkra stepped around from behind the carriage, a bulging cloth pouch held in each hand.

Salmaara's heart rose. "Is that what I think it is?"

"Why don't you open one and find out?" She tossed one to Salmaara.

Heart pounding, Salmaara bit into the cloth, tearing a corner free. Some of the magenta powder from within hit her tongue and gelled.

For the first time, Salmaara eagerly downed the foul powder. It never satiated as water did but was so much more than nothing.

"There's food, too. Not much, maybe four days' worth if we're really good.

"Watch out for selti. I hear they aren't the loyal type. If something happens to us, they'll stand there and watch. Probably what happened to whoever owned this coach. But I bet we could tell them to take us somewhere and they'd do it. Selti don't ask questions from my experience," Gjordkra said, taking more powder.

Salmaara tucked her pouch under her arm and walked to the back of the coach, rifling through the open compartment. She extracted some dried meat and bread. "You don't suppose they know how to take us toward Kaskahai?"

"Probably. They know the land better than most of us do, I've heard. Haven't been around them that much, though."

Salmaara offered the food to Gjordkra, who snatched it and bit into it furiously. Then, forcing her hunger to the back of her mind, Salmaara approached the selti. Both lay on the ground with wings folded against their backs and tails wrapped around their legs.

"Excuse me," Salmaara said.

They looked up with yellow eyes to meet hers.

She tore her loaf of bread in half and offered the pieces to them. "Hungry?"

They stared at the bread as if in confusion for several moments before the nearest one accepted the food. He sniffed it and bit into it. After the first bite, he took more in rapid succession, the fangs that filled his mouth tearing it easily. When he had devoured it, his companion accepted the other and ate it, as well.

"We need to go to Kaskahai for food, and then west. You know Kaskahai?"

The selti looked at one another then back at her, regarding her flatly.

"Sorry! I don't mean to—"

"Mau," the nearest said with a whip of his tail.

The other nodded. "Mau."

"Mau?"

"That's *home* in untainted," Gjordkra said, walking up behind her.

Salmaara turned. "Untainted what?"

"Mauviasen. You speak the tainted tongue. It's a mix of Mauviasen and southern. Jhaill's native tongue is untainted. I know lots myself, thanks to him."

Both selti finished eating and stretched luxuriously.

"Oh. So, Kaskahai is home for them?"

"Guess so."

Salmaara turned from the winged men, climbed into the blood-stained carriage, and sat on the bench, away from the dark stain on the cushion. Gjordkra sat beside her, unperturbed, and then Salmaara pulled one door shut and Gjordkra the other.

The selti started forward and broke into a run. They ran faster than any horse Salmaara had ever observed.

She slouched down on the bench, stretching her sore feet out in front of her. "What do you think happened to the owner of this carriage?"

"Probably ran into a cannibal band somewhere in or around Tzu Tihas. There are tons of them in the north, but people who know anything don't go up there. There aren't any cities; just nomads. But they know where our roads and cities are. That's why you don't travel without an escort. At least, that's what I hear. Of course, I've never traveled before … that I remember."

Salmaara grimaced. *Cannibals? What will be next in this place? Perhaps it's for the best that these people stayed separated from the people southward for so long.*

Leaning back, she fixed her gaze ahead at the backs of the selti as they plunged over the invisible ground toward the Destroyer's City.

CHAPTER TWENTY-TWO

KASKAHAI,
MAUVIAS

Eight shifts between dim and dark passed outside the selti-drawn carriage. Monotonous wilderness crept by day after day. Dust, ash; dust, ash. Dust-trees springing up; dust-trees falling. The selti running; the selti sleeping. The food and hydration powder depleting until it vanished. Hunger making Gjordkra unbearable company.

Salmaara lay with her cheek against the cold, metal wall beside her, staring dully ahead, trying to forget the gnawing pain in her stomach, when she saw the land drop sharply ahead. The mountain that sprang from the valley below the plateau they traveled on was too large to take in at once, its heights obscured in the ash cloud that spanned the surrounding wilderness. Rutilant veins of lava scoured the volcano's rocky slopes.

Salmaara leaned forward, lips parted. "Gjordkra, look."

Gjordkra sat up with a sullen glare before she, too, saw Mount Kaskahai, and her eyes rounded in awe.

"That's probably it," Salmaara said, her dry lower lip splitting with her speech. The blood didn't make it down her chin before the air claimed it.

"Probably," Gjordkra said with a nod.

Wind stirred ash from the valley floor and buffeted their small carriage but slowed the selti little.

"Gjordkra, we can't ride into the city. We have to get out here before we're seen." Salmaara looked down at the stretch of sharp rock between them and the mountain. *We are going to have to walk that.*

Gjordkra scowled but nodded.

Salmaara forced herself to her feet then knocked on the front window as loud as she was able.

The selti didn't react as they hurtled the carriage down the slope, toward the volcano.

She turned to Gjordkra. "Come on!"

Forcing one of the doors open, she leaned out of the carriage. The wind pelted her face with filth, too much to keep her eyes open.

She steadied herself with one hand on the carriage's roof and the other on the flapping door. Clearing her throat, she shouted, "Stop!"

The eldritch creatures either didn't hear or ignored her, keeping their pace.

I don't have anything to throw at them this time.

Jump. We have to jump.

She pulled back into the carriage and looked at Gjordkra, who shook her head.

"When we get to the bottom, we have to jump. They're not stopping."

The slope ended a short distance ahead, the passage down opening into a broad, flat plain littered with shards of volcanic stone.

Salmaara didn't let herself think of the landing that waited. Her leg had healed enough to walk on but still pained her.

She turned back toward the door. *We just have to do it.*

Gjordkra muttered curses under her breath to Salmaara's back. She heard "lunatic" and "die."

We aren't going to die.

When the carriage leveled out, Salmaara thrust the door open again. With a final yell at the selti, who sprinted blindly ahead, she took a deep breath, crossed her arms over her chest, and leaped from the carriage.

The ground hit her like a hammer, the impact knocking the breath from her lungs. She rolled and rolled, through ash and glassy volcanic rock, then stopped.

Lifting her head, she craned to see the retreating carriage that plowed ahead, toward the volcano, its doors open. An abandoned carriage, just how we found it.

Forcing the stinging pain that was her body to the back of her mind, she rose to her knees and crawled toward a black-haired, unmoving heap not far away.

Salmaara reached Gjordkra's side, and Gjordkra looked up at her. The wedding gown, already in a tattered condition, barely covered Gjordkra's bleeding torso. The air greedily lapped up the blood, and a miniature dust-tree forming around her.

"This is your not-getting-caught plan? Breaking every bone in my body so I'll end up crawling in there, helpless? They'll probably just kill us and take our bones, anyway. There used to be more civil people in Kaskahai before the southerners killed most of them. Those left are supposed to be crazies with sorcerous powers—the people who bred my master. The Shazrah."

Salmaara tore strips from the hem of her robe to bind the worst of Gjordkra's wounds. "I know, but we'll die if we stay out here. We have to find powder at least."

Gjordkra took a deep breath. "All right, I've followed you this far."

Salmaara finished tying off the cloth on Gjordkra. She then wrapped another strip around her own middle and tied it. "First, we have to get up and walk. Hopefully, anyone around will be distracted by the carriage's arrival long enough for us to slip in. I didn't see any others, so it doesn't look as though many people like a day trip to the Destroyer's city." Salmaara took a shuddering breath and took to her feet.

Gjordkra did the same, swaying. Salmaara offered her a steadying hand, which she swatted away. Together, they started forward.

"Say we do make it to the city and, by freak chance, make it out alive with supplies," Gjordkra said as they dragged across the rocky plain. "Remind me again where we're going? You said there is an escape route west. I'm not so smart as to guess what is west that could lead us south." Gjordkra tripped, and a sharp stone sliced through her tattered silk slipper and jammed into her foot.

She didn't react as far as Salmaara could tell, didn't even blink. Salmaara didn't know how the girl could stand it.

"The sea is west, Gjordkra. We can follow that south."

"The sea?"

"Lots of open water. I suppose we'll have to get there and see."

She squinted ahead at the massive roots of the volcano. Among them, she counted nine large openings, each with a road leading into it. "We must almost be there," said Salmaara. Which road to take?

As the faint light of the suns, hidden above the ash cloud, faded from the sky, they rounded another bend and stood at the head of a path that disappeared into the haze floating around the mountain. Hours earlier, they had diverged from tracks left by the carriage that led around to one of the openings in the mountain.

"Destroyer"—Gjordkra stopped short—"you actually got us here."

Salmaara ignored her, crouched down, and brushed the scorched path with shaking fingers, removing a soft layer of ash. She squinted at the pale material that paved the road and sucked in a deep breath. "What is this, Gjordkra? It's so smooth."

Gjordkra knelt beside her. "How should I know?"

Salmaara crawled forward. It was an immense relief from the sharp rocks. Little remained of the black slippers Yezhr had put on her.

She wiped more ash from the path as she went, feeling the different sizes and shapes of the path's constituents. Her fingers then fell on something rounded and recognizable. Part of a skull.

"They're ... They're bones!" Salmaara said, stumbling back to her feet, repulsed. It was bad to touch bone, Illun had always told her. He believed it could shorten one's lifespan by years.

"Does it surprise you? This is the road to the Destroyer Goddess's city. A queen of death," Gjordkra said, unperturbed. "How don't you know, having read all those ... books ... you're always going on about?"

Salmaara wiped her hands on her grimy robe, stomach twisting. "There was very little about Mauvias in them. Mostly they were about Kalitoomba and King Yulari." She took several trepid steps, grimacing.

I can't stand another step on that volcanic glass. I'll take my chances with the bones.

Yezhr did say something about liths being returned here when they die ...

Salmaara made her way down the bone road that wound around the volcano's side until it led to a pair of colossal gates. There, she froze, and Gjordkra mimicked her.

Unlike the dirty path, there was no question that the gates were made of bones.

Random knees, arms, and even whole skeletons of species that Salmaara didn't recognize formed an artful, albeit macabre, lacework.

The bones' yellowing surfaces had the well-loved texture of countless scrubbings—they seemed to glow in their ashy surroundings. Each gate formed half of a great semi-circle.

The gates stood open, daring the girls to see what lay ahead.

Gjordkra slipped in, motioning for Salmaara. "Quit gawking and get moving before we're seen," she hissed.

Tearing her eyes from the morbid gates, Salmaara followed.

A broad tunnel stretched out before them, the floor inlaid with flecks of bone. They followed it until it turned into a flight of stairs. Salmaara climbed them, her curiosity overruling her throbbing body.

As they emerged from the entry tunnel, they reached a broad landing. Salmaara gazed over the Destroyer's city as heat and sulfur arose to embrace them in its stifling arms. Malice seemed imprinted on the hot air, coming from every direction.

Her breath caught again, part in awe, part in defense against the fumes.

Inside the hollow volcano, rivers of magma oozed among thousands of winding stairs and dilapidated buildings constructed mostly of bones. Five tiers of yellowing buildings crawled up the interior sides of the volcano, one above the other. A magnificent palace of red granite sat on a sixth tier, looming over everything.

There wasn't a living thing in sight.

Salmaara hesitated before turning to her companion, heart racing.

After a moment's silence, Gjordkra spoke quietly. "I don't see or hear anyone. But they're probably here."

"Perhaps they're all inside or something. You never know. I mean, it is hot out here," said Salmaara, trying to keep the mood light.

She wiped sweat from her brow as it evaporated. Although the bone city sounded and appeared deserted, Salmaara could sense multitudes of people on the tiers ahead. At that realization, her heart sped. *We can't turn back now.*

Her stomach snarled once more.

Salmaara started for the largest flight of stairs that led to the city's first tier. "Any ideas as to where we should begin? It could take us days to find the supplies we need."

As she put her foot on the first step, it went through what appeared to be solid stone. Salmaara toppled forward with a horrified shriek, her heart pounded deafeningly in her ears as nothing but hot magma filled her vision.

Gjordkra caught her ankles. "Don't. You. Dare. Die!" she grated, her voice sounding very far away.

As Salmaara felt Gjordkra's weak hands slipping, she swallowed and flailed her arms. She tried to grasp something, anything, as she attempted to swing herself toward solid ground. Blood from her throbbing feet ran down her legs, evaporating before it reached her thighs.

Salmaara stared upward, heart pounding. From its underside, she could see that the staircase was only half substantial.

Gjordkra's hands shook as she attempted to get a better hold.

Salmaara bent, straining up toward her feet. She snatched Gjordkra's hands, and the girl screamed as she yanked Salmaara back to solid ground. Both collapsed at the base of the stairs.

"Bloody Destroyer. Reeking, bloody Destroyer!" Gjordkra said, rambling for several minutes, mostly curses that Salmaara had never heard, eyes fixed upward.

Salmaara swallowed and turned to Gjordkra. "How was I supposed to know half of it was an illusion? It looks perfectly solid."

"If you'd just looked at it, you would have seen one side is completely worn from use, and the other—the one you stepped on—isn't! Don't you dare leave me here alone. Not after what you've put me through. I'd hunt you down in the afterlife and see justice done!"

"Sorry." Salmaara swallowed another excuse. "I'll be more careful." *Not that it will help here,* she finished in thought.

The emptiness and silence did not offer any comfort now.

Salmaara felt eyes on her and knew they were not alone. She could feel many signatures in the buildings around them, even in the street, but could see no one. *Why don't they show themselves? There are so many. We're no match for them.*

"Are you all right?" she asked Gjordkra.

Her comrade glared. "Yeah."

Salmaara sat up and crawled back to the stairs. There, she prodded the more worn side of the staircase, the side that appeared substantial from its underside. It felt solid. However, she bought her fist down on the first stair to be sure.

"Who came up with this? Half leads to the city, half to a fiery death. Waste of space," Salmaara said, trying to make light of it and hide her own unease.

She turned back to Gjordkra, who only shrugged. She still lay limply behind Salmaara, eyes narrowed and lips pursed.

I need food soon. I'm not thinking properly. The stairs are obviously worn ...

Salmaara used the step to push herself to her feet. She mounted the remaining stairs and found them as solid as the first, but only on one side. *Still, what nasty trap!*

Gjordkra trudged up behind her. Both then looked in every direction, seeking any sign of life. Nothing.

The half-perilous stairs led to a broad street with unpaved, ashy ground underfoot and lined with bone houses, ranging from one to three stories tall, most dilapidated and apparently abandoned.

As she left the stairs to inspect the grotesque structures, she spotted a large pair of softly glowing, blue footprints that began in the street's center and walked away from her.

Heart quickening, she turned to her companion. "Gjordkra, look here."

Still displeased, with lips pursed and arms folded, Gjordkra stepped daintily from the stairs and onto the ashy street, joining Salmaara. Looking down, she raised a brow. "What?"

Salmaara crouched and pointed to one of the footprints, each as long as her hand and forearm combined. "Footprints."

"You're mad for real this time."

Frowning, Salmaara looked up at her. "How can you not see them? They're glowing!" she said slowly, looking back at them.

Gjordkra crouched beside her, violet eyes fixed on the ground, searching where Salmaara's finger rested in one of the footprints. "I see a patch of filthy ground. Some rocks, some dirt. No footprints. Doesn't look as if anyone's been here in forever."

Am I the only one seeing this? Salmaara rested her hand in the footprint. *How can she not see?*

Something about the glowing prints pulled her irresistibly. Straightening, Salmaara said, "I think we should follow them. They go down that alley over there."

She didn't wait for Gjordkra to reply before she made her way after the footprints, which went between two buildings made of carefully arranged arm and leg bones. Open, octagonal windows set into the buildings' sides stared blackly at the girls as they passed.

Beyond the alley, the footprints led to a winding stair set into a sheer wall of rock. The stairs themselves, however, were made of bones, not stone.

Rock flanked them on both sides as they climbed. She trailed her fingers along the wall and watched the large prints on the ground.

What sort of foot impresses on bone, stone, and dirt alike, and glows so brightly?

The stairs led them to a flat landing, where the footprints walked straight into one of the rock walls surrounding them and disappeared.

"They go into this wall," Salmaara said, stepping up to it.

If the stairs are intangible, why not this wall? But, what if it leads to a horrible death? If we can't find food ...

She sucked in a steadying breath and placed her hand against the wall. She gasped when it slipped through the stone as though it were air.

Staring at her wrist in the wall, she poked her head through.

A square shaft filled the small space before her, just large enough for the two of them if they stood side by side, and a metal platform on a chain and pulley system waited.

She pulled her head back. "There's a platform in there that goes down."

Gjordkra shook her head, still scanning the ground uneasily. "I really don't see any footprints."

"We need to see where it leads." Salmaara extended a leg through the wall and pressed the old platform with bloodied toes to see if it was solid.

It would hold.

Salmaara slipped her other leg through the wall and rested her foot on the platform. The remainder of her followed, encumbering the platform with her full weight.

The platform slowly started downward, picking up speed as it went. The platform was sound, but the chains were not. They clacked and slid from the pulley, sending the platform, and Salmaara, tumbling to the bottom of the shaft. A scream caught in Salmaara's throat as she dropped.

The crash of metal on stone echoed ahead, through a large space. Salmaara rolled forward onto cool stone with a grunt.

As chilly air cooled her arms and face, she thought it odd that anywhere in a volcano could be cold. She rubbed her arms, which shook, probably from the shock of the fall.

The sensation of being watched vanished, but the malice magnified. Casting her eyes about for anything to explain the sensation that something would snatch her from behind at any moment and finding nothing, Salmaara climbed back to her feet, looking around in awe. There was no similarity between this place and the macabre city above.

A grand chamber, entirely of sleek obsidian—floors, walls, and ceiling—faced her. It constituted an oval antechamber, with ornately carved arches and pillars framing two doorways on the opposite wall. Detailed reliefs and murals etched into obsidian walls and pillars decorated the room, along with a calligraphic language that Salmaara couldn't read but bore some similarity to the one in her father's books. Bright silver light illuminated the chill room from marble sconces set into the pillars.

Standing there reminded her of the dry fountain in the decaying square back home. Although of different material, it felt the same. It had been carved with great care and skill and seemed from an age long gone.

She turned back to the shaft and stepped onto the lift, looking back at the top. Frowning, she wondered why Gjordkra hadn't looked through the wall after her, particularly after the ruckus she had made.

"Gjordkra?" Her shaky voice echoed up the shaft.

Silence answered her query.

"Gjordkra, can you hear me?"

She examined the lift. The chain lay in a heap on top of the cracked platform. Looking back up, she sighed. The shaft had to have been at least three stories tall.

I won't be going back up that way.

"Gjordkra, I can't get back to you. I'll have to find another way out."

Salmaara turned back to the room and staggered across it, examining the images among the text as she followed one of the rounded walls. The first she came upon was taller than she. A woman in ornate plate armor, holding a broadsword aloft in one hand and a small object in the other, stood surrounded by corpses and broken fragments that may have once been buildings. The item in the armored woman's hand drew Salmaara's eye. It was an octagonal stone, the size of the woman's gauntleted fist, and had a slash through its center, much like the symbol on the Mauviasen flag.

She passed several murals that depicted one violent scene after another. Beheadings and disembowelments surrounded the largest image of a group of people apparently choking up their insides. A woman stared in alarm at her intestines as they oozed from her mouth, while a man lay beneath her in a puddle of his brains. Salmaara looked quickly away from them, as they brought back Günhai.

She strode away from the murals to one of the pillars, a hand to her belly. She touched the relief that adorned it. The entire pillar appeared consumed in stone flames.

A choking grief fell heavily on her breast.

She pulled her hand away, and the sorrow vanished.

She gasped for breath and turned from the pillar, shivering. She limped into the left-most of the two doorways that led from the ante-chamber, where a carved hallway opened into a sunken room, smaller than the antechamber, with vaulted ceilings and more silver lights. A narrow staircase spiraled down from the landing at the end of the corridor to the room's floor.

From the top of the stairs, Salmaara could see that a bier occupied the room's center. It rose seamlessly from the floor, apparently made from the same piece of obsidian as its surroundings. Flames curled around its top edges and the woman who lay on it without scorching or consuming either.

The oppressive malice that suffused the remainder of the tomb radiated from the bier and its occupant, growing stronger the closer she came, until it felt as though the very air were made of it.

Even from where she stood, Salmaara could feel the body's heartbeat. She could feel its power. She had never felt so tiny.

The feeling of the person permeated her as though it would overtake her. Her heart sped in fear, but she could not shy away; the moment Salmaara looked upon the woman, it was if invisible cords pulled her closer.

Salmaara proceeded down the stairs, her heart hammering loudly, but the steady beat that filled the room drowned it out by far.

Nearing the carved altar, she looked at the body. The black silks covering the woman's form fluttered at each inhale and exhale, rising and falling over strong curves. The high collar and cuffs of her burial robes were embroidered with silver thread, their strands forming the same alien language as the many inscriptions in the antechamber.

Her face was beautiful yet harsh and a pale olive. She had high cheekbones, full cerise lips, and heavy lids covered her eyes. Her muscled arms lay across her powerful form, and a crimson sheen covered fine, black hair that fell to her waist where the light touched it. Salmaara would have run had she been able.

The heartbeat's force jarred Salmaara. She still couldn't tear her gaze from the gorgeous woman.

"My husband's, Blue King, hands are most able to build such a place by themselves, aren't they, child?" a sensual woman's voice echoed in the chamber.

Salmaara jumped back from the body, looking around for the speaker.

A pearly phantom materialized across the bier from her.

It was the woman.

Salmaara uttered the curse she had heard so many use in this land since her arrival:

"Destroyer!"

CHAPTER TWENTY-THREE

KASKAHAI,
MAUVIAS

Salmaara stood face to face with Vias the Destroyer's soul.

The Goddess's still-living body lay between them. Salmaara blinked in disbelief, but the pearly apparition did not waver.

Vias' waist-length hair floated on a spectral breeze, she kept her hands folded in front of her. Her lips twisted in indulgent amusement. Most stunning of all were her deep crimson eyes beneath heavy lids. Ancient, and burning with a light of madness.

Salmaara gasped and tried to back down the stairs, but the Destroyer's gaze held her fast. One of Vias's brows arched at Salmaara's curse.

"So some have called me."

"You're—" Salmaara said. Her voice caught in her throat. She shook her head. "You're Vias the Destroyer."

"Indeed. And you are?"

"Salmaara."

"Salmaara of Zamazcus, and more I see," Vias said.

Salmaara nodded dumbly. The Destroyer's power engulfed her. She didn't feel the ground under her feet or see the ornate room anymore. Vias was all she could see and feel. The destroyer's signature was both deadly and alluring, reminding Salmaara of standing in an eternal grassy expanse, surrounded by roaring flames that offered a chance for new life even as they devoured the old. Like those flames, it licked at her, at first warm, and then blistering, until she thought she would burn away. Although she tried, she couldn't look away, and she felt weightless and yet pinned.

"Why has your empress grandmother never thought or spoken of you?"

Salmaara's heart sped. She hadn't thought of the connection between her queen mother and the empress. "She doesn't know me."

"Why is that, do you suppose?" the Goddess asked. She looked amused, as though she already knew the answer.

Salmaara couldn't think of an answer. *What game is she playing? King Yulari described her as a 'woman lacking reason.' This is the woman who destroyed an entire world and then tried to do to the same to this one!*

"How did you find the ancient entrance?" Vias's crimson eyes bored into her. Salmaara broke from the onslaught of thoughts that threatened to overwhelm her before they began.

"I followed footprints," Salmaara said. "It was easy. I thought you were hidden where you couldn't be found."

Vias smirked. She drifted around the body on the bier. Her fingers trailed over something Salmaara couldn't see that prevented the goddess from touching her own body.

"To doubt the security of these chambers is to doubt the abilities of His Greenness Esthadya and dear, dear King Yulari Lordian himself. A very select few have access to my dwelling here. The blood in your veins, or the very spirit in your body, determines your admittance. And you came in the back passage. That way has not been used since my...righteous...husband abandoned me here." Her ghostly locks floated around her face.

Salmaara frowned. "I don't doubt their competence and—"

"It does not matter. I will ask my first question again, child. Who are you?"

She knew my full name, my lineage…Daughter of Queen Kusae would mean granddaughter of Empress Velanoma. She doesn't need me to tell her who I am. She knows—her Xin'Dai gifts are legendary, even separated from her body as she is now, it would seem.

"What do you mean?"

Heat rushed to Salmaara's face. She didn't know what she was supposed to say. Nor could she believe that she was there, speaking with the most feared deity in the world.

Thinking of her family summoned memories of Illun, of her life in Bhevir. She missed everyone desperately. Struggling to stow her grief, she said, "I am who you have said, Vias the Destroyer, and no more."

The goddess scoffed, and drifted to her body's feet, falling silent.

Uncomfortable with the silence, Salmaara cleared her throat and spoke, although her voice trembled. "I have some questions that perhaps you can answer."

"Oh?"

"I met my grandmother, when I was captive in Günhai. She couldn't hear my thoughts. Actually, no one I have met can hear them. But I can see theirs if I wish. Why?"

Vias chuckled, musical yet bone-chilling within Salmaara's mind. "Not even my chosen servant can access you, hmm? I'm certain you have vexed her waking hours ever since. I shall surely hear of you when next she calls," Vias said distractedly. "Perhaps because you do not wish them to share in your thoughts, they cannot. It is not unusual for strong bearers of the gifts to naturally shield themselves from others. You, however, are blessed with more than a potent shield, I sense."

"What do you mean?"

"Salmaara, young dear, have you considered the possibility that you could change the thoughts of those who surround you? Their memories, desires, dreams—the way they perceive you and the world? To put it as you would understand—truth is clay in your hands. Reality is what you make it. I sense this ability in you, and many, many more."

"I … have never thought of that. I never would have thought of it," Salmaara whispered. Her stomach turned at the notion. *It goes against everything I believe in. What does a person have if not the ability to choose what they will believe and desire? And for me to be able to choose that for them? That is evil.*

Vias smiled eerily. Salmaara wondered if the goddess was listening to her thoughts. "It is my own gift granted me by the universe. Until this moment, I thought myself alone. I sense enough power in you, even to overwhelm my chosen empress. Explore your abilities, listen for others. Know that you can hear them upon your desire. Hear them and bend them."

Vias's presence in her mind intensified, like sharpened nails, prying. It felt as if it would take her over. Salmaara could feel her seemingly in every pore.

"Take me as your master, and I shall give you the world, and you will do greater things than in all ages past."

Salmaara shrieked, anger and panic filling her. "No!" She wanted nothing more than to be free of the destroyer's hold. She clawed at the invisible bonds that held her and took hold of them, tearing them from her body. Vias's hold fell from her, body and mind.

The force of the separation sent Salmaara staggering backward down the stairs from the bier and the living-dead body that lay on it. She toppled to the obsidian floor at the bottom of the stairs. The ghost remained still with a cruel smile on her full lips, but her eyes were wide with surprise.

I must get out of here. Find Gjordkra! Salmaara shoved herself to her feet and ran for the stairs opposite the ones she had used to enter.

"Until we meet again," Vias's sensual voice followed her up the spiral stairs and up the hall ahead.

Salmaara fled into the antechamber, glanced toward the broken lift, and ran into the middle of the three doorways. Ahead, a flight of stairs twisted upward. *Climb, I have to climb! I have to get away from here. I will not... I just escaped Vias the Destroyer. How did I do that?*

Salmaara charged up the stairs, around and around until she came to a landing that ended in a wall. Extending her hands, she pushed through the wall, falling onto a bone-paved stairway outside. Her heart pounded, and muscles burned. She curled up and gripped her head with both hands. *Vias... the Destroyer...*

"Destroyer, stupid girl! What did you do?" Gjordkra's angry voice filled her throbbing head. Her companion squatted beside her and shook one of Salmaara's shoulders with both hands, rolled Salmaara onto her back. Gjordkra's face softened when Salmaara looked up at her.

"Are you hurt?" Her brow creased. She took one of Salmaara's hands.

The potter's daughter shook her head slowly, her heart still racing.

"You sure? What happened?"

Salmaara wrenched herself up. "I don't know."

"Sal—"

"I. Don't. Know."

Gjordkra cleared her throat. "Fine. Anyway, I have exceptionally wonderful news." She hoisted a bulging satchel into Salmaara's view.

"While you were busy behind that solid wall, I found this sack just around the corner. Food, powder, the works. I guess we're going to live a little longer after all."

Gjordkra opened the bag and extended a charred bit of bread to Salmaara. She accepted it with quaking fingers.

"Thanks." Her voice came out in a barely audible rasp. Lifting the bread to her mouth took the most effort she could recall expending. Even so, she devoured it in two bites. Tearing one of the powder sacks open, she poured a swallow of the magenta stuff into her dry mouth.

Salmaara still hated hydration powder. Gjordkra had mentioned that Salmaara must have some Mauviasen blood to live so long on it. True southerners couldn't use it for multiple months at a time without significant deterioration or death. Salmaara's heart lurched. *Mauviasen blood... I have more of it than I could have imagined.*

Finishing her small ration, Salmaara's mind caught up, realizing what Gjordkra had just said. "You said you found this bag of food just around the corner? Just...sitting there for the taking?"

Gjordkra nodded solemnly. "You disappeared into the wall, way up there." She indicated a flight of stairs. "I couldn't get through, so I decided to look around a little bit, staying close so that if you came out...Anyway, just up the stairs, there was another street of houses. Found the bag leaning against one."

The story chilled Salmaara's blood and distracted her from her recent encounter. "That sounds like it could have been a gift. I know there are people here....I can feel them watching. Why would they help us?"

Gjordkra shrugged. "My master never said much about his people. That's one topic he avoids like nothing else. From the little I do know..." She shrugged. "It makes no sense. We should be dead."

Heaving to her feet, Salmaara looked around at the deserted landing they occupied. A broad street lined with bone structures stretched out in front of them and curved from sight. *Why are they hiding?*

"Well," Salmaara said grimly, fixing her gaze down the street ahead. "Shall we see if they will let us leave?"

Gjordkra cinched the drawstring on the supplies satchel and stood with a nod. Together they made their way down the street, and to one of the staircases that led down to the next tier.

Salmaara started down the stairs. *Can I really do the horrific things Vias suggested? Can I change people's minds, memories, desires? I'm sure I can hear them. I know so little of the gifts of Xin'Dai … How did I get her out? Why couldn't she hold me? Perhaps her power has been dimmed by the separation from her body…*

A fretful voice within begged her to forget the encounter.

But Salmaara wanted to know more. She took a long, steadying breath and asked Gjordkra's mind to yield its content to her. Nothing. The girl continued walking with furtive scans of buildings as they passed them.

Salmaara's mind felt stretched for a moment, until another presence filled it. It was the feeling of Gjordkra, and it reminded her of a closed flower spreading its petals in the sunlight for the first time. Unlike others she had encountered recently, like the liths, Vias, and the empress, it felt less intense, much in the way that Rianne's and Illun's had always been. Gjordkra's silent voice spoke. *"I hope she knows where we're going. I can trust her—maybe. Yezhr and Jhaill can't be far behind. Something feels strange."*

Blushing, Salmaara withdrew. *I can't practice on her without her knowledge. Focus. Focus on the task at hand.*

Salmaara and Gjordkra left the Destroyer's City the way they had come in. Although Salmaara sensed people all around them, she still couldn't see anyone.

CHAPTER TWENTY-FOUR

WILDERNESS SOUTH OF
KASKAHAI, MAUVIAS

"*Awake, my beloved, and watch what I will show you.*"

Yezhr's mind rose easily from slumber at the familiar, sensuous tones of his goddess's voice. A shiver of pleasure went through the lith's entire being, from his head-feathers to the tips of his fingers and toes, and even into his very soul as his signature, the sense of who he was, the whole of his very soul, was swept away and encompassed in hers.

As the final vestiges of sleep fell away, Yezhr became aware of his body, still resting beneath a coverlet, with Rimse's softness beside him in the tent they shared. He kept his eyes closed and his form utterly still.

"*Greatest Mistress, I await.*"

Vias showed him then that his Salmaara, his Prey, had come to her, had gained entrance to her tomb, something which left his heart pounding and mind racing. He had suspected great power in her, but it appeared that he had severely underestimated it. Then Salmaara had spoken with the goddess.

As he viewed the exchange that had taken place, he felt a twinge of irritation that the girl had still not learned how to respect those greater than she. It was a poor reflection on him that she had treated his goddess so.

He forced his attention back to the vision playing in his mind. Vias revealed what Yezhr had not failed to extract from his willful ward in months. *She is of the accursed, corrupted line of Zamazcus. Granddaughter of Velanoma, Kusae's child. Who, then, is her father? Kusae has always been alone …*

"*How did such a one find her way to Bhevir, to be raised by a humble potter?*" Yezhr remembered the man, whose resilient mind he had emptied of information as he had sought a way to find the girl. In a feeble attempt to divert Yezhr, he had filled his thoughts with clay and pots. If only Yezhr had pressed for her identity … perhaps the sulmai creature, Illun, had known.

"*I know not. And, as you saw, the girl either knew little of it or hid it from me.*"

A spike of fear chilled Yezhr's heart. "*Hid it from you, my Mistress?*"

He had sensed the power lurking in the girl from the first time he had connected to her mind when he had delivered the empress's message to the people of Bhevir. When she had run and her signature had vanished, Yezhr had decided to hunt and take her with him.

"*Indeed. As you believe, her power far surpasses what you suspected.*"

He had never been one to ignore what might become a valuable tool to Mauvias. Thus far, he had chosen to take Salmaara's training slowly, as trying to break something so fine at the wrong moment could ruin all. To turn her properly from a stubborn, insubordinate, and indoctrinated child into an equally passionate servant could only be done with his well-honed set of skills and done gradually.

What had made it such a challenge thus far—oh, but so pleasurable a challenge—was that he could only connect to the girl's signature if he could *see* her. Interestingly, Jhaill suffered from the same struggle, as did the governor's daughter, Pezra. Others, such as Yezhr's Rimse, couldn't ever find it.

Thus it was that Yezhr could not use his ability to perceive where a person had been by their signature to track the girl. Tracking them by Gjordkra's, however, was only too easy.

A recent memory suddenly leapt to the forefront of Yezhr's mind from the wedding.

"*She wished to know about Asha's gnome servant.*" He conveyed the creature's performance to his goddess and the girl's angry recognition of him. Then he told his goddess of his pet's need to speak with the gnome.

He now wished he had pressed more to learn why she needed to speak with him. Yezhr had suspected for some time that an ancient enemy of his lurked in that gnome's form, tiny and beneath notice to most. If that foe had any interest in Salmaara, then Yezhr had to secure her before she fell into his clutches.

As Yezhr considered the wine incident further, he thought the entire thing bore that chaos-monger's mark. Still, Yezhr did not worry overmuch. The last time they had clashed, the lith had emerged victor. That the Velanoma Zamazcus who ruled the world at present did so, and not another, was proof.

"*Reclaim the girl, Yezhr, my beloved, and bring her to me. That is my command.*" With those words, the superintendent felt the goddess leave his mind.

He opened his eyes and sat up. Rimse's signature, soft, like a feather brushing against his cheek, waited for his to accept it. He did so, and then his mate trailed a finger along the curve of his bare back from where she lay.

"*What is it, master?*"

"Information and instruction from the Greatest."

"Oh?"

"I must speak with Jhaill."

"Do you require me, master?"

"Not at present. Rest."

Yezhr let her mind slip from his as he stood and dressed himself in black pants, a tunic, and boots. He secured three knives in one of his boots then made his way to the tent flaps, which had been tied securely against the night's howling wind. He untied enough to slip out and swiftly made his way to the next tent over, where Jhaill was supposed to sleep, not that he did. He had never been a creature of the light.

Beside that one, a third tent housed those the governor had managed to assemble to aid in the hunting and capture of the two runaways.

Yezhr connected to Jhaill's mind as he untied the entry to the other lith's tent.

The governor of Günhai looked up from where he crouched over a small cauldron that filled the tent with a pale green glow. As the party had travelled, he had provided them with brews to protect them from the harsh climate and give them extra vigor to cover more ground each day than was natural.

They would have caught the girls already had the pair not chanced upon a selti-drawn carriage and pulled away. Not only did selti run faster than dragons but could do so for longer. In their cursed state, dragons could run well, but they had not been created to run. They had been created to fly, and the accursed Green God had taken it from them.

Jhaill raised his scarlet stare to meet Yezhr's amber one. The wound that Salmaara had dealt Jhaill was healing but still stood out, red and puckered on his grey scalp.

"*We have many matters to discuss and plans to make before the suns rise,*" said Yezhr. "*Will your brew be ready to carry us swiftly to our quarry?*"

Jhaill scowled, his mangy black head feathers quivering. "*Of course it will.*"

Yezhr sat across the cauldron from the other lith. "*Then let me begin.*"

CHAPTER TWENTY-FIVE

WESTERN LESSER T'SKEL, MAUVIAS

Five days following their flight from the Destroyer's city, Salmaara and Gjordkra stared at another black mountain face that soared into an equally dark sky, the Lesser T'Skel of the West. The only obstacle between them and the sea.

"These don't look too bad. We can get over them. Sometimes you just have to take it a little at a time," Salmaara said, desperate to break the exhausted silence, although she didn't believe her own words.

"Sure, whatever." Gjordkra scowled at the jagged rocks that seemed to reach forever upward as she folded her arms.

"Over we go, then," Salmaara said. She marched forward with as much enthusiasm as she could muster, despite her swollen legs and feet. Her shoes had disintegrated two days since, and the makeshift foot coverings they had made from the top of the food satchel provided little defense against the rocky wilderness.

"You are out of your Destroyer-be-damned gourd, as usual." Gjordkra sighed as she dragged her own bloody, numb feet up the mountain after Salmaara.

"Out of curiosity," Gjordkra panted, "did you connect to my mind in Kaskahai?"

Salmaara blushed. "I think so. Sorry."

Gjordkra narrowed her eyes. "So, you do have the gift! Anything else you want to tell me?"

"I don't know."

Gjordkra lowered her voice. "You don't know? Either you do or you don't."

"I don't understand my ... gifts. I don't know what I can or can't do."

"Well, when we find a good place to stop, you know, when we aren't so bloody exposed, maybe we could see what you've got. It's not good to go around not knowing."

Salmaara nodded as a bead of sweat drifted from her temple into the cursed air. She tried to maintain outward calm for her paranoid company, but inside, her stomach clenched and her heart sped.

King Yulari always warned that a man with a weapon he doesn't know how to use is a great danger, not only to himself but also his comrades in times of need. I do not want to harm anyone, but I will not be able to ignore this—it is part of me. Besides, even though everyone I have met in the empire uses the gifts for control and harm, I know it can be used for good. So many of those things I did at home that must have been done with my gift ... they were good, I think. She thought of knowing where Rianne was in the fire, of being able to sense impending danger. *But it wasn't good enough ...*

She turned her thoughts away from Bhevir when they summoned that familiar ache that she kept deep within her heart.

Salmaara climbed onto a ledge, kicking, and then stared into a deep shaft that led to a cave set into the mountain. She had a feeling that the way she wanted to go was into the darkness.

Salmaara squared her shoulders against her qualms. *This sense has not yet led me astray. I should follow it.*

Gjordkra joined her. "You think this could go through?"

"We would be fools to hope, but I think we should try it." Salmaara sat and shimmied down an ashy wall of rock that led into the shaft, Gjordkra following.

A round tunnel of smooth rock laced with dimly glowing emerald veins waited ahead. The tunnel stretched on for a long way before it plunged from sight.

As Salmaara started forward, for once, Gjordkra did not object to their predicament.

Leading Gjordkra into the glowing tunnel, Salmaara had never seen the like of the luminous emerald that crisscrossed the dark rock walls and parts of the floor like a gigantic spider web. And as they drew near, she could sense an ancient presence emanating from it, as though it were alive.

She meant to ask Gjordkra if she knew anything about the odd stone, but Salmaara's companion spoke first.

"I've been wanting to ask you about Kaskahai. You scared me nearly to death disappearing like that, and then coming out and rolling around like your head was on fire. I thought maybe the Shazrah got you." Gjordkra folded her arms tightly under her breasts. "And that wall was perfectly solid, according to my fists. First, the invisible footprints, and then the wall."

Salmaara shivered and rubbed her arms. "I don't know why I saw the footprints, or even whose they were. As for the wall, someone told me that it was because of blood or the soul. I don't know what they meant."

Gjordkra shrugged. "Most things with the Shazrah have to do with blood."

Salmaara paused and reached out to brush the glowing wall. "I wonder what all this green is."

Gjordkra snatched her wrist, wrenching her hand away. "Don't touch it!" she hissed. "It's inside all the T'Skel Mountains—north, south, east, and west. I've heard stories about people who touch that stuff. Their eyes turn green, and they go insane within a week. They just start killing people—family, friends, strangers. Whoever. Don't always kill everyone they see. Usually ends in them killing themselves, though." Eerie green light shone on Gjordkra's pale face.

Salmaara swallowed and reclaimed her hand. "Why?"

Gjordkra started forward again and shrugged. "I don't know, but Jhaill's pretty obsessed with some creepy old things. Some I overheard, and others he told me. I have a theory. According to him, the T'Skel weren't always here surrounding Mauvias."

Gjordkra stepped carefully among the veins on the ground. "Once, most of the mountains spanned the eastern coast of the continent, through Yendu, north and south, when Southern Yendu was actually south of Northern Yendu and the Shadowlands. The rest were in Arvitra. The name T'Skel, means *the split*.

"Lady Destroyer tore them from the ground and dropped them where they are now, around Mauvias, to forever set us apart from other peoples. So, I think all this green stuff is the result of her unnatural act. Cursed the very rocks of these mountains when she took them for hers, like she cursed our air and us, her people."

Salmaara nodded, shying away from the glowing emerald veins.

A passage she had read came to mind. It described something similar found in the barrens of Northern Yendu. Instead of mountains and caves filled with emerald light, it was said to bear great craters dug out of the earth, crisscrossed with the emerald veins until the ruined land met the sea. The author had mentioned that those who went into the chasms returned mad. *And I was going to touch it ...*

"I feel like it hates me. It seems alive," she said.

Gjordkra smiled wryly. "Like I said, cursed."

They pressed onward, avoiding the emerald curse on the floor and keeping away from the shining walls.

CHAPTER TWENTY-SIX

WESTERN LESSER T'SKEL, MAUVIAS

Rock was pressing into Salmaara's side when she woke and saw Gjordkra crouched with her back to the potter's daughter, rocking back and forth on her heels.

Gjordkra rarely held still and, at times, Salmaara wondered if she slept at all, even when she was lying down.

Green light from all around them bathed Gjordkra's dark hair. The emerald veinless spot they rested on had taken some finding. It had been days since they had descended into Western T'Skel.

Salmaara sat up.

"Finally." Gjordkra turned to Salmaara and offered a scrap of dried meat that they had procured in Kaskahai.

Salmaara accepted it and tore a chunk off as Gjordkra chewed her own in silence. When she finished the meat, she reached into the remains of Gjordkra's ash-stained satchel for a pouch of hydration powder. She ripped the top open and poured it into her dry mouth. As soon as the powder turned to sludge, she swallowed. Salmaara could hardly recall the feel of water on her tongue, but she knew she wanted it as much as she wished to see the full light of the suns again.

Gjordkra took some powder, too, swallowed it, and stood.

Salmaara shouldered their pack then joined her as they started forward in silence. The tunnel floor steadily rose beneath her feet in a steep incline. She smiled to herself. *We're ascending. Perhaps I didn't doom us after all.*

Gjordkra froze beside her, but Salmaara continued forward, looking over to see why her companion had stopped. Therefore, she didn't see the chute until she toppled into its opening.

She cried out as she slipped down the smooth tunnel and heard Gjordkra curse when she missed catching her arm.

Salmaara skidded down a long ramp on her back, surrounded by rock on three sides. Then she rolled off at its end and into another tunnel below.

"Salmaara!" Gjordkra called frantically from above.

Salmaara's pounding heart soared into her throat, and a feeling she thought she would never experience again flooded her ashy skin.

"Gjordkra, do you feel that?" With pleasure, Salmaara took a long, deep breath.

Gjordkra slid into view, feet first. "What?" the girl asked as she dropped down beside her with a frown. Then she stiffened and gasped. "What is this? Is it dangerous?"

"This is humidity from water. It's salty. We must be near the sea, and we're alive!" Salmaara replied with a grin, smelling the salt.

Although the hills sheltered Bhevir from the sea that bordered it to the east, its scent had never been far away.

Ahead, Salmaara saw a white prick of light that marked the end of the cavern.

"Let's go!" Salmaara leaped to her feet, and they clambered toward the light, dancing around the cursed emerald veins.

"You'd best hurry up, or I will see this sea first." Gjordkra lurched forward giddily as she sprinted through the remainder of the tunnel, dodging the veins easily.

Salmaara ran after her.

Gjordkra burst from the cave well ahead of her, and Salmaara laughed as she finished the short climb, refreshed as the humidity thickened and kissed her face.

"Salmaara, no!" Gjordkra's panicked voice jolted her from her jubilation, but it was too late.

Governor Opthonne snatched Salmaara's forearm in an iron grip as she emerged from the tunnel.

She stumbled over uneven ground as he dragged her out of the mountain's shadow and onto a vast, barren clifftop. Distantly, she could hear the roar of waves and felt sea-spray spiraling madly through the air, like frenzied dancers forming numberless tiny funnels as the curse bubble undulating high on the black mountainside behind her pulled them into its oblivion. The suns sank toward the horizon ahead, bathing the black expanse of rock bloodred.

Where, but a moment ago, she had felt the fire of elation, ice now spread through her from where the lith clutched her arm, and goose bumps rose in a flood. She looked from his scarred hand, up to the lith's face, meeting his burning, scarlet eyes. Just above them, she couldn't help noticing the jagged wound that she had dealt him on his scalp.

She wrenched her arm, trying to loosen his grasp, but he only tightened it. Then she felt the governor connect to her mind, his touch like thin wire wrapping around her head, slowly constricting.

"*Hello, Prey.*" Had he been conversing aloud, Salmaara would have described the acerbic way he spoke the name as "spitting."

He strode away from the tunnel mouth, dragging her behind him. She tugged, twisted, and kicked, but he was too strong by far.

"You have led us on quite a chase, but it is done now. You will receive the punishment for all that has transpired, including the loss of my wedding night. There will be much you will see that you might learn what you must."

Not two paces away, Yezhr stood calmly with his hands folded in front of him. He wore the same set of woven black leather armor and kamas that he had when he had led his army to destroy Bhevir, murder Illun, and take her as his prisoner. He regarded her imperiously, his amber eyes ablaze with pleasure—at his victory, no doubt.

Fear and loathing rose in her at the sight of him, and the creature that she kept caged within her pressed urgently on the walls that she kept around it, desperate to howl, to bite, to be the animal that Yezhr regarded her, as if only it would spare her having to return to Günhai.

How can this be happening? How did they find us? How did they know where to cut us off?

Behind the superintendent, Gjordkra struggled to break the hold of three powerfully built male liths. Her thrashing didn't shift their grips or balance in the least.

Two others stood to the side, observing all in silence.

Salmaara clenched her teeth at the sight of Gjordkra's duress and the governor's recent threat. *Even if I can't, she must escape!*

When they reached Yezhr, Governor Opthonne twisted Salmaara's wrist and wrenched her down. She tried to remain standing, but he forced her to her knees. Both hit the black rock beneath her with twin cracks. He then let go of her arm.

Heart hammering, Salmaara tried to stand, but Jhaill stepped on her ankles from behind. She grunted in fury and pain as she managed to twist enough to see what Gjordkra's vile groom was doing behind her.

The fading sunlight fell upon the links of a gold chain. A gold chain attached to a collar. The lith's nimble fingers unlocked the catch on the collar, and it fell open, at the ready.

"No!"

Salmaara raised her gaze to Yezhr. She felt him coming for her, that sensation like the blade of an axe at her throat. Something lay between it and her, however. The smooth, dark, invisible barrier reminded her of one of Illun's ceramics, and it conformed perfectly to the lith's body like a second skin. Like a vase, it thinned at his neck.

Hoping that it would prove a weak point, she lunged at it and grasped it with ethereal hands, applying pressure there.

Nothing happened.

Determined, she doubled her efforts and felt it buckle then crack. The crack expanded, allowing her to slip through and reach Yezhr's axe-like signature. She encompassed it whole in herself.

She looked down at herself through Yezhr's eyes. She could feel fear, but it was not her own.

Where she had fused herself with the lith's signature, she could feel him struggling to end the bond, to separate his blade-like self from her. Salmaara, however, pushed back and secured her hold.

She was in his mind. Terror and exhilaration blossomed in her at once. The control over the lith who had striven to be her master was intoxicating.

The first thing she noticed was darkness, exactly like she had perceived in Jhaill the first time she had seen the monster. That darkness permeated Yezhr's being, a darkness that she sensed lay upon his very soul for the lives he had taken or destroyed. A darkness that matched the desires of its master's heart.

Yezhr's darkness made Jhaill's seem like a puddle compared to an endless sea.

Salmaara waded through it, and then she gazed upon her captor's thoughts. At least, she assumed his thoughts would be contained in the convoluted labyrinth that sprawled before her. The ever-present darkness hovered in the maze's passages like a perverse fog, obscuring anything inside from her view.

Setting her jaw, Salmaara entered the maze. The blackness that reached to her ankles and covered her feet shifted and surged upward. Like one of Mauvias's dust-trees, it formed a pillar that blocked her way, writhing wildly for a moment then taking shape. The potter's daughter recognized the figure the dark mist had formed.

A spectral Yezhr loomed over her, barring her from going any farther into the maze. Glowing pinpricks in deep red, like one of Günhai's lanterns, regarded her from where the lith's eyes should have been. When he spoke, Yezhr's voice sounded from every direction.

"Prey must leave at once."

"If I do, you must let us go."

Through the superintendent's physical eyes, Salmaara could see Jhaill still leaning forward with the collar. Only, he moved so slowly that it could scarcely be said that he was moving at all.

"It is not its place to make demands. It is its place to obey," Yezhr continued.

Something fluid writhed within the maze around the Yezhr's wraith. Salmaara focused on it for a moment before recognizing it as anger. Near it, she sensed something else—fear.

Shifting her attention back to the lith's inner-incarnation, she said, "Gjordkra and I are not going back. Ever."

The fear substance increased, spreading up the walls of the maze behind Yezhr. She then felt him try to throw her out again, to sever the connection she had created between them.

He applied pressure on where she had joined her own signature with his. She felt him push and tear, attacking from many angles. It was not enough. Not nearly enough.

It was not two people fighting on equal terms. The hold Salmaara had secured was like a mother sitting on a querulous child. The child thrashed, and railed, and pounded, but it moved her little. She just had to wait for his energy to ebb.

The sensation ceased, and the Yezhr's shade folded its hands. "Perhaps, if Prey only understood what I have chosen to give it—a place in the world, a purpose—it would cease being unreasonable, and be honored, as is correct." The lith then indicated behind him with a hand made of darkness. The walls of the maze shimmered, mirror-like, and Salmaara recognized herself pictured there.

In that moment, she saw how Yezhr viewed her. Yes, as a clever pet of which he was proud to be in possession, of how he had been unable to sense her signature that night in Bhevir, how he had chosen to hunt her and claim her for his own. Through the lith's perception, she realized that he viewed her as incapable of making worthy decisions, that she needed him to make them for her.

In those images, she saw Yezhr's ambitions for her. He had planned to spend years persuading her to serve him willingly. He thought her rebellious-ness and passionate nature to be more assets than flaws and had not wanted to extinguish those aspects of her if he didn't have to, for he believed such could be used against enemies of his goddess to potent effect. The lith even showed her that he had chided himself for losing his temper and overdoing her first whipping, as if it would convince her that he hadn't really meant to hurt her.

Yezhr planned to take her back to Kaskahai, to Vias. Together, goddess and lith would erase all she had been and remake her to suit their vision. In that line of thought, she perceived that Yezhr had done such things before, to more individuals than she could comprehend. He believed he had taken lowly lives and elevated them to greatness, and this was what he wanted for Salmaara.

"Does Prey see now?"

Salmaara balled her ethereal hands into fists and drew herself up. "I am *not Prey, and I will not be a prisoner of Mauvias in heart and mind as I have been in body! My name is Salmaara Zamazcus, Yezhr Terrich. I am the daughter of Queen Kusae Zamazcus, who fights the empire and its goddess, and you. I can and will make my own choices and will suffer the consequences, good or bad.*

"The ability to choose our paths for ourselves is the most precious gift given to all living beings—what we dream of, what actions we will take, and who we will become. They are each person's to decide, and theirs alone. How dare you presume otherwise?

"As for a purpose? You cannot give me a purpose, only I can find such a thing for myself. Do you know who taught me that?"

The shadowy lith shifted but said nothing.

"A potter named Illun Sultos, my father."

Images of Yezhr's minions capturing Illun drifted over the labyrinth's wall. The superintendent had tortured him and procured little information about how to find Salmaara. She watched through the lith's eyes as she returned on the llama's back and crawled to her dying father's side. He had walked up behind her and waited for the potter to die before he had spoken his first words to her.

"This is the first time I captured Prey," Yezhr said. "Does it remember?"

How could she not?

She again resisted the cry of those she grieved, keeping them in the place deep inside her heart.

"Above all things, surely Prey understands that it belongs to me. Even if Prey were to escape this day, I would find it yet again. I will never stop hunting it, not until it has fulfilled all that it must. It will come with me to Kaskahai. It will submit to the will of the Greatest of the Four Creators, just as Gjordkra will return to Günhai and accept what it must."

In the face of his threat, the people that Salmaara had kept caged inside herself since she had been taken, the people whom she loved, burst free.

She allowed memories of Illun patiently teaching her his art, comforting her when she cried, always thanking her for being in his life to fill her heart. She remembered his gentle face, his cyan eyes, and how, although they carried sadness, they also held love. He had loved her, and she had loved him.

She let her girlhood with Rianne playing beside her come forth, and the adventures they had enjoyed, pretending to be explorers or warriors in the woods near Salmaara's home, of times when they had fallen from trees or come home muddy for a scolding from Mirana. Rianne had been the first of Bhevir's children to decide that someone should be a friend to that weird, pale redhead.

In her heart, Salmaara also found Gjordkra. Gjordkra, who had chosen to help her instead of letting her drown in Günhai's evil on her own, who had decided to stick with her no matter which direction she ran. Gjordkra who, despite all she had endured in her own life, had made room for Salmaara. The potter's daughter couldn't stand the idea of her having to suffer any more.

A burst of brilliant light shot out from Salmaara and into Yezhr's darkness, dissolving the phantom lith. It kept going until it filled the corridors of the lith's maze-like mind. In that moment, the logic of the tangled labyrinth of Yezhr's thoughts became clear to her, as though she had traversed the maze many, many times before.

Mixed in with Yezhr's thoughts, mad, colorful eddies swirled on the floors and walls. Some lay almost still, while others jumped around in droplets or little streams but always in motion. From what she had felt moments earlier, she recognized them as Yezhr's emotions.

She perceived a rush and looked forward. A gush of the colorful fluid surged toward her, like a river freed of a dam, and swept her up in it, tossing her head over heels.

Salmaara felt what Yezhr felt. Triumph and excitement melted away into *fear and anger. Within that powerful swirl, she sensed possessiveness. The possessiveness that had arisen when he had declared that she belonged to him, that he would never give her up.*

Mixed in with the possessiveness, she sensed protectiveness. She could pick out colors within the torrent that were separate, yet she recognized them for what they were. In their current predicament, Yezhr was protective at once of Jhaill and of her.

On the outside, the governor lined up the open collar so that he could close it on Salmaara's neck. Aware of Yezhr's thoughts, she learned that the accursed thing had been coated with one of Jhaill's potions, a substance that would make her very compliant for the journey that the liths intended she take—a journey back to the Destroyer's city and into its goddess's power.

Forcing her own rage and panic to stillness, she returned to Yezhr's need to protect his Prey, in whom he had invested much care; and Jhaill, favored among his grandchildren, whom he had created, as well, raised from infancy and honed into the tool that now served its purpose.

Salmaara envisioned the viscous emotion substance as a rope, and its threads were her and Jhaill. She reached for her thread—the smaller of the two by far—and pulled the feeling toward her and away from the other. There, she took it between ethereal palms and, as she had to many a length of clay, she rubbed it between them, lengthening it, little by little. She added to it, as well, transferring protectiveness from the length belonging to Jhaill to her own, and rolled and rolled until her thread became a monstrous worm that overwhelmed any other sensation in the lith's body.

Letting her creation drop, she commanded, "Save us!"

A dagger hung at Yezhr's waist, which he snatched. As one, he and Salmaara easily dove over the potter's daughter and onto Jhaill. Together, they slammed the dagger down.

Salmaara blinked and let her connection to her lithian captor go. She returned to herself as Yezhr plunged his dagger into Jhaill's shoulder. The chain and collar tumbled to the ground.

The governor stepped off her, staggering backward, and with his physical departure, she felt his mind lose touch with hers, as well.

Thus freed, Salmaara scrambled to her feet and turned to view the strange altercation between the two liths.

Jhaill thrust the superintendent away from him, blood raining down his side. Yezhr struck him twice more in the torso.

The two liths not holding Gjordkra shook off their shock and rushed to aid their governor. They tackled the superintendent, but he threw them off easily. He had left his knife in Jhaill's middle.

Behind Yezhr, the scarlet-eyed monster that Gjordkra called "master," crumpled, gripping where the knife stood out from him.

Yezhr drew the pair of kamas hanging at his belt, holding one in each hand. Their wicked, crescent blades shimmered as he returned to where Salmaara stood, keeping his back to her.

Salmaara sprinted to Gjordkra who hung limply between her captors, staring at the spectacle, open-mouthed. Salmaara, hoping that Yezhr might set upon them, as well, should they try to impede her, hooked an arm around Gjordkra's middle and pulled her free. It would not have worked had Yezhr not attacked the three that had been holding the other girl, but her captor-turned-protector whirled into them, kama blades flashing when they lurched after the girls.

Together, Salmaara and Gjordkra raced toward the cliff's edge, away from the lithian party. Once there, Salmaara gawked at the roiling surf that battered the cliff far below.

If we jump, we die. Return to Kaskahai, and then probably Günhai, and live as prisoners until we die, or be smashed on razor rocks …

She saw the current, the rocks, felt the chill burning, burning, burning in her lungs. She took a step back.

Gjordkra joined her, paling. "This is your miracle escape route?"

"Yes!"

The violet-eyed girl threw a glance over her shoulder, and Salmaara looked with her.

Jhaill lay in a heap, while four liths struggled to hold Yezhr down and the remaining one ran toward them.

As Gjordkra set her jaw, Salmaara took a panicked breath and said, "We jump." She offered her hand to Gjordkra.

Her companion looked at it. "The day we met, you said friends call you Maara." Gjordkra took her hand with a firm nod. "I guess I'm going to jump with you, Maara."

They leaped together, plummeting from the sheer cliff toward the churning surf below.

CHAPTER TWENTY-SEVEN

FORGOTTEN VALLEY, NORTHERN YENDU

Rain and wind clawed the walls of a twisted fortress. The ancient building stood in a shale-littered valley of deep gray, sheltered by the southernmost roots of the T'Skel Mountains, three days' ride northwest of Kalitoomba. A still lake lay to one side, reflecting the fort and the stones that surrounded it.

The castle's keep looked like a cube, twisted at its foundations and top and cinched at the center. Many slanted windows radiated from the narrow point. A myriad of zigzag towers struck out from the keep, topped with silver turrets that shone in the flicker of lightning that darted through the clouds.

Kisoni Lordian observed the weather from a seven-sided window with a deep frown, his chin resting upon his hand, marred by a coiled scar that twisted around his forearm and ended on his palm. King Yulari had given him the serpentine wound millennia ago when Kisoni, then brash and idiotic, hoped to slay the Blue King on behalf of Vias, his sister. When Yulari had healed him, the king had also helped him broaden his vision. Now he sought to please Vias and his parents no more.

Kisoni wore the disguise of an old man. A snarled wig and thick beard reached past his elbows. The mane of storm-gray hid his ebony hair and flawless ivory skin beneath. He had keen, emerald eyes, likewise concealed by a pair of bushy brows. A simple brown robe adorned his body.

Why he still bothered with the disguise after all this time alone, he didn't know. Habit, perhaps.

Those in his family were masters of disguise. There was no Lordian in their true form that did not command the attention of all for miles around wherever they walked. They were gods, after all.

His eyelids drooped. Yet another long day of dusting and sorting books, like so many thousands of years full of dull days before this one.

He couldn't leave the valley. He didn't know who had created the barrier, only that one day, about a century ago, he had been propelled hundreds of feet backward and into the lake for trying to leave. He had tried several more times with the same result.

Kisoni had sworn to guard the books of his own volition. Even if he'd had a choice, he wouldn't have forsaken his task after giving his word. He was Keeper of Souls, and now Keeper of Books. He never abandoned those things entrusted to him.

But he wondered who wanted to keep him here and why.

He missed his forays to Kalitoomba with its soaring glass towers and their bright colors glowing in the suns. He missed the ancient northern quarter with its stone and brick buildings under Castle Errasitka's guardian gaze. He missed roast meats sold on skewers, rolled in a sweet, yellowy powder. Above all, he missed the city's vigor and constant hum of life. Kalitoomba never slept.

Something had gone wrong, though. None of his family had been to visit since his internment. Perhaps, as he couldn't go out, they couldn't come in.

The voices of the trapped souls of Digaria, his home world, hummed in his mind, never silent. Clamoring, pleading for release. Release that he could not provide from worlds away. Instead, they were doomed to wander among the living, unable to pass on.

He squeezed his eyes shut against the pain their cries caused. He couldn't do anything for them now. All the Keeper of Books could do was occasionally read aloud from the volumes to stay madness, to drown out the souls.

He inhaled deeply to calm his heart, which ached suddenly. Then he heaved to his feet and mussed the wig of tangled hair as he walked toward the door, illuminated by the periodic blue flash of lightning outside. Perhaps a new stew recipe was in order. He couldn't afford to sulk.

Pushing his spectacles back into place from where they had slid down his nose, he stepped into the circular hallway then marched down an undulating stairwell that ended in his modest kitchen.

The chamber was as uneven and twisted as the rest of the castle. Its floor slanted into a fireplace with a skewed mantel. A battered table of the same silver tsin wood occupied the chamber's center, while the floors and walls were of shale slabs from the surrounding valley. A large pantry occupied the wall opposite the hearth. From inside, he dragged a violet cauldron and scooted it across the smooth floor to the hearth.

He grunted, lifted it by a narrow handle, and hung it on a hook over the fire. Wandering over to a pump set into the wall by the pantry, he then filled a bucket before adding several portions of water to the cauldron.

Hoofbeats.

He froze. Then he strained his hearing, waiting to catch the sound again.

It can't be.

Hoofbeats.

He grinned. Perhaps Elloerr, the universe, held some kindness for him after all.

He mussed his hair again for dramatic effect, searched for a staff, and hunched himself.

Yes, there were hoofbeats, he was certain now.

He rushed to the castle's front doors, wrenched one open, and searched the pluvial dark beyond for the oncoming traveler.

The formidable Lastauk stallion and its burdens materialized from the downpour at a full gallop, mud flying around it in thick waves.

Kisoni snatched a lantern that sat beside the door, hastily lighting then waving it. "Ho, there!"

The horse slowed as it arrived, huffing, and stopped just short of crushing his feet. He felt the stallion's hot breath on his ratty wig. Kisoni, from his height of almost eight feet, looked into the horse's broad snout.

Two dark shapes sat on the mount, both clad in heavy cloaks—a man and a child. Kisoni moved aside as the man secured the child to the horse, leaped from the beast like a shade, and then led it into the doorway. Kisoni stumbled back to avoid being trampled.

Light fell on the magnificent animal, whose hair was uniformly deep indigo, and his mane was tied in short knots down the back of his strong neck. A purebred built for battle, huge and heavily muscled in the lower thighs and legs, which lent the elegant creature an aspect of ruggedness and raw power. The stallion was one of the finest specimens that Kisoni had ever seen and, he estimated, the creature stood twenty-five hands at the withers, at the least. The incredible beast must have cost his riders a fortune.

The horse stared down at the Keeper of Books with proud, intelligent eyes, waiting for him to make another move.

"We need food and shelter, old man," the rider said with a harsh edge, speaking Mauviasen. The accent was from somewhere around Kaskahai, Kisoni thought. Perhaps there was a hint of somewhere else, too, but he couldn't be sure.

"We have ridden for a week with little rest," the man said, glancing up at the child who sat on the drenched horse.

He patted the snorting Lastauk's neck and murmured something to him. Then the stranger turned back to Kisoni, standing hunched over and gasping with each breath. "We seek a safe harbor," he managed.

"You've come to the right place," Kisoni said. "Come in and warm yourself. I will find you some dry clothes. Your Lastauk shall also be welcome to stay by the fire until I can warm a place for him." Kisoni beckoned them forward and escorted them into a vast den adjacent to the entry.

Several armchairs cushioned in deep green velvet were clustered beside small tables around an enormous hearth, large enough to be a room by itself. By a stroke of luck, he had lit the fire an hour earlier to warm the chamber.

"May I take your cloaks?" Kisoni said.

The man nodded, unfastened a silver brooch that held his closed, and then handed the cloak to Kisoni.

The Keeper of Books observed his new guest as he took it from the man's callused hand. The man's silver hair, partially pulled from his strong face with a black clasp, fell to his shoulder blades. He wore a deep frown and had weary, violet eyes. Rich olive skin, tinted gray with ash, like any Mauviasen's, covered a strong build. The darkness of his complexion suggested a mixture of blood, however. Mauviasen tended to be fair, due to the suns' filtered exposure. Kisoni wondered if the man possessed Shadowlandish blood, as well.

"Come along, girl," the man said. With the horse's reins still in his hand, he reached up and hoisted the child from the quivering beast, grunting and swaying as he did so. He then set her on the floor.

The man knelt to remove the child's cloak then placed it Kisoni's waiting hand. The orange light of the torches glinted on metal fingers as they surrendered the fabric.

Kisoni accepted the cloak and saw that the man had not only a metal hand, but his entire right arm, beginning at his shoulder, also appeared to have been lost and replaced.

Kisoni's guest kept his attention on his little companion, whose jaw quaked violently. Her bright emerald hair rested against her back in a tight braid, contrasting with the pitch black of her skin. Her almond-shaped eyes, the same hue as her hair, were wide with fear and bewilderment. Diamond-shaped pupils, much like a dragon's, sundered the green. She could not have been older than ten by Kisoni's estimate. He had never seen her kind before.

"Over here, Agaria," the man said softly. He sat her on the hearth, placing his metal hand upon one of her small shoulders, the other pressed into his middle. "Good girl."

Once she was comfortable, he turned back to Kisoni. Their Lastauk, too exhausted to stand any longer, shook his head and lay down near the girl.

"Stay here a moment. I'll start some food," Kisoni said before he strode briskly through a door on the chamber's far side, which led into the kitchen.

"Where are you from?" Kisoni called back to the traveler as he flitted around the kitchen, gathering herbs and vegetables. He would have to raid his stores for some meat later.

"What do you mean?"

"Where have you ridden from in such a hurry?" Kisoni clarified, tossing a handful of energizing herbs into the pot. Kisoni then piled the vegetables on the table—silver onions, cabbage, and long, narrow udai. He plunged a knife through an onion and into the tabletop, chopping it into thin slices in short order.

"We hail from Tzu Tihas, from the fortress of its prince. The girl is of great value to the empress," he said. "I rode here knowing of nowhere safer in the world and having little notion of what I will do next."

Kisoni finished cutting the vegetables then dumped them into the stew. He returned to the adjacent chamber where his guests waited.

The man sank into one of the armchairs, his hand still firmly pressed to his side. Kisoni saw blood seeping between the quaking fingers.

"You're injured."

"Yes. I tore the stitches riding." He squeezed his eyes shut.

Kisoni returned to the kitchen and found wrappings and a bottle of alcohol in a drawer. He grabbed several glass tubes of antiseptic and pain suppressant as well.

He returned to the armchair and knelt before his guest. "Let me see it," he commanded.

The man removed his hand with a distrustful look.

His side was a gory mass of cloth and mangled flesh. Tangled remains of stitches protruded.

Kisoni set about cleaning the wound, which appeared to have been caused by a sword. He steadied the stranger's arm, which kept moving protectively back toward the nasty gash, and then the Keeper of Books pulled the remainder of the ruined stitches free.

"Stars, what a mess you made."

"You try stitching yourself while holding onto a struggling child and riding at a full gallop on a Lastauk. Out of Tzu Tihas. At night," he said with a grimace.

"You're a brave man."

"You aren't what I expected," the man said as Kisoni doused the torn flesh with the alcohol. He gasped out raggedly, "You're not at all like your sister, Kisoni."

"Right you are. She'd use your blood to stain the walls and hang you on it for decoration. She rather likes those visceral colors. Who are you that you know who I am?" Kisoni asked, raising his bushy eyebrows.

The other chuckled quietly. "I do know and revere my wicked lady well. I maintain her prison, as is my station."

"And what station is that?" Kisoni murmured, continuing his work.

"Prince of Kaskahai."

"And you're running from an empress?"

"Yes, the Empress of Mauvias. I got past her hotheaded consorts and stole away one of her most prized possessions—the girl."

There is an Empress of Mauvias? What else has changed?

"You didn't have any trouble in the pass, did you? How did you know where to find me?"

"No. My daughter—now dead—once chanced upon you here and told me of you. Of course, she did call you by another name. Seash the Sorcerer?"

Kisoni nodded.

Content that the wound was clean, he prepared a needle to sew the deep laceration closed. He crawled over to the fireplace, careful not to disturb the slumbering child and horse as he held the needle in the flames.

A vision of a young woman with perfect Shadowlandish features—dark hair and eyes, and light olive skin—came to his mind. She had been one of his last visitors.

"Oh yes, I remember her. The curly-haired mapmaker," Kisoni said sadly. "I am sorry to hear that she is gone."

The prince's jaw tightened. He swallowed, anger quickly replacing his upset, and looked away. When he looked back, his eyes were hard. "Yes, that's how I knew where to find you." His hands tightened into fists.

Kisoni readied the antiseptic, which he had in a needled glass tube. He wiped the neatly stitched area clean again.

"What may I call you?" Kisoni asked, plunging the needle in then emptying the tube into the prince's body via a small button on the top before the man could blink. When he was finished, he bound the wound, content that the stitches would hold.

"I once wanted to be called Laniter ... but that man is dead now, no more than a dream. His family killed. Wife and daughter executed. Home taken. I am damned to be Prince of Kaskahai, Vadik Asenar, forevermore." He leaned his head back against the armchair's cushion.

"Rest a while, Prince Vadik. I shall have some stew prepared soon. I will watch over the girl. Agaria, you said?" The Destroyer's brother smiled, and Vadik nodded, closing his eyes.

Kisoni threw a blanket over him and turned toward the child who, awake again, crouched like a frog before the fire. She stared at the tongues of flames with her glassy eyes, delight mirrored in them.

As the Keeper of Books approached her, she sprang into the flames, and they engulfed her small form, burning her wet clothing away.

Kisoni gasped, lunging after her, but stopped short.

Agaria sat facing him, unharmed. She smiled luminously, her black body glowing like an ember. Now that her heavy clothes were gone, he could see that she had a thick tail which, like her eyes, reminded him of a dragon's.

"You mind the heat, don't you, little one?" he chided with a small smile. "Now I must find you new clothes. Then you may help me make food for your weary guardian." He glanced over his shoulder at the Prince of Kaskahai.

The child nodded and crawled from the fire. She extended a small hand, which he took.

They left the room together and walked through the kitchen. One of Kisoni's white cotton tunics hung over a chair by the fire. He dressed the naked child in it. It reached to her ankles.

"There you are, little one."

She nodded and twirled.

"Now, let's see if we can find some tylis herb. It should help your friend heal faster."

The dragon child merely nodded again and took his hand, her tail snaking behind her. Something about her round face was distinctly predatory, as her glassy eyes didn't leave his face.

He dropped her hand, fetched a basket from the mantel, and extended it toward her. "Carry this for me, will you?"

She took it.

An arched door was set into the wall across the kitchen beside the stairs that led to the castle's upper levels. Three, semi-circle grooves adorned its center. It had no apparent handle. Kisoni led the child to it and stroked the grooves—the center, the left, then the right. They shuddered under his touch and, with a series of snaps, released. The door creaked open, away from them.

He took Agaria's free hand and stepped through the opening and onto a landing on the other side. A draft of frigid air hit his face as they left the cozy kitchen.

A town could have fit inside the chamber below. Circular, its green marble walls drew up into a tremendous dome. Titanic tsin bookshelves covered its white marble floors.

Currency required for a single branch of silver tsin could feed an average family for a month, if not more. Kisoni had neither built nor furnished the castle. He had taken up residence when his dear friend, Esthadya, had asked Kisoni to take on guardianship of the books to divert his mind from the clamoring of the souls. He had always assumed the materials a gift from the Shadowlanders, who admired Lord Knowledge.

Each bookcase spanned the width of five men from shoulder to shoulder and stood ten stories tall. Shelves at the chamber's fringes reached the ceiling, over twelve stories high. A crooked staircase descended to the white floor and the labyrinthine library.

Kisoni led Agaria to the bottom then turned aside to follow the wall that supported the stairs.

He felt the child shiver and frowned as she leaned into his side. He draped his arm around her shoulders and rubbed her arm as they passed several shadowy bookcases to a glass door that led into Kisoni's gardens. As a wash of humid air hit them as they entered, Agaria perked in his arm.

Green marble paths wound through several large planter boxes, each filled with dark-leafed herbs and vegetables. Rain splattered a lopsided glass dome that formed the ceiling above several fruit trees that lined the path.

They strode in silence to one of the stone boxes, in which Kisoni grew his medicinal herbs. He spotted the *tylis* he sought, a broad-leafed herb with charcoal leaves edged in pink. It originated in Arvitra, to the west, and had extraordinary healing properties.

The girl's emerald eyes brightened at the sight, filled with curiosity.

"They don't have these where you come from, do they?" said Kisoni warmly, crouching beside her to pick several *tylis* leaves from the planter. He then placed them in the basket clutched in the girl's hands.

"Why are you sad?" Agaria asked so quietly that he almost missed it.

He frowned, taken aback. "I'm not sad. Do I look sad, Agaria?"

"Yes." She twirled the basket in delicate fingers, her gaze fixed on it.

"Don't worry about me," he said as brightly as possible. He would be fine now that he had guests.

The return journey to the kitchen yielded no more conversation. The two of them walked side by side, the eldritch girl clinging to the basket.

They prepared the stew together, Agaria stirring under Kisoni's instruction. The child's eagerness and curiosity warmed his heart.

She sniffed the leaves he held up for inspection then shook her head and hissed in displeasure.

He offered her the last scrap of dried meat from a jar, which she snatched and devoured. He smiled.

How strange. She really does seem like a little dragon trapped in a two-legged form.

Kisoni returned to the sitting chamber where the prince of the Destroyer's city slumbered. His face had an unhealthy pallor, and his breathing was unsteady. At least the bleeding had been staunched.

Kisoni knelt before Vadik, resting a careful hand on one of his shoulders. The prince's violet eyes sprang open and, for a moment, Kisoni feared that he might have to stop an attack.

When his weak guest relaxed, Kisoni said, "Agaria and I have food for you."

Agaria entered the room with a steaming earthenware bowl cupped in her small hands.

The weary prince nodded then straightened himself to receive it.

"You are kind, Kisoni. I had begun to believe the world was sapped of any mercy," Vadik said and sipped the stew carefully, still suspicious despite his flattery.

Apparently satisfied that it would cause him no harm, he began to devour it with urgency, as though he had never eaten in his life.

The Keeper of Books took the empty bowl from him and refilled it.

The prince ate it.

"Can you move?" Kisoni asked, his green eyes flicking to the newly applied bandages. "I have a bedchamber that I would relocate you to."

"I can try," the prince replied. He tried to fully straighten and failed, his face paling further.

Agaria rushed to his side and took one of his hands, and Kisoni offered his arm as Vadik pushed to his feet.

Kisoni caught him as he fell and pulled Vadik's natural arm across his strong shoulders.

"Are you ready?" Kisoni asked with a quick smile.

Vadik winced. "It's worse trying to move now that I've rested."

Kisoni led him through the kitchen and up the crooked stairs to the upper floor with the dragon child in tow.

"What happened, if you don't mind my asking?" Kisoni panted out as they reached a small chamber outfitted with a bed and table.

Vadik collapsed onto the bed and bit back a yelp. "As I was escaping with Agaria, having dealt with the Prince of Tzu Tihas, I was attacked. I didn't see my attacker or the implement of my wounding, nor did I stop for a chat. I had to keep moving, carrying Agaria on my back. I'm grateful no harm came to her."

"Rest now and regale us later with the tale. I would love to hear of it. Matters in my sister's nation never fail to remain interesting." Kisoni smiled, wondering how he could still have a place in his heart for that most wretched of women, as he closed the door and entered the hall.

That was when the presence hit him.

The man occupied the sitting room on the lower floor—Kisoni could pinpoint his location precisely. It seemed that the force of the man's presence would overtake the very stones of the castle that tried to contain it. If one could get past that, it had the distinct sensation of standing in cool moonlight, full of memory. It was another reason so many like him, the zermai, disguised themselves.

Kisoni shivered as he made his way back to the stairs, hesitating but irresistibly drawn, as though a thick rope were attached to his rib cage, dragging him toward the man.

Nothing for a century, and now three visitors in one day. The Keeper of Books now knew whom to blame.

Kisoni made his way to the cavernous sitting room adjacent to the front entry and stiffened when he stepped into the doorway. Not a speck of dust lay in the chamber, and everything within had been arranged into pristine order. Even the rug under the armchairs lacked a single wave, and the mud from Vadik's horse had disappeared, along with the animal itself. Kisoni did not worry for the animal—he knew he would find it comfortably stabled later on. The fire blazed high in the grate, every other flame precisely the same height, alternately high and low.

The source of the overt orderliness sat in one of the green armchairs, idly leafing through one of Kisoni's books.

Kisoni took a deep breath of the too-clean air and, drawing himself to his full height, entered. He gingerly sat in one of the chairs opposite the one the man occupied. Most who sat in those chairs made them seem luxuriously sized. However, the man's imposing height of over nine feet made the chair seem fit for a child.

A robe of black silk embroidered with silver threads accentuated the strong lines of his muscular body. He carried no weapons with him, for he needed none.

Kisoni had always thought it unfair that one like him was as handsome as he was powerful. Women throughout the ages had found him irresistible, at least in this, his zermai, form. The man's ink-black hair, reaching to his shoulders, was swept back from his young face in a silver clip inlaid with ivory. His piercing eyes, which Kisoni thought could freeze ice, were a mixture of red, blue, and violet.

"So good of you to join me," Hazc said. The book in his hand closed and drifted through the air to settle on an immaculate stack, seemingly of its own will.

Kisoni scowled. "What do you want?" He tried to retain composure, but hatred mingled with fear roiled inside of him. Despite his change of allegiance, Kisoni had never been able to overcome the emotions that he had associated with this man since the former's infancy. Kisoni's mother had even used Hazc as a threat who would come and turn him into something horrid if the boy didn't do as she or his father had commanded. Now he knew that was silly—Hazc didn't waste time on such things. Still, the deep-rooted fear remained.

Hazc smiled. "I have a task for you, naturally." A sharp *pop* punctuated his statement as a crack in the table between them mended itself.

Kisoni flinched.

Hazc didn't look away. "You will soon have more visitors, if I have read the clime well."

Kisoni didn't know how Hazc could see what happened all over the face of multiple worlds and predict events as he did, but it terrified him.

Kisoni was zermai, like Hazc, but considerably lesser, and he knew it. *That, and the gift of foresight is lost to him ... Everyone knows that.*

"Is that so?"

"Two, traveling together, to be precise. One a young girl possessing red hair. I will come searching for her, and when she strikes me down, you will give me this." Hazc produced a glass vial from his cloak. It drifted across the table into Kisoni's waiting hand.

He wanted to gasp aloud and hurl the thing away, but he merely wrinkled his nose instead. "This? You want me to give you *this*? Don't you—"

Hazc stopped him with a musical, bone-chilling chuckle. "I hate it when I interfere with my work. I must be stopped. Asha, as well, this time."

Staring into the black substance in the vial, wishing he could make it disappear, Kisoni grimaced. As much as he disliked Hazc, he wasn't sure he could give this to anyone. It wouldn't kill Hazc—nothing that Kisoni knew of could without the other man's leave. One could cut Hazc's head off, and he wouldn't die unless he decided to leave his body. *But the pain it would cause …*

As though he could hear his thoughts, which Kisoni knew he could not, Hazc said, "You will do as I have instructed?"

A bitter taste filled Kisoni's mouth, but he nodded and tucked the vile stuff into one of the concealed pockets in his robe. "Asha will have my hide for it," he muttered.

Hazc nodded. "I imagine so."

Both men turned at a scraping on the stones behind them.

Agaria made her way toward them, dragging her feet with every step, her emerald eyes fixed on Hazc as though in a trance.

"And now, for the second item of business." Hazc extended one of his hands to Agaria.

The girl's dragon-like eyes lit at the sight of him, and she hastened to him, kneeling at his feet.

Hazc reached into his cloak again and produced a fist-sized emerald with many octagonal faces, each with a vertical slash through it.

Kisoni recoiled.

Luminous, emerald veins spread over Hazc's hand and up his arm until they covered him entirely, even until his eyes glowed the same hue.

"I'm not touching that!" Kisoni said fervently.

"No? Well, fortunately for you, it is meant for her," Hazc said, patting Agaria's head.

Even having the emerald near disgusted Kisoni. It had cost him his freedom once, not to mention the lovely blue eyes he had been born with. He remembered his rash idiocy every time he saw those emerald eyes looking back at him in the mirror. Even had it not so impacted his existence, it was still an unnatural object. One that should never have been made.

One that he had taken part in making.

Agaria accepted the emerald and hugged it to her like many girls her age would a doll. When he released it, Hazc returned to normal.

Kisoni clutched the arm of the chair. "Hazc ... you don't plan to give this power to mortals and ... You're not going to summon ..." He couldn't bring himself to say their names. "... *them* here?"

Hazc settled back in his chair, making it seem a throne, with the green glow illuminating his chilly smile. "Oh, yes. Yes, to all."

Kisoni stared at the eldritch child, groaning within himself. *He has no mercy left*, he thought bitterly.

CHAPTER TWENTY-EIGHT

OFF THE COAST OF ARVITRA, TAUS SEA

R ope dug into Salmaara's back as she drifted upward, away from the cold water. Salt crusted her lashes, and two bright orbs floating in a blue sky blinded her. Her body sung with pain—sweet, stinging pain, as though fire licked every inch of skin.

Indistinct voices buzzed loudly in her ears, and her head felt as though someone had taken a hammer to it.

Up she went. *I'm alive … I'm alive.*

A deafening, scratchy voice sounded right next to her. "Got another one, Cap!"

Two men dumped her from the net onto the deck of a ship.

She groaned and tried to move, but her limbs refused. She couldn't seem to think enough to discern where she lay over the pain pounding in her head.

She coughed once, water running down her chin. It didn't evaporate but ran down her body in cold rivulets.

"Wake up!" A bucket of freezing water doused her body.

She gasped and scrambled to her knees, her surroundings coming into sharper focus.

She knelt on a deck stained black, worn smooth by the constant passage of feet. A narrow mast with a square sail of deep azure blue rose from the middle of the sleek caravel, of which Salmaara could easily see both ends from where she knelt. Atop the mast, a banner flew, black folds with an emerald octagon undulating in the rising breeze—*Maliem Esculis.*

She quickly counted some fifteen men standing around her. All, save two, were brown and weathered from days toiling in the suns, their sleeveless coats a myriad of patterns and colors. She wondered if they were from Arvitra. The remaining two wore long-sleeved shirts and pants that brushed the tops of their feet. Cloth was wrapped around their heads to form hats. Salmaara recognized their pale, olive skin and dark eyes—like the smugglers she had seen in Bhevir. All the men wore the same dark expression. Not hostility as she had expected, but suspicion, like children caught stealing sweets. Several had curved swords in their hands.

Wind chilled Salmaara's naked skin. What little remained of her thin robe from Mauvias, the sea had stripped away.

She sat back and pulled her knees to her chest in a feeble attempt to hide from the stares of the scruffy faces around her. Then Salmaara spotted Gjordkra's crumpled form a short way across the deck through the men's legs.

The man with the scratchy voice, the one who had pulled her up in the net, stared with narrowed eyes. "We should put 'em back."

A second, spindly man with a thick blond beard covering his neck and one eye missing nodded vigorously.

Salmaara took a sharp breath and, fighting down her embarrassment and headache, thrust herself to her feet, hoping she had the right idea.

If I can convince them ... "How dare you speak of me in such a manner! Do you not know who I am?"

The ring around her instantly expanded as the men stumbled back in surprise. Only the two smugglers didn't move, but they did regard her warily.

Salmaara shivered and wrapped her arms around herself when the wind brushed across her, raising bumps all over her skin. Several scrapes oozed blood down her torso.

Fighting down the insistent headache, which was making it difficult to keep her feet, she pointed toward Gjordkra. "Fetch clothing for me and my sister, immediately."

Her friend lay in an unmoving heap, but Salmaara could see her breathing.

The men remained frozen, gawking.

She drew herself up indignantly. "Well? This is no way for subjects to treat a high lady of Tzu Tihas. I have connections you cannot fathom!" Her heart quailed at the thought.

Flinching, the one-eyed man took off his brown tunic and edged forward, offering it with a grimace, as though she were a deadly snake coiled to strike.

She accepted it with a grateful nod.

Murmurs of "lady" sounded through the little cluster of men.

The ship rolled under her, and her stomach with it, as she pulled the shirt over her head. Her legs wobbled as though made of jelly, but she kept her feet, trying not to think of what caused the motion. *So much water ... tossing, tearing, shoving, burning ...*

She looked back to Gjordkra and could see blood seeping through her friend's fingers.

Fighting the headache, which seemed to grow stronger every moment she remained on her feet, Salmaara added, "Do you have anyone who can see to an injury?"

One of the sailors, with his head shaven bald, pointed to Gjordkra with a thick finger. "Get 'er to that fix-it man in the brig. He'll know what to do."

The shaven-headed man's shipmates regarded him sullenly, none of them moving. Finally, one of the smugglers stepped forward and picked Gjordkra up with disdain in his dark eyes, as though she were caked in mud. He carried her to the back of the ship, where a door led inside.

Salmaara straightened, eyeing the men as imperiously as she could. "I require help, as well. I will go with her."

The bald man stepped forward, awkwardly offering a blanket. "Allow me to take you, my ... lady." He said the title as though he had never used such language in his life.

She accepted the blanket, wrapping it around her shoulders. The man then led her into the interior of the ship where the crewman had taken Gjordkra.

Within, two ladders climbed in different directions, one up and the other down. The man helped her down into the belly of the ship, where a long hall filled with narrow hammocks waited. At its end, he unlocked a barred door and stepped in, holding it for her.

"If there's any trouble from that scum, you call me, you hear? You call for Captain Pol." Not waiting for a reply, Pol turned and left.

Within, the well-muscled smuggler stood over a cot, where Gjordkra lay, his bulk blocking another man from Salmaara's view.

Salmaara gripped the door when the ship rolled. The motion felt stronger here below decks. She then made her way forward, staggering in a zigzag.

The smuggler stepped away from the bed and, with a slight bow as he passed her, took up guard inside the door.

Salmaara turned her gaze back to the bed.

An old man with a grizzled mane of silver hair had half turned on a stool by the cot to look at her. He wore a leather jerkin over a worn, cotton shirt and soft pants of some creature's hide. She had never seen a face so lined. His was darkened by years in the suns. He had a sharp nose and almond-shaped, blue eyes that shone brightly from his gaunt face, like twin sapphires.

He heaved to his feet with a grimace and walked four steps to her, clacking with every step. As he drew nearer, she could see he was more metal than man at his joints—knees, elbows, shoulders, and fingers.

With a stern smile, he took her arm and led her to the cot. "Sit," he said.

She sat back heavily on the edge of the bed.

He fished a white ball, the size of his thumbnail, out of one of his pockets. "Eat this. It'll help with the stomach."

Salmaara took it, frowning. Manacles, lacking chains, hung around his bony wrists, and red welts covered them where the metal rubbed.

She ate the white ball and sighed when her stomach stopped leaping up and down with each roll of the ship beneath her. "Thank you, sir," she told him.

"*Sir?* Just call me Takin. No need for sir and all that." He laughed.

Salmaara looked back at Gjordkra, wondering at the sight of her asleep. Several new cuts from the fall laced her face, but she breathed steadily.

Takin stood, indicating his chair.

Salmaara shook her head. "So, you're a doctor?"

"Me? Nah. I know a little medicine, but I'm a blacksmith." He sat back down and took a rag, dabbing at some of the cuts on Salmaara's face. "*Once was Grand Engineer, now blacksmith ... Blacksmith! Lords, how I've fallen.*"

Salmaara smiled. "Grand Engineer? What does that mean?"

Takin jerked in surprise and froze, lips quivering. "Uh …"

The smuggler spoke from behind them. "A high-ranking heretic of the old world. We're taking this miscreant to his execution in Arakamda, my lady," he said in a smooth voice.

Salmaara turned to look at him for a moment. His dark eyes glittered with a cunning light. He did not fit among the unpolished men above decks. Suddenly, she was very uncomfortable having him behind her.

Salmaara didn't remember trying to listen to the old man's thoughts. They had just come to her, as though he had said them aloud. The connection was there one moment and gone the next.

Takin maintained his smile, but it did not reach his resentful eyes. She wished she could apologize.

He bound her wounds in silence, but she heard his voice in her mind. *"My Lord, my King, can you even hear me anymore? Don't you care how we suffer without you? Can't you hear the servants of the enemy blaspheme your name?"*

Salmaara's heart ached as Takin's ached, as though a fist gripped it. She yearned for what had been taken from her.

She lost her connection to him and, as quickly as the pain had come, it left her as though she had never felt it, but she still had to wipe a tear from her cheek.

Outwardly, Takin appeared unaffected. She wanted to offer comfort, but couldn't, not with that smuggler standing behind her.

At least I didn't take him over, like Yezhr.

The memory of that frenzied moment returned to her in a flood. Yezhr and Jhaill catching them on the cliff, planning to take them back.

What did I do to Yezhr? Did I really do as Vias said I could? What am I?

The thought chilled her.

"If you are feeling tended, allow me to show you above. Such filth as this is unsuitable company for milady. I will bring your sister when the ... prisoner ... is satisfied she can be moved," the smuggler said with a neat bow.

She stood and walked to him on wobbly legs. *A smuggler who doesn't know medicine? That is what they are known for, isn't it? All the ones who came to Bhevir were healers.*

He offered a heavily muscled arm when her knees buckled at the door. She took it carefully and allowed him to lead her up the ladders to a sturdy door of black-stained wood. He twisted the knob and let the next heave of the ship pull it open the rest of the way.

They stood outside the door of a small cabin. A broad hammock woven of blue-stained cord swayed with the motion of the boat, and heavy bolts pinned a wash table to the floor.

Captain Pol tossed the remainder of his ratty clothes into a chest. He bowed when he saw her and tucked the chest under one of his arms, hurrying forward to hold the door while Salmaara entered.

"I left some of my clothes for you. Not much, but I hope it will satisfy," the captain said, wiping a grimy hand across his forehead in an effort to remove some of the sweat that ran down his face and neck. Then he turned back to the room behind him and pointed to a pair of long shirts draped over a crate beside the wash table.

Watching the hammock sway and thinking of having to sleep in it stirred Salmaara's gut again, despite Takin's medicine. *I'll just have to get used to it.*

She managed a smile for the waiting men. "Thank you, Captain."

"I'll have someone bring food.

"Kaman! Go get some food for the lady," Pols said sharply, noticing the smuggler's presence for the first time since they had entered.

Wordlessly, Kaman stalked away with a
lurching floor beneath his bare feet. Captai.
door closed behind him.

Salmaara slipped into a pair of rough brown

As she sat in the hammock, Kaman returned
pickles and strips of dried white meat that had
maara wasn't sure what it was when the man pl.
hands but thought anything that stank so strongly
eaten. Still, it was better than anything she had eater

Salmaara cleared her throat. "Kaman?"

He looked back, dark eyes glittering. She thought sh
in them. "Milady?"

"Where are you from? I know of men who look like y
who know medicine."

Kaman's mouth quirked in an almost smile. "Smuggler:
the lands of the Lady Gracious, the Shadowlands. A Sh
Medicine is widely known and practiced there, especially in
our destination. Smugglers …"

Not a smuggler. A Shadowlander.

As Kaman turned to leave, Gjordkra stumbled into the doorw
in a brown blanket. She staggered past Kaman to sit beside Salma

A thought from Kaman slid over Salmaara's mind as the man
hold of the doorknob. "*… not ladies. Not well-educated enough. The*
look Mauviasen, especially the red-haired one. She clearly has lithian bl
in her. But they must be low, if not fugitives. I will not let them slip awa
The truth will be mine." The Shadowlander left, pulling the door shui
behind him.

Salmaara stared after him. *Not good …*

When he was gone, Gjordkra lay back in the hammock. "This is your

f escaping Mauvias? You saw the flag above decks," she said, wrin-
her nose.

maara raised her brows. *So, she was awake … How did she see any-*
g without getting caught?

We're lucky they're a bunch of simpletons and bought your Mauvi-
n nobility story. They took to it too quickly if you ask me."

almaara nodded, setting the bowl of salty victuals in Gjordkra's lap.
e then took to her feet and collected the second shirt for her friend
fore returning to the hammock.

"And what's wrong with your head? You haven't let it go since you got
ere."

Salmaara lowered her hand, realizing that she had been cupping her
throbbing head. "Oh, I have a little headache. I'll be fine." Salmaara lay
back beside her friend and offered her the shirt.

Gjordkra selected a strip of meat with one hand and accepted the
garment with the other. Gjordkra swallowed. "They're acting like they've
got something to hide. I wonder if that old man is really what they say
he is. They're probably after reward money, and if we are who we say we
are, they'll think we can give them just that, or our family can, at least,
especially if they return us safely."

Salmaara took the bowl while Gjordkra dressed. Pushing the meat
aside, she took a pickle. "They might, but that Shadowlander, Kaman,
doesn't believe it. He wondered if we are fugitives and intends to hold us
until he finds out who we truly are. We may be able to fool the others,
but not him."

Gjordkra bit into another strip of the white meat harder than was
necessary. "You listened to his thoughts just like that? What are we going
to do? This is a small ship on a lot of water. We can't run, can't hide."

Salmaara opened her mouth to reply when a series of loud thumps

and shouts from outside froze the words on her tongue. The ship shuddered under them.

Through a wooden grate above the hammock, she could see the helm. Men raced about shouting in panic, throwing buckets of water at one another and the deck. An orange glow flickered just out of sight, followed by the scent of smoke on the sea wind.

Gjordkra gasped when a flaming cinder floated down through the grate above and settled on her lap. Her eyes widened.

The girls looked at each other and yelled, "Fire!"

CHAPTER TWENTY-NINE

OFF THE COAST OF ARVITRA, TAUS SEA

Exhaustion forgotten, Salmaara and Gjordkra scrambled from the hammock, sending the bowl and remaining food tumbling to the wooden deck.

Salmaara reached the door first, stuffing the last of a pickle in her mouth. She felt intense heat through the wooden planks and metal door handle. Covering her nose and mouth with a hand, she opened the door.

Flames from outside squirmed through the cracks in the door at the bottom of the ladder, and smoke filled the small space between the captain's cabin and the ladder down into the belly of the caravel. Beside her, Gjordkra shook her head.

Still covering her mouth, Salmaara slid down the ladder then ran down the second.

Gjordkra cursed and hurried after her. "Wait! We'll be trapped!"

Salmaara didn't look back. "We can't leave the old man! We should at least give him a chance," she said, continuing forward. We have to save him. *He doesn't deserve to die, and he loves King Yulari, too. What must he know of the old world?*

Salmaara sprinted between the hammocks below, avoiding the sailors that darted around, screaming and gathering more buckets. One tried to stop her but didn't return when she shoved him away as hard as she could.

She reached the brig door and shouldered it open, panting.

Takin tossed his manacles onto the bed and rubbed his wrists as she entered. He turned, with a long knife in hand.

Salmaara's knees buckled as the ship surged up beneath her.

Gjordkra arrived in the doorway, scowling, and stopped just short of falling over Salmaara, her violet eyes wide with fear.

Takin lowered his knife and offered Salmaara a gnarled hand with several metal fingers. She accepted, and he pulled her up.

"You girls showed up at the worst time. I've had this set up for days. I won't go quietly to my death at the hands of these Shadowlander traitors, nope. Get yourselves overboard and you won't die. The final one should go off in a couple ticks. Can't stop it. Should supply us with plenty of flotation, yep." He didn't wait for her to reply, pulling her by the arm from his prison and leading her back through the pandemonium among the hammocks and to the ladder.

Salmaara tossed several quick glances over her shoulder at Gjordkra, who kept up on remarkably steady legs for one who had never been on the ocean.

Takin released Salmaara's arm and climbed mechanically, cursing his metal limbs under his breath. Salmaara and Gjordkra followed him quickly.

The girls froze in front of the flaming door, but Takin barged past them and forced it open with a metal shoulder, grunting as a cascade of cinders fell on him from the doorframe. He didn't wait for them, disappearing into the milling bodies and flames that engulfed the deck ahead.

Salmaara and Gjordkra hopped through the door, trying not to burn their bare feet.

A singed stump stood where the caravel's mast had been. A hole that four men could have jumped into gaped in the foredeck, flames leaping wildly from it. Several men still tried to extinguish the flames, and two others dove overboard while Salmaara watched.

"We're going to have to jump into that again," Salmaara said grimly.

Gjordkra nodded. "I survived it last time … somehow."

"Takin said something about *plenty of floatation.* If we end up in the water, find something to hold on to." Salmaara shoved the image of the choppy ocean waters from her mind. She couldn't think of it, or she would never do what she must.

Through her headache, which caused spots over her vision, she looked to the smoky sky, at the suns. It was late afternoon. Very few hours remained until dusk and then dark, and she could not see land in any direction.

As they moved out on deck, she looked for Takin. The old man felled two sailors with one sweep of his blade and scrambled onto the deck railing. Once on top, he turned back toward the ship, gripping a bit of loose rigging. Some of the men, having quelled the fire on deck, turned toward him.

Salmaara made her way forward. She wanted to explain her and Gjordkra's allegiances before it was too late, and that meant staying with him.

He didn't take his eyes from the men on deck, regarding them with a wicked grin. "Hail King Powerful!" he bellowed then leaped backward from the railing and out of sight.

Salmaara turned to Gjordkra. "We have to get off. He said something would—"

She didn't finish her sentence. An explosion in the ship's hull blew the vessel in two, timbers and men alike shrieking as it tossed them into the air.

Time seemed to slow as the black planks beneath Salmaara's feet buckled and propelled her toward the gray sky. Splinters drove into her skin like needles, and rope whipped wildly around her. She tried to see Gjordkra through the surreal cloud of debris, but her momentum spun her instead to face the heaving gray swells of the Taus Sea.

CHAPTER THIRTY

VEKAN'S HOUSE,
NORTHWEST ARVITRA COAST

A series of cliffs enclosed an oval bay where waves broke over a gravelly stretch of beach, two days ride south of Mauvias's border. Afternoon faded into a flat dusk. No clouds loomed in the darkening sky as the tide rose.

On the precipice of the highest rugged cliff, situated across from the gap that led to the Taus Sea, a house on four rock stilts reached for the sky.

Vekan of the Sirens, too exhausted to weep anymore, knelt on the gravelly beach beside a carved boat that would return his mother, Legacy, to the sea for the last time. He surrounded her with tiny candles to keep her warm on her voyage.

She lay in the shallow craft, her wild hair braided to either sides of her brown face. Her feathered wings were folded about her voluptuous form, never again to take flight. Scales appeared where the froth of surf fell upon her.

A century before, King Yulari had commanded Vekan's mother to stop drowning sailors and sinking ships and begin rescuing them instead. She had raised her son to heal, and he had never had a violent thought in his life.

Smooth brown skin covered his well-muscled body. He possessed a head of silver hair, windswept from years of soaring over the sea in search of flounderers. Bird-like eyes of royal blue peered from a youthful face, with a firm jaw and hooked nose. A feathered pair of silver wings sprouted from his broad back. He wore a loose cotton shirt and brown trousers.

Vekan was now the last of his kind.

He pulled the tail of a squirming firefish, and a small puff of flame came from its thick lips to light the candles surrounding Legacy. He then pushed the boat into the waves until the water covered his waist then his shoulders as the flames slowly spread over his mother's body.

Arkarias's conical snout rose from the surf, metallic green above and white below. When Vekan was in deep enough, the shark helped him nudge the craft into the bay with a single thrust of his great tail. As Legacy's pyre drifted away, the massive shark returned and came up beneath Vekan.

Watching his mother go, the siren sat atop Arkarias's broad back, leaning back on the creature's fin, which stood at least a head taller than Vekan.

The shark had been around for the entirety of Vekan's brief twenty-six years. Sirens far outlived the land folk, such as sulmai, who had once easily enjoyed half a millennium of life. Had the sirens and their offspring not been hunted to their ends, they would each have lived through three generations of land folk—a millennium and a half.

The shark had served as his guardian, and as his mother's before him. Now Arkarias was all that he had left.

Vekan wasn't sure how long Ark's kind lived, but he knew his friend was getting old.

Legacy's floating pyre drifted farther and farther away.

"She's free, Ark. Free of the pain," he said in Inarian, the old tongue. His melodious voice hummed among the cliffs in the bay, a soft and mournful sound.

As he watched the flames disappear through the gap in the ring of cliffs, his keen bird's eyes spotted something—a splash of auburn near the foot of the cliffs, bobbing in the evening surf.

He sat up, shook the water from his wings, and pushed off Ark's back. He flew over the bay to where a girl drifted in the waves.

He waited for Arkarias to catch up then pointed to the unconscious girl. The shark loaded her onto his snout.

When the water became too shallow, the siren relieved his piscine companion of his burden and dragged the girl onto the gravelly beach. He knelt beside her and put an ear to her bosom.

A gentle heartbeat echoed through her chest.

He smiled wanly. "She's alive."

Vekan scanned her for injuries with a practiced eye. Splinters, cuts, and bruises dotted her, but she looked surprisingly healthy. She breathed easily but did not wake.

Vekan carried the girl from the beach to a path that switch-backed up the cliffs to his house fifty feet from the water.

His mother had originally constructed the house some four centuries earlier. All had been replaced many times over, piece by piece, thanks to its exposed location, but it still looked much the same.

It was a long, wooden rectangle with a single room inside, and it had a steep, cobalt roof with eaves that curled into wooden statues of drowning figures reaching skyward. A rounded stone chimney rose from the side facing the water. Three shuttered windows lined each of the two longest sides of the building. Four colossal stone stilts supported it, elevating it three stories to keep it out of reach of the brutal waves the Taus produced in winter months. Vekan had added a veranda that encompassed the outside of the house, as well as spiral stairs wrapping around two stilts leading up to it.

A forest of fragrant redwood and alder bordered the property and covered the nearby hills, their black foliage rippling in the ocean breeze, like a second sea. Neat gardens surrounded the house, and paved paths wound among planter boxes and three small animal pens filled with geese.

The garden ended when it reached the edge of the cliff. There, Vekan had constructed a wooden walkway that jutted from the cliff's edge, suspended over the bay. A long springboard stuck out from a flight of stairs situated at the walkway's far end.

Vekan reached the house and entered. He laid the girl in one of twelve hammocks that hung along the sides of the room. Then he made quick work of her wounds, pulling the splinters free with experienced hands.

"Gjordkra ... Ship exploded ..." the girl murmured without fully waking.

Vekan rested a hand on her shoulder and nodded. "I'll be back."

He ran back outside and toward the platform that hung over the ocean. Breaking into a sprint, he thrust himself into the air from the springboard and plummeted toward the roiling surf. The wind yanked at his hair and whipped his clothes. As he was about to hit the water, he spread his wings.

The siren flew parallel to the water, the tips of his wings brushing the surface. He couldn't hold back when others needed him. Besides, the retreating suns would soon take the light he needed with them.

He pumped his wings harder, the strong beats on the water attracting Ark's attention as Vekan passed overhead. The shark's dorsal fin sliced the surface as they set out into the open sea through the gap in the cliffs.

When they emerged, the ocean pushed the remains of a small caravel against the outer rock wall. The shredded vessel looked as though someone had smashed it with a huge fist.

She said exploded. Were they attacked? I've never heard of it. Not that it couldn't happen.

Vekan hummed three undulating notes. One for water, one for the flotsam, and one for the sailors he hoped to find. He received his reply through the wind, in an ancient language that only the tides and fish understood. *Windsong.*

The water had drowned a crew of eleven, which it still held. He would recover them later.

The bits of decking and rigging that bobbed on the water's darkening surface were harder to discern. He saw a bloated man, hours dead, though hadn't drowned. A piece of wood ran though his stomach and out his back. Vekan frowned.

As the red light of the retreating suns faded from the horizon, he winged up a little higher to better oversee the shattered vessel.

The ill-fated ship's crew had most likely been fishermen from Arvitra, judging by their woolen tunics and pants. He hummed a note to the sea—living.

Nothing.

He would try one last time. He sang two additional notes—woman and hidden.

Ark began to thrash vigorously near a large section of wooden decking and broken rigging. A feeble cry sounded from within it, which brought a smile back to Vekan's face.

He descended on the heap, cast the ropes, sails, and boards away, and froze as a terrified but enchanting face came into view.

Soft, ebony hair was spread around her face in a voluptuous veil, and her violet eyes, surrounded by thick lashes, were wide with alarm. Her full lips parted.

The tattered remains of a tunic clung to her in a few places. He had never seen someone so disfigured.

Her collarbones zigzagged toward her shoulders, one of which was slightly higher than the other. He traced her narrow waist, broad hips, and the curve of her full breasts. All were etched, every inch, with scars, thick and thin.

For the first time in his life, Vekan blushed at the sight of a woman, and she wasn't even naked. Despite the scars, she was the most beautiful he had ever seen. He had stopped breathing.

He realized he was ankle deep in ocean and, with three beats of his wings, he recovered himself, landing lightly beside her then slicing her free of the rigging that held her fast to the wreckage with a small knife.

"Your comrade bade me find you," he said in tainted Mauviasen, fixing his eyes on her unblemished face, trying to ignore the heat coursing through him, particularly below the waist.

She recoiled at the sight of the shark's conical snout. "Get away from me!" She drew one of her legs back as if prepared to deliver a blow, whether to Ark or Vekan, the siren couldn't tell.

"He's perfectly friendly. He found you. We're here to rescue you. Ark doesn't like the taste of the two-legged, anyway! He's going to help me get you ashore." Vekan indicated the cliffs.

She stared at him incredulously.

"On you get. He'll carry you."

She shook her head and blurted, "No!" Her eyes darted between him and the beast with mounting distrust. She edged farther from them, stark terror in her eyes.

He stumbled as the floating bit of decking shifted with her movement.

Then she lost her balance and toppled over into the dark ocean.

Vekan shook his head slowly. "She's going to get too cold, Ark." Flapping his wings to maintain his balance, he squatted and extracted her from the water by the arms.

She spluttered and shivered convulsively.

"Please?" Vekan frowned. He pulled her back onto the floating wood.

"Can't you carry me?" she muttered.

"I suppose I could, but it would make me very tired, and you need someone to look after you." He backed away from her so that the wood wouldn't tip again.

"I am not getting back in there," she glanced at the water, "let alone near that!" She stabbed a finger at Ark's shiny snout.

The shark mouthed the corner of the wood that they stood on with serrated teeth as big as Vekan's hands.

"So, if you're here to rescue me, you'll have to carry me." She folded her arms under her breasts and turned her nose toward the deepening night sky above.

"I …" Vekan sighed. "As you wish," he said with a frown, scooping her up with one arm under her knees and the other supporting her back.

She leaned her face into his chest as he spread his silver wings.

Vekan seldom flew with weight, other than his own, and didn't understand why she disliked Arkarias so. He had never known a sweeter, more trustworthy creature. Even when he was an infant, the shark had taken him for numberless rides and hunts. He couldn't have asked for a better guardian.

The siren hoped he would make it. No one had ever forced him to carry them before. But this one was coherent. Most of those he found were drowning, drowned, or badly injured. They didn't have the presence of mind to argue with his instructions.

"Off we go," he said, pumping his wings hard and managing to lift just a few feet above the water. He headed back for the bay, as Ark slipped silently through the water after them.

As they rounded the cliffs, Vekan saw an orange glow at the foot of the cliff below his stilted house.

Curse this woman's obstinacy, he thought. He was already exhausted and the night would be long.

"What's that, under the cliffs?" she asked, her soft lips brushing his chest as she turned her head toward the smattering of flame on the water.

He focused on pumping his aching wings. "The locals. Hill gnomes, intent on taking my house from me. Most likely led by one Gwenapid the whatever," he panted out.

Taking several rapid breaths, he lurched forward, pumping his wings ferociously, but still sagged. He then launched his burden ahead with the last of his strength before he hit the cliff edge with his chest.

The scarred beauty cried out as she skidded through the abrasive gravel that covered the ground above, safely on the cliff top. Then she hurried back to him and gave him her hands. He took them, scrambling from his hanging position to safety.

The woman sat beside him, bleeding.

"I'm sorry," he said, driving his fingers into his hair. *How could I have been so impatient? I ought to have landed on the beach and walked her up …*

"For what?" She covered herself with her arms and scrunched legs.

"Throwing you like that. I hurt you." His heart faltered, and his stomach turned at the fresh scrapes that covered her.

She blinked. "You're really … apologizing?" She shook her head slowly, her brows furrowed.

He frowned. "Of course! I wasn't careful enough." He looked over her once more, at the wretched scars that covered her body. "But then, it doesn't appear that you came from a genteel lot." He managed to tear his eyes from her.

"You're funny," she said with a roll of her violet eyes.

"I'm Vekan."

"And I'm Gjordkra. You said my friend sent you after me? Salmaara? Is she all right?"

"She's alive, but got cut up, too. She'll mend, though," he said.

He needed sleep. He would fall asleep here if he didn't move soon. It seemed so far. He'd had an unduly emotional day already, which hit him harder than the physical exertion.

"She's resting in the house." He pointed to the stilted house, a few steps away.

Gjordkra nodded and strained to stand.

He scrambled to his feet and offered his hands. "Let me help you."

She stared at his hands. "Why?"

"Because it's the right thing to do."

"You are a strange bird-man," she said. Though she took his hands, distrust pooled in her narrowed eyes.

He helped her stand then escorted her up the nearby stairs to the house. His exhaustion was the only thing keeping him from staring at her.

Thank the creators for that, he thought.

As they entered the house, Gjordkra followed Vekan to a wicker chest by one of the round windows. He opened it, revealing a pile of salty-smelling clothes.

"Here," he said, extending a blue tunic with large holes cut in the back.

She pulled the remains of Captain Pol's wet tunic over her head and accepted the new one.

When she looked back up, the siren stood with his hands over his eyes, his cheeks flushed.

"What?"

"Nothing ..." he said. "Are you all right?"

"Yes."

Gjordkra wandered over to where Salmaara lay snoring in a hammock. The girl looked a little pallid but not deathly.

Behind her, the winged man collapsed in the largest hammock of all, his eyelids falling shut. The chamber filled with the sound of his deep breathing, as well.

Watching her slumbering comrades brought to her attention that she wasn't tired in the least and in want of a walk. She didn't know what lay outside, so elected to quietly pace the house.

The fresh wounds did not bother her. Most were in areas where she no longer felt anything.

When will I awake from this dream? Pleasant things didn't last. Surviving an exploding ship, and then being rescued by a winged man.

He had apologized for hurting her. No one had ever apologized for the wounds they inflicted. And the way he had looked at her? There was something so different about it. Her heart fluttered.

She would soon wake and Jhaill, her husband, would be waiting.

Jhaill ... What happened on that cliff top?

One moment, Yezhr had been holding Gjordkra prisoner, faithfully awaiting his governor's orders, and the next, he had lunged at his superior with a frenzied gleam in his amber eyes. She had never seen the aloof superintendent display any deep passion. She had thought him incapable. She knew he had intended to kill Jhaill in that moment. And yet, there was none whom he served so loyally.

The way he stabbed Jhaill, who might have fought back if not for his own shock at such uncharacteristic behavior, had been savage.

If there was a being in the world that the horrid Governor of Günhai called his favored, it was Yezhr. Yezhr who would carry out any task his governor commanded without question. Yezhr who must have led her groom across the Mauviasen wilderness in pursuit and knew how to avoid Kaskahai and where to cut them off. And yet, he'd turned on the other lith in a moment without a word, allowing their quarry to escape.

And Yezhr never allowed his prey to escape.

Gjordkra spun on her heel when she reached the far wall by Vekan, beginning another lap.

Why now? Before jumping from the cliff, she had caught sight of Yezhr's face as Jhaill's other henchmen had held him down. Thoughtful was the only way to describe it.

Salmaara.

Nothing seemed to flow naturally in the girl's presence. None escaped Günhai. None visited Kaskahai. None escaped Yezhr. *But we did.*

Salmaara had bested Jhaill and Yezhr, Gjordkra's lifelong tormentors and masters.

This overly trusting, heretical lunatic.

She stood before Salmaara's hammock, eyeing the redhead's youthful face as she ruminated. Then Gjordkra turned to the window, where a faint orange glow near the cliff's edge caught her eye. She craned to see it, frowning.

Vekan mentioned some malicious gnomes, didn't he? Why is he sleeping if they're coming to attack?

She remained and watched as the first of the tiny, shadowy forms rolled gracelessly onto the cliff top. A torch fell from its hand.

She wondered if she ought to wake her rescuer.

Biting her lip, she looked at him where he still lay deeply asleep. Then, turning back to the window, she gazed out onto the moonlit cliff face, where a small rabble, barely discernible, assembled.

The group of twenty strong tiptoed forward in unison, in an apparent attempt at stealth, toward the house.

Gjordkra folded her arms and watched as the mob proceeded through knee-height grass—knee-height for Gjordkra perhaps, but tall enough to cover the invaders.

As they emerged, they were promptly set upon by a small gaggle of honking, flapping creatures. Birds of sorts, Gjordkra guessed.

Even from behind the wooden wall and glass, she could hear the gnomes' muffled shrieks as they were viciously bucked and pecked from their feet. The long-necked, gray and black birds lashed at them with sharp beaks, and the gnomes writhed, their tiny fists pummeling their assailants to no effect. Then, once some of the gnomes escaped the fray, they began slinging rocks at the birds, which effectively dispersed them.

A yawn sounded close behind her, and Gjordkra turned to see Vekan stood there, also watching the small-scale battle.

"I wonder what they have for me tonight," he said with marked fondness as he moved to stand beside her.

"Not much. They're pathetic."

"Of course." He grinned, his handsome bird's eyes fixed on the badly ruffled horde as they scrambled to regroup.

"Would you like to come out and watch with me? I can usually conjure a few tricks of my own if the occasion calls for it." A devious smile tugged at his lips.

Gjordkra shrugged. "Will Salmaara be all right?"

"I don't know." Vekan drooped in mock anguish. "By the breaking of the dawn, we might all find ourselves overrun by the genius of

Gwenapid, slain by his inescapable hand."

Gjordkra stared at him incredulously.

He cleared his throat. "I jest."

What a strange man.

When she remained silent, he spoke. "I wasn't serious. Anyway …
your friend will be safe." He grinned again. It was very becoming.

She smiled.

"Do you want to stay here and rest or get acquainted with the locals?"

"Do I look tired to you, Master Vekan?" She placed her hands upon
her hips.

"N-no!" he stammered.

He seemed to think he had offended her.

"Let's get on the roof," he said, offering his hand. She accepted it.

They exited the house onto the veranda via a window on the opposite
side from where the gnomes approached. Vekan then boosted Gjordkra
onto his shoulders, and she grasped one of the carved, wooden drowners
and pulled herself up. He followed her with one sweep of his silver wings.

They crept up the steep roof, Gjordkra following the siren to the pitch,
where they lay on their stomachs, side by side, to peer over at the party
gathered on the cliff edge, around the boardwalk that hung over the dark
water ahead.

The torches, now jammed into the ground, illuminated the little scene
that showed the gnomes endeavoring to haul cylindrical objects up with
rope to stack them.

The gnomes themselves were unsightly little brutes, each a foot or two
tall, with coarse hair that sprouted in sporadic tufts from their scalps.
Their noses protruded from their round faces, long and bulbous. Gjordkra could hear their squeaky grunts as they hauled the cylinders.

A mad scramble broke out as all present attempted to form a line and haul the rope with their combined strength, then lurched backward. Several of them fell piteously to the ground. Their efforts were not in vain, though.

The gnomes who still had their feet pulled a squirming form over the edge to stand among them with a collective grunt. By far the most hideous of the lot, gut wobbling, the newcomer squinted toward the house. Although he stood far away, Gjordkra thought she felt an immense abhorrence radiating from him.

He stepped forward, a torch in one fat hand, illuminating his unfortunate choice of a striped tunic and puffy, thigh-length breeches adorned with spots. The shades of green, yellow, and brown clashed, even in torchlight.

"Unholy daemon!" he screeched in a high, whiny voice, raising his arms and the torch toward the starry sky. "Come forth from your lair that you might finally be slain and this land restored to its rightful owner! I, Gwenapid the Sixth, on my great-grandfather's, Gwenapid the Great, grave, swear to destroy you, as did my father before me and his!" he cried with such immense passion that he swayed where he stood on the tips of his toes while waving his arms fanatically.

Vekan snickered and looked to Gjordkra, who pursed her lips.

"What did you do to his family?" she asked.

"Nothing, of course," Vekan replied.

"What are they going to do?"

"Wait and see," Vekan murmured, his wings unfurling slightly as he peered over the pitch.

"Have they ever even come close to hurting you?" Gjordkra asked, amused by the mass of little bodies below.

"Once. Gwenapid the Fifth got inside somehow and waited behind my hammock with a knife. When I sat in the hammock, I got a nasty prick in my right shoulder." Vekan reached back, pulling at one of the wing holes in his tunic. He lifted it up slightly so she could see his back.

Gjordkra saw a jagged scar above his wing, far more than a prick. It was the only imperfection in his suns-browned flesh. She touched it carefully, curiously, while Vekan watched her unblinkingly.

"What?" She realized she was still caressing him and removed her fingers, her cheeks growing hot.

"Oh, nothing," he mumbled, returning his attention to the paltry band of would-be assailants.

Vekan sighed and shook his head. "It appears they intend to fire upon us, fair lady," he moaned with a grin.

Indeed they did. Gjordkra tore her eyes from him to receive a gooey blow from the first projectile. She slid a ways down the pitch of the roof with a startled yelp. She hadn't realized she had been sitting up far enough to have been spotted.

Vekan extended an ankle for her to catch, which she did with one hand, while the other removed the brown mush from her eyes.

"What is this?" She shuddered.

"Mushrooms!" Vekan said as he received one in the side of the face.

"Are they meant to hurt us or shock us into submission?" she asked, crawling back to him then peeling it from his smooth cheek.

"I don't think I'll ever know," Vekan replied.

"Looks like we won't have to break out the good traps tonight. We can sit back and see to your friend," he said.

Gjordkra slipped farther down to the edge of the roof then ably swung down to the porch, where the sound of the mushroom barrage pounding the opposite side of the house became clearer.

Vekan landed gracefully and soundlessly beside her, where he stopped in front of the open window, bent over, formed a cradle with his hands, and waited for her.

She raised a brow. "So?"

He cleared his throat. "May I help you up?"

"Oh." She blushed as she used his little step to slip inside.

He followed her and closed the window behind them.

The mushrooms rattled the door in the wall across from them and smacked the windows but did not harm the glass. Gjordkra wondered how Salmaara could sleep through such a commotion.

She gazed out at the line of gnomes below where they loaded their gooey mushrooms into the long objects they had pulled up earlier then blasted the house with them.

"What happens when they run out of mushrooms?" Gjordkra asked as she slumped into Vekan's hammock to get more comfortable but could still watch the futile assault.

Vekan sauntered over and sat beside her. "They go home," he said, enfolding her with a feathered wing, "to plan the next assault."

"When will you see them again?"

"Who knows?"

A final mushroom slid down the window in front of them, and all went still.

CHAPTER THIRTY-ONE

FORTRESS T'VULUS,
MAUVIAS

In wake of Kalitoomba's fall, Tzu Tihas became the world's largest city. A century later, its economic prowess reigned unmatched. It was the seat of Mauviasen power, and that meant the capital of the world.

The metal city rose up from Mauvias's eastern plains, just north of the T'Skel. Once, Tzu Tihas had been no more than another Mauviasen settlement that struggled for what all of its countrymen did—survival.

Three hundred years later, it dominated the plain and ran into the base of the T'Skel. It shimmered pale green with flashes of violet through Mauvias's chronic dimness. The city's coloration arose from widespread use of the precious metal, starsya, in construction.

Prince Soar discovered a wealth of starsya in the ground surrounding the city near the beginning of his long reign. The metal was slick and pearlescent, colored deep violet, with bright green highlights. Most incredible, however, were the metal's cooling properties.

A building covered in starsya plating was like walking into an icebox. It wasn't long before the commodity couldn't supply the demands of clamoring Mauviasen nobles. Prices climbed until the metal became only the pleasure of the very rich. It became even rarer when it caught the interest of southerners, and then the Prince of Tzu Tihas, against all custom, opened trade with them. His boldness was responsible for Tzu Tihas's initial growth and eventual success.

Class divided the city in half—east and west. Officials and royalty resided in the east. The west, which faced the open wilderness between Tzu Tihas and Günhai, was reserved for the less fortunate.

A crenellated stone wall ran the perimeter of the city, in imitation of Kalitoomba's. Tzu Tihas had never required the walls for utilitarian purposes, but their prince had a taste for things southern.

A new wall was added outside the farthest settlement every few decades as needed to accommodate the city's burgeoning populace and expansion. So far, eight rings divided the older sections from the new.

In each of the western-most walls, the crenellated stone peeled away and formed nine open arches, supported by starsya pillars that looked like unraveling ropes. These arches were the only way in and out of the city. They were not fitted with doors or barriers, for the city had never suffered or feared attack.

Fortress T'Vulus dominated Tzu Tihas's eastern cliffs, which bore the castle's staggering visual weight like a broken back. The opulent building was solid starsya, a testament to its master's unshakable wealth and power.

Slender towers topped by shimmering turrets composed most of the fortress. The towers around the perimeter were shorter and grew in height as they reached the center. Battlements ran the full perimeter, and the massive keep could be glimpsed through the center.

Wind jostled the sheer curtains leading to a round veranda that protruded from T'Vulus's central tower overlooking the city and surrounding wilderness. The red light of afternoon played on the smoky eyes of a man who leaned lazily against the starsya railing. He admired the city sprawled before him. It was as much a part of him as his arm or leg. It was his greatest pride and his life's work.

Prince Soartagmon Tarrke smiled contentedly at the city. He was a man of mixed races, sulmai and lith. Unblemished skin covered his imposing musculature. His face did not betray his three hundred and ten years. It was proud, with a firm jaw. He had sensual lips from his Sulmai father, and large corneas that nearly filled his eyes from his mother. Feathery black hair grew to his shoulders. He wore a translucent green robe that hung open, its sash fluttering in the breeze.

Soar heard the pest's mind before the man's pattering feet scooted into the bedchamber behind him. The fool was thinking that he had better guard his thoughts so that he didn't betray the ill news before he was able to speak it. He also hoped that Prince Soar wasn't listening.

"Yes, Ghu?" Soar said softly without turning, his tone dripping with honey sweetness. The prince never raised his voice, for there was no need. His servants understood the consequences of wasting his time or disobeying him.

"I ... I bring tidings, my p-prince." The little man sweated despite his cool surroundings.

Soar turned to him, and the creature jumped, swallowing a shriek.

"Kage would have your tongue for supper if you interrupted me merely for your sport," Soar murmured.

"M-m-my prince—"

"Proceed."

"I received w-word from Günhai, m-my prince. The governor was nearly assassinated in a recent hunt for a pair of escapees."

"Oh?"

"By Superintendent Yezhr, to be exact, m-m-my—"

"Enough. Continue."

Ghu cleared his throat and wiped a quaking hand across his pasty brow. "The s-superintendent bore the governor home from the wilderness, west of Kaskahai, where he was barely saved. Yezhr hasn't s-spoken since. None have been successful in extracting a-anything. He will not explain himself. The g-governor requested that the e-empress herself come and inspect the man in question."

"She returns this evening. I shall convey your message. We are ready to receive her, I presume? Her journey will have been long."

"O-of course. The kitchens and the throne room are ready for her."

"Is that all?"

Ghu froze, his little mind emptying as terror took hold. Soar didn't wish to play with him for the moment.

The prince squatted down slowly with a cool smile. "Ghu," he purred, looking into his servant's glazed eyes.

The orange-eyed man leaned in tremulously, readying himself for a blow.

"Go away," Soar said.

The pasty creature jolted into motion and fled the chambers, slamming the door behind him.

Yezhr turned on Jhaill? That isn't possible.

Soar had known both men all his life. Yezhr was a simple man who lived to serve his governor, his empress. He only looked for the next hunt to fill him. Men like Yezhr didn't harm those who made his lifestyle possible.

The prince leaned on the desk and reviewed the images garnered from Ghu's mind: Jhaill Opthonne locked in his office, heavily bandaged on a shoulder and his torso. Many of the smaller nicks around his collarbones and stomach were stitched. Given the placement of the wounds, Yezhr had missed his victim's vitals by a small margin. They were erratic, unskilled blows. There was an older gash on the lithian man's head.

If not for the ridiculous empire and its hotheaded empress, Soar would have gone down to Günhai himself to investigate such an intriguing matter. As things were, Velanoma expected him to remain in Tzu Tihas unless she gave him leave.

Jhaill would have requested Soar's opinion before the empress rose out of nothing and declared that Vias herself had chosen her. In recent years, the governor seemed concerned only with earning a place in Velanoma's good graces. *Your worst mistake, Governor.*

Soar had obtained her favor easily and became more disgusted by the day. He tolerated her because he worried their *Xin'Dai* prowess was matched. If he erred in his attempt to subdue her and invoked her hostility instead, it could be his end. He knew the opportunity for her removal would come.

He was a man of patience. He had turned a wild rabble of cannibals into the greatest city in the world. *Surely, I can remove a little country girl playing empress.*

Soar strode inside the tower behind him. Furniture of carved, dark wood from Arvitra filled the chamber. A canopy bed the size of a minor noble's drawing room sat against the outer wall, flanked by exquisitely carved tables. His favorite piece, imported from Arakamda, capital of the Shadowlands, was a silk rug of mostly red, cream, and black, that lay beneath everything over the cold floor.

An arched door near the bed opened into a short hall and Soar's bathing chambers. T'Vulus was the only place in Mauvias with water. The prince had struck a bargain with a Kalitoombian merchant to acquire the underground spring. The channel and piping had taken nearly one hundred years to complete. A door to a conference chamber was set into the left wall.

The prince tied his robe and stepped into the hall. Flickering lanterns lined the broad corridor.

Due to the empress's absurd desire to erase Kalitoomba's memory and all it stood for, she insisted that Soar remove the bright silver lighting he had acquired from the fortress. It irked him every time he passed the primitive spots of flame. *One more thing that will change.*

The Prince of Tzu Tihas glided down a winding staircase to the tower's base and into a similarly grand corridor. He passed through a door at its terminus, which led into the great hall. Chairs formed rows before decorative pillars on either side of the hall, and immediately to his left, centered on a raised dais, was an ornate starsya throne, hammered to look as though it was made of gnarled wood. Soar mounted the stairs and sat on the throne.

He could hear all minds in his castle and the city beyond. None were of any interest. All was as it should be.

Then he felt her.

The empress's signature felt like an abrasive length of rope constricting around his throat. All possessing Xin'Dai had their own signature, some stronger than others. Velanoma's was strong. And unpleasant.

Soar stood and strode toward the doors at the hall's far end.

Ghu skittered from a side chamber and fell in behind him as the prince threw the double doors open and descended the straight flight of stairs to the keep's entry.

The metallic floors curved seamlessly up, forming slender pillars, which connected with the vaulted ceiling. Curtains of sheer red fabric hung from the arched ceiling in tasteful swags.

The doors at the bottom of the stairs groaned open as Soar descended, and Velanoma swept in.

The rubies in the crown that floated around her head caught the light from the suns as they slipped toward the jagged peaks of the T'Skel.

She wore a conservative silver dress that reached to her knees and riding pants beneath it. As with all her wardrobe, it had been tailored to suit the missing section of her stomach.

She made her way to him before he took another step and kissed him long and passionately, tangling her fingers in his hair. He returned her affections, pulling her against him.

"Welcome home," he said.

"How are affairs here, my love?" Velanoma asked, caressing his face and hair. Her crimson eyes burned with desire.

"I received word from Günhai—"

"After a bath, hm?" She stole another kiss, silencing him.

He forced down his annoyance.

As she broke from him, her face drained of all passion. She resumed her stately poise with hands folded in front of her, as always when in the presence of servants.

Soar looked to the door as her companions entered. First came Asha, Velanoma's Mu'Zhai. A sour expression marred her beautiful face, her upset no doubt stemming from her pitiful and omnipresent gnome servant who puffed up the short flight of stairs behind her. Asha silently fumed about some imprudent remark the creature had made moments earlier. What that was, Soar couldn't discern. Her thoughts darted around, difficult to follow.

Hazc came in at her heels, dragging the empress's starsya trunks behind him. Soar couldn't hear his mind, but it did not concern him. No gnome that Soar had ever seen possessed a signature. He assumed their minds were as empty as they were small.

The third of the empress's favored party entered last, burdened with a simple medical pack. Rexus Danvi, bastard son of the late emperor and also the empress's physician and mortician. Why she permitted such ilk in her midst vexed Soar beyond words.

Asha had a temper but could be managed. The gnome did not concern him. The worst the helpless creature seemed capable of were wounds of wit, and he never spoke to Soar or the empress. His usefulness as a footstool kept him alive. Rexus, however, overstepped his bounds far too often.

Soar kept his attention on the man. He had storm gray hair, which he kept in a neat tail that touched the nape of his neck. He possessed a severe face with angular features and light olive skin. His eyes were so dark they seemed black, which belied his Shadowlandish lineage. He always wore a grave expression, as though he were the bearer of dire news. He wore a thigh-length black jacket with lace accents on its lapels, a garment favored in Arakamda, of which the man was native. Underneath, he wore a white cotton tunic and black breeches. Black boots reached to his knees.

Soar turned from the servants and led Velanoma through the door behind the throne and up the tower to their chambers. As he reached the door that opened to the conference room, a thump sounded behind him. He turned.

The gnome stood behind him with the empress's luggage.

The tiny fool bowed before their eyes met. He could never have guessed how a creature with such diminutive legs kept pace with them.

Velanoma waved a dismissive hand. "Leave them here," she said.

The two-foot gnome did as instructed, trotting from sight.

"Now," Velanoma purred, "where were we?"

"Liberating you from that stifling dress," Soar responded, slipping one of his arms around her incomplete middle then pulling her into the chamber and closing the door. He swept her off her feet and carried her past the bed to the bathing chamber.

The room was the only one in the castle that was not of starsya. It was solid green marble, because moisture did not agree with starsya. It had a series of elegant, fluted pillars surrounding the octagonal bath set into the floor that was large enough to accommodate sixteen men. A series of curved marble faucets and handles, each the length of Soar's forearm, lined one side.

Soar set the empress down, kissed her hand, and then strode to the bath and activated the faucets. Water roared from them in a gushing flood that began to evaporate as it fell.

Soar had spent many hours gauging how much water should be flowing into the bath to keep it full. Although a sizable vapor cloud hovered over the bath, the water flow was still enough to fill it quickly before the air could claim it.

Soar poured a bucket of sweet-scented salts and oils into the flow and turned toward Velanoma, who stood admiring him near the bath's stairs.

She stepped from her slippers and waited as he shifted behind her to deftly unlace the strings of her gown then smoothed it from her fair shoulders.

"You need not trouble yourself about Asha, Hazc, and Rexus. They have been nothing but devoted and useful at every turn. They could never hope to bring you, Soar, to grief. They have no power," she said.

"I don't trust them, my empress. I never will."

"As you see fit."

"Did you find success in your southern endeavors?" Soar murmured.

She stood nude from the waist up but didn't turn. She was a beautiful woman, despite the missing portion of her torso. It was astonishing how she survived such a wound. Unblemished skin pulled tightly over it, long since healed. Although he had tried to get an explanation more than once, she always evaded the subject.

Velanoma was slight but strong from years as a warrior yet pleasantly curved. Her full right side created a delightful slope before filling out into a full hip. He ran his hand over it and continued downward to remove her riding pants.

When her clothes lay in a heap at her feet, he moved to free her hair from its tight bun.

"No," she said in response to his query. "Despite resorting to methods I did not wish to employ, we gleaned nothing of the whereabouts of Vadik or the emperor. The only success was Yezhr's, for which I was not present. I shall never tire of witnessing Bhevir's destruction."

Velanoma had taken to ordering the city's demolition whenever she deemed she had allowed rebuilding to go on long enough. She had quarantined it, letting new settlers rebuild where they thought themselves out of her grasp. Then, when it suited her, she ordered its destruction anew. Since the beginning of her reign, she had done so three times. Little remained of the original great city once ruled by Esthadya Lordian, one of the four creators. Velanoma hated the place.

It had been her childhood home.

"And I loathed every wasted moment I endured there. Its opulence, its vanity," she said in response to his thought.

The empress had only recently retaken the land from her daughter's grip and learned, to her great delight, that it sat on a motherlode of several varieties of gems that her fickle Shadowlandish subjects prized highly. Retaking the land, removing the settlement, and mining it would not only serve to remind those who had forgotten the empire to whom their allegiance was owed, but would also please the Council of Grace, who provided Velanoma with the armies she needed to maintain stability in the southernmost parts of her empire.

"Let us talk and think of something else. You mentioned Günhai?" she said, turning toward him as her crimson hair fell free over the curve of her pert breasts and to her waist.

She untied the sash on his robe, and he shrugged it from his shoulders before letting it fall. Then she kissed him.

He took her hands. "Yes. It is appropriate that you should mention Yezhr. Word arrived that he attempted to slay Governor Opthonne."

"And this report is accurate?" Velanoma raised her fine brows.

Nodding, Soar escorted her down the stairs into the rising water. "Ghu has been to see the governor himself. Jhaill looked very sorry indeed. He requested that you inspect the superintendent personally. No one has been able to extract anything from the traitor. He has been in a stupor."

"Then I shall examine their case soon. I wish to tarry here a few days. You have been missed."

Soar swallowed a twinge of irritation. If she didn't want to go immediately, he would.

"Now, now, my love. I shall certainly not abandon them. They are cherished assets, after all," she purred.

"Of course," he said. He then kissed her throat and brushed his fingers through her silky hair.

"What of Kusae?" he asked as his lips touched her ear.

Velanoma shuddered.

"My army took the South of Arvitra from her a week past. She now has one holding, and it is poor."

"The basin?"

"Yes. The basin. She was a fool to dismiss Sethmar. It will be her undoing. She has never understood war."

Despite how he truly felt about the news, Soar smiled. The fugitive emperor had been the only thing between Velanoma and victory for the sixteen years since the split. Over the past year, since Kusae had sent her father away and ordered his execution, reclaiming Northern and Southern Yendu had been as easy as taking a breath. But Velanoma still expended massive efforts to keep the Yendus under control.

Kusae had been a soft ruler. No one had added to her strength sufficiently to slow her inevitable fall. Velanoma had pushed the rebel into Arvitra Basin then plucked her commanders from her, one by one, only to supplant them with traitors created in Günhai.

The basin was a nasty trap, and only four days south of Mauvias's border.

"What will my empress do when she floods it with her might?"

"I shall leave her to drown, as she would have me." Velanoma rested her face against his chest then kissed it.

She went rigid.

"Soar ..." Velanoma looked up at him, her lips parted in surprise. "Yezhr tried to kill Jhaill Opthonne?" she asked slowly.

"Yes."

"What of that little girl, his latest pet?"

"Girl?" Soar searched the memory he had gleaned from Ghu and found what he wanted. "They were pursuing her and Jhaill's new bride when the attack happened. On the other side of the Western T'Skel, past Kaskahai of all places."

"I must go to Günhai immediately." The empress set her jaw as she pulled away from Soar.

He smiled coolly in her wake.

She strode up the bath stairs then stood still while the water evaporated from her body. The prince stayed in the water as she clothed herself.

Soar watched her thoughts. The girl's face swam into focus. She had curly auburn hair and, although terrified, power lurked in her young gaze. Velanoma had been unable to access the child's thoughts, nor had Jhaill or Yezhr.

Something about her face unsettled him. There was something familiar about it.

"I shall return," Velanoma said as she strode from the chamber.

Soar watched her go, waiting for her mind to disconnect from his own. When it did, he submerged to his neck in the bath.

He couldn't force the girl's face from his mind. He wondered that she had concerned Velanoma so. She was just a teenage girl. But Yezhr attacking Jhaill … It took great restraint not to chase after Velanoma and demand to accompany her. He knew, however, that nothing incurred her wrath like perceived insubordinate behavior, even from him.

His thoughts shifted back to the girl.

I know her, he thought, inhaling the scents rising from the sweet bath. *Who is she?*

GLOSSARY

Agaria (Ah-gar-ee-uh): Curious Princess of Dragons. She is a dragon trapped in a two-legged form, transformed by the Dragon's Eye (see Sijin Baeir) in her mother's womb. She has tar-black skin with emerald hair and eyes that glow at times.

Arakamda (Arr-achk-am-dah): Capital of the Shadowlands, ruled by the Council of Grace, although they gave their sovereignty to the Mauviasen Empire. Arakamda is built on the Elin River Delta and boasts many structures of black or white alabaster. Its people are the best healers in the world. Structure of Note: Arakamda Sanctuary.

Arvitra (Arr-veet-ruh): Heavily forested nation situated between Mauvias and Northern Yendu. Arvitra is Queen Kusae's last hold in the world. City of note: Basin City of Arvitra and Sunad.

Asha (Ash-ah) Umgalásha (Oom-gall-ah-shuh): Empress Velanoma's Mu'Zhai (see Mu'Zhai).

Batal (Bay-tall): Prince Vadik's Lastauk (see Lastauk).

Bhevir (Beh-veer): Salmaara's hometown in Southern Yendu.

Castle Errasitka (Err-ass-it-kuh): King Yulari's castle on the north end of Kalitoomba. Its name means "Dungeon of Memory." It is said to have been haunted.

Castle Taraterrum (Tar-ah-terr-um): Built in Arvitra Basin by Velanoma, pre-empire. She hoped to build a new capital city there to help their people forget King Yulari and Kalitoomba. Queen Kusae lives there.

Dragon: Carriage-sized creatures used by Mauviasen, especially in war. They are well-muscled with a barrel-shaped torso and smooth back.

They have short necks that line up with their spine, allowing them to ram through many thick and heavy obstacles. Dragons are highly venomous. After the Destroyer's incarceration, Esthadya cursed the dragons as punishment for their part in the war, taking their wings and voices from them, dooming them to become little more than beasts of burden.

Digaria (Die-gar-ee-uh): Home world of the Lordians, the elder gods, and destroyed by Vias.

Elloerr (El-oh-air): The universe.

Esthadya Ophrahai Lordian (Ess-thad-yah Oaf-ra-hie Lord-ee-an): One of the four creators. Also known as the Green God, so named for his green hair and eyes. Kalitoombians called him Lord Knowledge more often than the common translation of his name, Esthadya, which is (Lord) "Knowledge." Esthadya ruled over South City, Kalitoomba from his keep, Castle Sahkmar. He appears to have died before Empress Velanoma's attack on his city that led to King Yulari's downfall. There is much mystery surrounding Esthadya's activities in the universe. He is known to have close associations with both Yulari and Hazc. Esthadya is married to Falyarah.

Falyarah Ettshca Lordian (Fall-yar-ahh Et-shuh Lord-ee-an): One of the four creators. Falyarah is credited with creating the suns. She is worshipped, along with her husband, Esthadya, in the southern nation of the Shadowlands. Falyarah in the common tongue means "Gracious." Mortals most often refer to her as "Lady Grace." The Council of Grace in the Shadowlands is named after her.

Forgotten Valley: Shale-covered valley in Northern Yendu where Kisoni Lordian (see Kisoni Lordian) has been banished for a century.

Fortress T'Vulus (Tee-vool-oos): Starsya fortress built by Prince Soartagmon. Located on the easternmost border of Tzu Tihas.

Gjordkra (Gee-ord-kruh): Girl who grew up in Günhai. She belongs to Jhaill Opthonne, Governor of Günhai.

Gnome: Small creatures ranging from one to three feet, generally seen in servitude. There are many varieties, such as hill gnomes, that live undisturbed in wild areas of Arvitra. Most are hostile toward other races.

Günhai (Goon-hi): Prison city of interrogation and torture that guards the way into Mauvias. Governed by Jhaill Opthonne.

Hazc (Hask): A mysterious being in a gnome body.

Inaria (Ee-nar-ee-ah): The name of the world.

Insha Doren (In-shaa Door-en): Flag of Yulari Lordian's Kingdom. Most commonly referred to as the Forbidden Flag in the empire.

Jhaill Opthonne (Jail Op-thon): Governor of Günhai. He possesses the Stolen Kaskahai Power of the brew.

Ka'Bahk (Kah-buck): A soul shield.

Kage (Kaa-gay): Prince Soartagmon's dragon.

Kalitoomba (Kall-it-oom-bah): Located in Northern Yendu. City of Wonders, called the Forbidden City in the empire. Kalitoomba was King Yulari's seat of power pre-empire, and capital of the world. It is illegal to look at it, speak its name, or especially to go there. An elite group called the Forbidden Guard lives in and around it, devoted to enforcing those laws.

Kaskahai (Kaas-ca-hi): The Destroyer's city, built into a volcano. Most buildings and roads are constructed from bones. The Kaskahai are said to have been hunted down to a select group possessing sorcerous powers.

Kisoni (Kiss-owe-knee) Lordian: Keeper of Souls in Digaria, Keeper of Books on Inaria, and youngest brother of Vias the Destroyer and Zephias.

Kotang (Koe-tong) of the Shazrah: "Beloved" of the Shazrah. High Priest or Priestess of Vias the Destroyer. He or she communes directly with Vias on behalf of his or her people and is chosen for the purity of their Kaskahai lithian lineage.

Krédaal (Cray-doll): Divine power of the physical plane.

Kusae (Koo-say) Zamazcus: Daughter of Empress Velanoma, rebel Queen of Arvitra, and Salmaara's mother. Kusae has waged a long war against her mother for the duration of Salmaara's life. A war she is losing.

Lastauk (Lass-tawk): Shadowlandish breed of horse characterized by incredible speed, intellect, and indigo coat.

Lethusi Yar Xced (Leh-thoosy Yar Said): Divine sword of Vias the Destroyer that hungers for blood. Its name means "Blood will Ever Stain" in Digarian.

Lith: Race created by Vias the Destroyer with Xin'Dai powers. They are characterized by a lack of mouth, head feathers, and eyes with overly large corneas. All liths have grey skin ranging from dark to light. Liths are also born with wings, but these are removed at birth.

Maliem Esculis (Maa-leem Esk-you-liss): Flag of Mauvias, also called Ensign of the Destroyer, or The Conqueror. It consists of an emerald octagon with a vertical slash of black through it on a field of black, which is a representation of the Sijin Baeir (see Sijin Baeir). Empress Velanoma added a coil of flame around the talisman when she marched on Kalitoomba.

Mauvias (Mao-vy-as): Northernmost realm and home country of the Destroyer's empire. Land created and founded by Vias the Destroyer prior to her incarceration by King Yulari. Well known for its liquid-destroying cursed air and Xin'Dai race (see Lith). Cities of note: Tzu Tihas, Kaskahai, and Günhai.

Mersa-Zermai (Mur-suh-Zerr-my): A blend of two Digarian races. The only known one is Asha.

Mu'Zhai (Moo-Jye): The empress's "protector." Asha serves as Velanoma's Mu'Zhai.

Pezra (Pezz-ruh): Dungeon Mistress of Günhai, also daughter of Jhaill Opthonne.

Raiva (Rye-vaa) Cliff: Highest of the five cliffs of Arvitra Basin. Castle Taraterrum is built on it.

Rexus Danvi: Doctor and mortician, native to Arakamda, Shadowlands. He is an illegitimate son of Emperor Sethmar Danvi and the High Priestess of the Council of Grace, Tearíshva Vodarin. He serves as Velanoma's personal physician.

Salmaara Zamazcus (Sal-mah-rah Zam-az-cuss): A girl raised by Illun Sultos in Bhevir.

Selti (Sell-tee): Enslaved Mauviasen people who are said to have failed their nation around the time of Vias's imprisonment. They have bat-like wings and long tails, with dark skin. They are most often used to pull carriages.

Sethmar Danvi: Fugitive former husband of Empress Velanoma. She still refers to him as the Emperor.

Shai'Kotang (Shy-Koh-Tong): "First Beloved" of the Shazrah. Yezhr Terrich holds this title.

Shazrah (Sház-rah): Ruling body of Kaskahai. They are lithian priests and priestesses of Vias. Their high priest or priestess is called Kotang.

Signature: The feeling associated with an individual's soul.

Sijin Baeir (See-shin Bye-ear): The emerald talisman. Also known as the Dragon's Eye.

Siren: People said to have been jointly created by Vias and Yulari. They have wings, bird-like eyes, and the power of Windsong. They enjoyed sinking ships and drowning seafarers until King Yulari commanded one of the very last of their kind that she, Legacy, would be a rescuer. Her son, Vekan, is the last of their kind.

Skol Mountains: Mountain range on the border between Southern Yendu and Shadowlands. They are a popular breeding ground for southern dragons.Soartagmon Tarrke (Sore-tag-mon Tark): The Prince of Tzu Tihas and lover to Empress Velanoma. Soar for short.

Stolen Gifts of the Shazrah: Refers to gifts "stolen" from other bloodlines outside of the Shazrah. One possessing a stolen gift has the unnatural blend of gifts from both Xin'Dai and Krédaal within their person at the same time. Although powerful, these individuals do not tend to live full lives and are typically unhealthy.

Sulmai (Sool-my): Dominant humanoid people of the world.

Sunad (Soon-ad): City on the Arvitra side of the border with Mauvias.

Takin (Tah-keen) Lor: Former Grand Engineer of Kalitoomba.

Taus (Touse) Sea: Ocean to the west of the Inarian continent.

T'Skel (Tee-Skell) Mountains: Mountain range that divides Mauvias from the rest of the world. Its name, T'Skel, means the "split" or "the divide." The T'Skel once bordered Northern Yendu's Eastern Coast, but Vias the Destroyer is credited with moving them to their current location as a declaration that her people were separate from all others.

Tzu Tihas (Su Tie-huss): Capital of the Mauviasen Empire. Started as a collection of cannibal tribes that Prince Soartagmon brought under control with the help of lithian allies. He built tremendous wealth from the mining and sale of the precious metal Starsya for which the city is well known. It is also known as a center for weapons manufacture. Location of note: Fortress T'Vulus.

Vadik Asenar (Va-deek Ass-en-are): The Prince of Kaskahai, thought to be dead, who has stolen Agaria, the Dragon Princess, from Empress Velanoma.

Vekan (Vey-khan): Last of the Sirens who rescues the lost at sea with the aid of his ancient guardian Arkarias, the shark.

Velanoma Privii (Pre-vy) Zamazcus: The Empress of Mauvias. She has ruled the known world for a full century and is credited with deposing King Yulari.

Vias (Vye-ass) Lordian: One of the four creators, but also the Destroyer goddess. Vias is best known for her astounding Xin'Dai abilities. She founded the northern nation of Mauvias, which simply means "Vias's Home." She resides in a prison tomb where her soul cannot unite with her body.

Windsong: A power specific to the Siren race that allows them to communicate with the winds, especially to summon storms or find lost things.

Xin'Dai (Shin-die): Divine power of spirit that deals with the mind, emotions, and soul.

Yezhr Terrich (Yay-zurr Terr-ick): Superintendent of Günhai and Shai'Kotang of the Shazrah (see Shai'Kotang).

Yulari (You-lar-ee) Digarious Lordian: One of the four Creators. He is known by many names: The Blue King, Lord of Storms, Lord of Sorrows, Lord of Inaria, Sethusmayhai (Lord of Storms) and, most commonly in his time by the translation of his name, Yulari (King) Powerful, because it was considered disrespectful to use a god's true name. Yulari is responsible for the creation of much of the physical world. Yulari has a long and tormented history with the Destroyer goddess, Vias, who is his wife. He fought a long war on their home world of Digaria but lost his people to Vias. Seven thousand two hundred years before Salmaara's birth, Yulari separated Vias's soul from her body and imprisoned her in the bowels of Kaskahai. After her imprisonment, he ruled Kalitoomba from Errasitka in peace until one century before Salmaara's tale begins when Velanoma's army attacked his city. He vanished after the battle, and none have seen him since.

Zam'anti (Zahm-ahn-tee): The realm outside of time.

Zephias (Zef-eye-as) Lordian: Fallen dark god to whom Rexus Danvi has sworn an oath.

Zermai (Zerr-my): Race of the gods native to Digaria.

Since I can remember, I have loved stories. I acted them out as I walked around the school playgrounds of Eastwood, Soldier's Settlement Matraville, and Oakhill Drive elementary schools in Sydney, Australia—a small stand of trees became a sprawling forest, and benches long balustrades surrounding a shining castle. Later, when my family moved back to America, I beg an to include other people in my stories. Sometimes they were characters, other times they were listeners. I loved to take a boring story and figure out how to make it exciting. Other children gathered around to listen to why we really had fire drills and had to learn math—both of which turned out to be quite sinister.

I wrote my first fantasy story in fourth grade. I had written other stories before, but there was something different about this one. It starred a group of characters living in a castle atop a high cliff overlooking a great basin. Over a great dividing mountain range, lived one of our character's wicked grandmothers who ruled the land. The girl wanted nothing more than to make friends with her grandmother and help her see the light. Okay, so the main character of the story was Bulbabee, a bulbasaur from Pokémon, who gathered his friends to find an emerald talisman that could stop the mountains from moving. But the girl on the cliff and her familial struggle stayed with me. I knew she wanted her own story.

So many people encouraged and influenced me in those early years. First and foremost, my parents, Jeff and Marianne, who read everything from books about dinosaurs and sharks to Tolkien to me at bedtime every night from the time I was an infant. My siblings, Jessica and Ryan, who played with me, and in one instance, allowed me to light a toilet paper tail on fire while we pretended to be foxes. I also had many great teachers who encouraged me to read, to be creative, and pursue writing, especially Pamela Smith, and Jan Rolan. Dean Mattson taught me to have a positive mental attitude, and "do homework first, and then something fun."

My first year of high school changed my life. While participating in physical education, I took two blows to my head that resulted in a traumatic brain injury. I lost the ability to read and tolerate light among other things. For six months I lay in darkness, sequestered from the world, sleeping up to sixteen hours every day. My mother never left my side, and never complained of the radical mood swings or the rain of tears. Many people in my life withdrew from me, but not my family, and not my Heavenly Father. Every time a doctor told us what I might not ever be able to do again, they supported me in saying, "Oh, yeah?"

That first six months was just the beginning of a slow road forward. I went to therapy to relearn how to read and remember things. I learned to drive when I was almost eighteen. I wore tinted glasses for years, and hoped to make it to maybe a full day of school per week. Almost every day, however, even though it hurt my eyes, I made my way to a computer, determined to write something, even if it was just a sentence or two at a time. By the end of high school I had completed a 420,000 word novel.

My father saw how much I loved writing, and found a seminar that was held in Pasadena California that year, taught by Kevin J. Anderson, Rebecca Moesta, David Farland, Eric Flint, and Brandon Sanderson. Going to Superstars Writing Seminars reformed my view of writing forever. I realized that I could do what I loved most as a job, if I could do it well enough. I remember leaving with the invigorating thought, "I can be an author!" Over the next couple of years, I took my writing to workshops taught by David Farland, whose invaluable wisdom and willingness to work with me gave me the tools I needed to take my